A Choice of Lightning

RUNNING IN PARALLEL
BOOK 2

A CHOICE OF LIGHTNING

WRITE
ON GIRL

KARA O'TOOLE TREECE

A CHOICE OF LIGHTNING

Write on Girl books are available from your favorite bookseller or from www.KaraOTooleTreece.com

Hardcover ISBN: 978-1-7371380-4-4
Paperback ISBN: 978-1-7371380-3-7
Ebook ISBN: 978-1-7371380-2-0

Library of Congress Control Number: 2021923617
Cataloging in Publication data on file with the publisher.

Layout Design: Rachel Thomaier

Printed in the USA

10 9 8 7 6 5 4 3 2 1

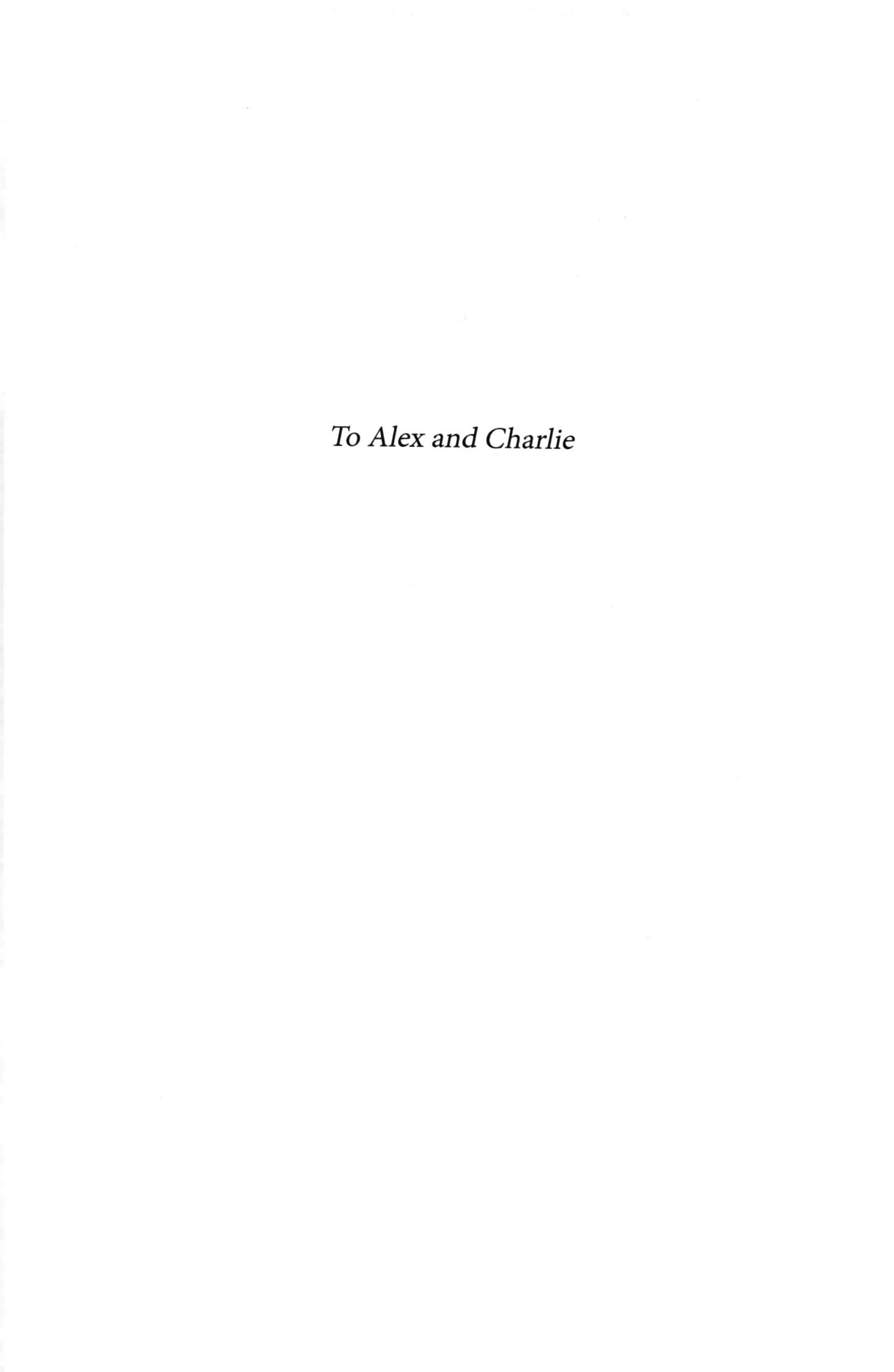

To Alex and Charlie

FARA 1

Midwest Territory, Present Day

I couldn't believe it. The Team was going to help me rescue Agent Hanlon from Barrington Park.

Rescuing him—successfully—wasn't something that I could do alone. I didn't know how to even begin to rescue someone; I had somehow missed that lesson in school. But I would try it anyway, if I had to. I would do whatever it took to get Agent Hanlon—Jay—back. It was my fault he was in this mess. I had left him and had run away to a parallel universe. Even though he told me to. Even though it was to keep my crazy ability away from Barrington Park. I still left him.

I had to save him.

As soon as the Captain agreed to help, Blu left the office to gather the rest of the Team so that they could plan Jay's rescue. I didn't know what planning entailed, just like I had no idea how I was going to help these warriors do anything worthwhile. I was simply a broke waitress who just so happened to open portals between universes. Not even successfully, most of the time. I could feel myself shrinking further into my chair in the Captain's office as the panic settled around me, and I struggled to shove it down as far as I could. I couldn't break down—not until I'd rescued Jay. After that, I could have as big of a meltdown as I wanted. Until then, I had to be strong. For him.

Eventually, the Team returned to the Captain's office. It took everything I had not to stare at them, especially at Ink. Even just carrying a tray of coffee and a box, he gave off a sort of coiled, dangerous energy that was nothing like Calum.

He caught me looking and smirked, which made me blush a thousand shades of red. I had to remind myself, again, that the Team were not my friends, even if they looked like them. How was I ever going to get used to this weirdness?

Ink tossed the box on the table and started handing out coffee. "I conned someone into giving me these."

Blu reached for the box and let out a moan.

"Do you like donuts?" Ink asked.

I nodded, afraid to speak for fear of letting loose the tears that were fighting to free themselves from my eyes.

"Then grab one before Blu eats the whole box."

Blu threw a napkin at him as I took a donut. They were the good kind—no crap sprinkles or dumb filling, just glazed happiness on a plate. Styx gave me an encouraging smile as I bit into my little slice of heaven.

"I'm not sure who Blu has had the opportunity to speak to," the Captain began, "but just so we are all on the same page, I'm going to start at the beginning, albeit a summary. Time is of the essence."

The Team settled into their chairs and turned their attention to the Captain.

"As Fara told us, Agent Hanlon of her government attempted to rescue her from Barrington Park, who is, as we've established, the Counselor's brother. When she escaped her captors, the agent was being held and tortured by Barrington at a secure location. After you left my office, Fara told us of her intention to rescue the agent and asked for the Team's help in doing so. That is our most pressing mission. Not only is he a personal friend of Fara, but he holds vital information regarding the Counselor's brother and could be an asset to us. Once we secure the agent, we will finish debriefing Ink and Blu's latest mission."

Styx smacked Ink's hand as he reached for the last donut. She grabbed it and handed it to me with a grin. Just like Adora. The Captain wasn't fazed by the interruption.

"Before we begin planning the agent's rescue, there is some additional information I want to relay. First, we believe that someone at Jurisdiction is able to open portals to other universes, although we are unsure who or how."

"Someone else can do what Fara does?" Jackrabbit was looking at me. It took everything I had not to shrink from his gaze. He wasn't Hewitt—not really, at least—but it was going to take some time to get used to it.

"Yes," the Captain said. "We are also positive that this person is unable to open a portal into Fara's world, which means that Barrington is stranded there. Therefore, it is of the utmost importance during this mission that Barrington does not capture Fara. Should he take her again, he will be able to return to this world. The brothers cannot be allowed to reunite under any circumstances. That is priority one: keep Fara safe."

"So," Styx said, "like, the first question I have is how in the hell are we supposed to get back to Fara's world? No offense, but it doesn't sound like she has control over the whole window-opening thing."

I couldn't blame her for questioning my ability. Up until just a few minutes ago, I couldn't open a portal if I tried. But I could open them when I wasn't trying, which was scary. And annoying. However, the Captain had asked me the same thing while Blu had gathered up the Team, and after a few failed attempts, I had managed to open up a portal on purpose. It opened to Calum's apartment, which felt right, somehow.

"It's OK," I said. "It's a fair question."

The best way to prove to them—and myself—that I could do this again was to open another portal. However, with everyone looking at me, I couldn't concentrate enough to do anything other than tremble a bit, which wasn't helpful. I closed my eyes and reached back into the memories of the past week, as horrible as they were. After a bit of letting the feelings out, I felt a portal opening.

"I'm opening a portal now." My voice came out small and shaky, which was exactly how I felt at the moment. I opened my eyes. Their heads all whipped around as I stood and turned, giving the Team a view of the window. I let the feeling of panic and dread flow through me. The window started to flicker, and I pushed my feelings toward it, asking it to get bigger.

"Whoa, Fara. That's crazy shit!" Styx turned in her chair for a better view.

Ink came around the table and Jackrabbit leaned across, each staring at the portal I was creating. Through the window was Calum's apartment again, and I breathed a sigh of relief—at least it was opening to the same place. There was also an origami swan on Calum's coffee table, which was just on the other side of the portal. I reached through and took the swan, then looked at the window and thought, *Close*, which it did with a hiss.

"What . . . was . . . that?" Ink said. He stared at the empty space where the window had been.

"I believe that Fara just showed you her ability," the Captain said.

Ink gently grabbed me by the shoulders. "Are you OK?"

"I guess."

"Where was that?"

I was flustered by the intensity of his gaze, especially since the breathy sexpot Ink from a moment ago was completely gone, but he also wasn't acting like Calum. His eyes scanned me, like he was cataloging everything about me. Was he making sure I wasn't injured? I didn't know, but whatever he was looking for, it wasn't something Calum ever did. Even if they were physically identical, they were not the same.

When he was done, he squeezed my shoulders—not hard, but enough to snap me out of it.

"Fara?"

"That is Calum's apartment . . . My Calum, not you, obviously."

"What's in your hand?"

"I think it's a note from him."

"Why would he leave you a note?"

"Because I left him one telling him I was OK."

"When did you leave him a note?"

"When I opened a portal a little bit ago."

I couldn't take the intensity of Ink's gaze, so I sat back down and stared at the folded swan.

"Can you stop interrogating the poor girl?" Styx said. "She just opened a frickin' portal to another universe. I think we can stop with the thousand questions."

The room was quiet, all waiting to see what the note said. Was Calum OK? Was he being followed? Was he hurt? I counted to ten and unfolded it.

F,

I'm not sure how you got a note in here, and I'm hoping you didn't risk your ass to do it. But just in case you come back, I'm leaving this here. I hope wherever you are, you are safe. Adora and Millie went to the police after you were taken. Barrington told them that you went with him willingly. Adora lost her shit, of course. I told her to hold off on trying to rescue you on her own. She still doesn't know. I won't tell her. Hanlon said the assistant has the device now, so she'll know if you do your thing. He went to find you but hasn't returned. Don't tell me where you are. If I don't know, I can't tell them, if it comes to it. Remember your promise. Stay safe. C

P.S. I told Douche you were sick. Adora is covering your shifts. I also punched Hewitt—wish you could see his face now.

I looked up to see everyone watching me with varying degrees of curiosity and concern in their eyes. "You all can read it if you want."

I passed the note to the Captain, who read it and passed it along.

As Ink read the note, he raised an eyebrow at Jackrabbit, a sly grin on his face.

"Is Hewitt the same person as Jack?" he asked me.

I nodded and his grin grew wider. "So, if I'm reading this correctly, my other me punched the other you in the face, Jack. I can only imagine you deserved it."

"Or you could just be an asshole in her world, like you are here. Fara, I hate to even ask . . . but why would your friend punch other me?"

I didn't know how to answer him without telling him the whole truth. And I wasn't ready to talk about that yet with these people. I wasn't sure why I felt embarrassed by Hewitt's treatment of me, but I couldn't help but think it was somehow my fault.

"Well, the Hewitt in my world is a bit of a bully."

"If I'm an asshat, then I'm glad I got punched."

"I'm absolutely sure that whatever it was you did, I was right to punch you." Ink winked at me. I looked away, uncomfortable. Calum never winked or joked like that, and watching someone who shared his face wink and smirk and generally flirt with everyone was disconcerting.

"All right," the Captain said. "Now that we've established that Fara can open a portal to her friend's apartment, we need to plan the details of this rescue."

FARA 2

Watching the Team plan a rescue operation was like something out of a movie. It didn't seem real, and I couldn't believe that I was part of it—that I had instigated it. But I was. And I had. And I was scared. I pushed down the fear. I couldn't give in to it. Not yet.

They peppered me with questions about the security and the building where Barrington was keeping Jay, and I tried to answer as best I could. I had spent hours captive in the mansion that Barrington had commandeered, keeping vigil from my window in an effort to stay awake, telling myself that the information I was gathering would be useful when I escaped. It never came to that. I'd jumped through a portal instead. But that information might come in handy to these professional rescuers. I forced myself to talk, to tell them everything I'd seen when I was there: the grounds, the guard rotations, where Jay was, the house's layout, Agent Smith, and the rest of Barrington's security detail goons. Anything that I could think of. I didn't know what was important—I had never had to rescue someone before. It was completely new territory for me, but apparently not for them.

"How are the security armed? Swords? Daggers?" Blu asked.

"They all have guns," I replied, to which I received blank looks.

"We don't have those here," the Captain explained.

That surprised me, but then the daggers everyone carried, and Ink's two swords, which were casually leaning against the wall, made more sense. If they didn't have guns, then they had other ways of brutally killing each other. All of it sounded awful to me. "I honestly don't know enough about guns to be helpful, other than get out of the way if they start shooting at you."

They asked me to draw a floor plan as best as I could so they could choose the safest way to get into and through the mansion. When I started drawing the second floor, Blu walked to the bookcase on the other side of the office. She sifted through a bunch of rolled-up papers, bringing a big one back over to the table and laying it out flat.

"Fara, is this the basic layout of the house?"

What was she talking about? How could she have a blueprint of a house from my world? There was no way that was possible. I took a moment to look at the layout—it was exactly the same.

"How?"

"Holy shit, B . . . Those are the High Governor's blueprints!" Styx said.

"I know, I had to memorize them, which is why I recognized what Fara was drawing. I don't know how it's possible."

Jackrabbit laughed. "Who knew that you'd be breaking into the same building twice?"

I didn't know what they were talking about.

"How?" I repeated.

"Our girl Blu," Ink said as he ruffled her hair, "infiltrated a big Jurisdiction masquerade party to steal some of their secret stuff, and the party was held at the High Governor's mansion—which I'm assuming this is."

That couldn't be coincidence, could it? But I couldn't worry about it right now. Right now, we were going to rescue Jay. I could worry about this after. I could freak out then.

"There's a service entrance by the kitchens," she said, "and if you're right, Fara, then your agent is being held in the area where I found the blueprints. We can get in through there."

The Team spent the next hour discussing the rescue plan. The *mission*, they kept calling it. I answered their logistics questions as best as I could, but otherwise I kept quiet and ate my donut. This was so far outside of normal to me that I had to stifle an inappropriate laugh. I was going to open a portal to my own universe so that a bunch of assassins from a different universe (who happened to look like me and my friends) could rescue a government agent who I had kissed. What the hell was even happening?

When they seemed to feel comfortable with whatever details they needed for the mission, we all verbally agreed to the final plan, and the Captain dismissed everyone but me so they could retrieve the gear they needed. She asked that I remain in her office in order to stay hidden, at least for now, as she didn't want anyone to suspect anything before we jumped to my world. And since there was a mole wandering around, she couldn't be too careful.

"Blu," the Captain called as they walked out, "after you get your gear, please stop by the armory to get Fara a dagger and some clothes. I'm sure they have extras around."

A dagger? My heart sped up, but I pushed the fear down. We were an hour away from attempting to do something that a highly trained federal agent had failed—break into Barrington's temporary home. But I had something Jay didn't. I had this team.

⚡ ⚡ ⚡

Blu came striding back into the Captain's office and handed me a clanking burlap sack. I had no idea what to do with most of the items inside it.

"There's a bathroom over in the corner for you to change into your armor," the Captain said. "Don't worry about the rest of the items in your bag yet. Blu can help you with those."

"Armor?"

"Unfortunately," Blu said, "Drake didn't have any additional armor, so you're stuck with regular clothes. But considering you will be away from combat, I think it should be OK."

I didn't know whether or not to be relieved that I didn't have armor, so I added that to the list of things to worry about later, and I went into the bathroom to change. I pulled the clothes out of the sack, which included a pair of black cotton undies. While I was a bit weirded out by the idea of some armorer making this underwear—or weirder, that I was wearing someone else's underwear—I hadn't changed my clothes since before I went to the gym yesterday (was it only yesterday?), and beggars couldn't be choosers. The new shirt had a built-in bra, so I could finally stop wearing the sports bra that had permanently molded itself to my body. My leggings almost walked away on their own volition because they were so filthy, and the tank top I was wearing wasn't even mine. Was it from here? Was that bedroom somewhere near? As soon as that thought ran through my brain, I shut it down. I could wonder all sorts of things once Jay was safe.

"Don't hold the dagger like that. You'll hurt yourself," Blu said as I walked out of the bathroom.

I realized I was holding the dagger between two fingers like it was diseased. I looked ridiculous. I sighed. I would not allow myself to think that I was an idiot for trying to save Jay, even though I had zero experience with daggers or rescues or missions.

"Don't worry about it. Everyone has to start somewhere. Here, let me help you."

Blu walked over and showed me how to attach the sheath to the belt and then buckle it around my thigh. The sheath was on the very last notch. I prayed that it wouldn't cut off circulation to my feet. Even my thighs were betraying how out of place I was.

"Mine is on the last notch too," Blu said with a grin, like she was reading my mind. Maybe she was. We were the same person, theoretically. "I've complained to the armorer that women need strong legs to survive, so he should make these for people of all shapes. I mean, all shapes need to protect themselves, not only skinny people. He said he'd work on it when he had time."

As Blu was adding the finishing touches to my ensemble, Ink sauntered into the Captain's office, dressed in the same black armor as Blu, except that it was almost indecently snug against his chest and legs. What was it with men and wearing shirts that were three sizes too small? Not that I was complaining when Jay did it, or Ink for that matter, since they both looked like they could be underwear models. But still.

Ink caught me staring at him and raised a perfect eyebrow. With his swords and daggers and unreasonably tight shirt and his hair perfectly disheveled, he looked like some author's description of a sexy assassin. The urge to inappropriately giggle was almost overwhelming. Exhaustion and panic were getting to me.

"I see you're armed," Ink said after giving me a once-over.

"Blu had to help me figure out all of this stuff. I had no idea what most of it was, much less how to use it."

"We'll teach you how to use everything if you stick around, but for now we can't have you unarmed. Just remember if things go to shit, the pointy end goes into the bad guy." That last part earned him a snort from Blu.

"Hopefully, things won't go to shit, and I won't have to use it," I said.

"Things always go to shit."

BLU 3

I studied Fara as we got ready. She was standing in the corner of the Captain's office with her arms wrapped around herself, her shoulders slumped forward and her head down as she stared at the ground in front of her feet. It was the same posture I had seen from some of the people we rescued from Jurisdiction. It was the posture of someone who had been beaten down. I knew Barrington (or at least his minions) had traumatized her, but I didn't think that was all of it. What had she gone through to get to this point, to look like she was afraid of her own shadow?

To be honest, I was worried about how she was going to react to the stress of this mission. She was holding herself together better than I could imagine, but she'd never done something like this before. She had never held a dagger. Never taken someone's life. She was determined to get this agent back for whatever reason, and she thought she was ready to do that. I just hoped her inexperience wouldn't get her hurt.

I was also worried about the mission itself. We were going into a different universe, and they had technology and weapons that we weren't accustomed to. The unknown is what always got us into trouble, and there were thousands of unknowns with this mission. The one thing I took comfort in was that I somehow knew the layout of the building where they were holding the agent. In and of itself, it was fucking weird.

"Everyone has their orders," the Captain said, once we were all geared up and ready to go. "Remember: get in, get out, and no unnecessary heroics." She directed that last part to me. I didn't know how things worked in that other world, so I couldn't promise I wouldn't burn the place down if I needed to. I gave her a thumbs-up, and she shook her head.

"Fara, are you ready?"

"Yes." She closed her eyes, and a bizarre silver line emerged from her forehead. I took it to mean she was doing her portal thing.

"You can only see the portal from this side," she said, not taking her eyes off the space right in front of her. "I'll try to make it big enough for everyone to squeeze through, but you'll have to go through it from over here."

I got into position. "I'll go first." If her Calum was home, hopefully he wouldn't attack someone appearing out of thin air who looked like his best friend, although I couldn't imagine how he was going to respond to all of this. Without killing us, I hoped.

I stepped through the portal. It felt a bit like walking through a bubble. Was that the membrane I was feeling? I didn't have a clue. Regardless, I took a moment to marvel at the fact that I had just walked into a different universe. I was standing in an apartment in an entirely different world. It was not how I had planned to be spending my day, but it was entertaining nonetheless.

Before going further into the room, I gave the area a once-over to scan for potential threats, more out of habit than anything else. Once I'd established that nothing was going to stab me, I stepped aside and looked around the space. This apartment was much nicer than anything we lived in. Her Calum had taken the time to decorate it with art. There were pictures of people on the wall who I didn't recognize, and paints and colored pencils lying around. There were multiple rooms, and I was now standing in his living area.

Jack was making his way through the portal when a door opened to an adjoining room.

Standing in the doorway was Ink . . . but not Ink.

This guy was thinner, with longer hair that hung just past his chin. He was wearing cotton pants that hung on his hipbones, and he had tattoos across his chest and up both arms. Looking at Ink—but not Ink—was beyond strange. How was Fara keeping her cool about all this?

Ink-not-Ink saw me, and his eyes widened in surprise. He rushed over, pulling me into a crushing hug, my face pressed against his smooth skin. I was too startled to react, so I let him hug me, breathing in his scent of peppermint—which was different from how Ink smelled. Weird. Then, as if he finally recognized something was off (maybe I smelled different from Fara?) he really *looked* at my face.

"What?"

He turned to see Jack coming through the portal, so he released me and stalked over to Jack, grabbing him by the front of his shirt.

"What are you doing?"

Then he seemed to notice the portal as actual Ink came through, and Calum

shook his head in confusion.

"I'm fucking dreaming."

Ink stared at him but moved out of the way so that Fara had room to get through. The portal closed with a quiet hiss, and I watched Fara's composure completely crumble, a sob escaping her trembling lips. She ran the few feet that separated her from Calum, throwing herself into his open arms. She buried her head in his chest, sobs racking her body. He hugged her and kissed the top of her head as his eyes scanned us in bewilderment. He didn't say anything or make any sort of quip—which is what Ink would have done. After not even a full minute, Fara took a breath, and her sobs, her tears, her devastation . . . just disappeared. It was like the whole thing had never happened. All evidence of her breakdown was wiped away before our eyes.

"So, yeah. Sorry to barge in like this. Um . . . So . . . We have a lot to talk about, but not a lot of time."

"Why are there two of you, and why is Hewitt here? And why is there a guy who looks just like me?"

"I wouldn't say you look *just* like me," Ink drawled.

"Really? Now?" I rolled my eyes. He smirked at me.

Calum watched all of this with equal parts confusion and wariness.

"I know, it's all weird," Fara said, "and we don't have much time. The short version is that they are from a parallel universe, which is where I've been hiding out."

"You've been hiding in a parallel universe? How did you do that? What happened?"

"I escaped Barrington Park by accidentally opening a portal into another universe—the universe these guys live in," she said.

I saw this turning into a lengthy reunion, and time was already against us. That agent might not stay alive for long if Barrington's men were torturing him. I knew that because that had been me once. I cleared my throat.

"Hate to portal in and run, but we need to go, Fara."

Calum stared at me and blinked a couple of times.

Ink chuckled. "I keep thinking that we'll get used to it."

Calum finally tore his eyes away from us and looked at Fara. "What are you doing here? I got your note, and I thought that was the last time I'd hear from you, at least for a while. It's not safe here."

"Barrington captured Jay when he tried to rescue me. They tortured him so that I'd give them the device they think

I have, but Jay reminded me of my promise." A look passed between them that I couldn't grasp. Something of significance. "Like I said, I escaped through a portal I created by accident, and landed in this group. Literally. They've agreed to help me rescue Jay, since apparently they know how to do that sort of thing. It's super complicated and I promise that I'll tell you more when I can. And really, I'm sorry to barge in like this, but for some reason your apartment is where my ability opens the portals in this world."

He pulled her back into a hug, talking into her hair. "It's OK. I'm just so glad you're all right. When Adora told me you'd been kidnapped . . . "

He didn't finish. He didn't have to. We all knew that feeling, probably too well. We stood there awkwardly for a minute.

"So, all of it is real? You actually made it to another universe? We were right?"

"Yes, we were right. And for some reason, my abilities open to the world they live in. And obviously you are there, since he's standing right here, and Adora—but they call her Styx and she didn't come with us, and me . . . and Hewitt." Her voice hitched at the last part. "But we have to go before they kill Jay."

"You think they'll kill him?"

"That's why we're here. I can't let them kill Jay, Calum. I can't. So I need to ask you a huge favor. Since my car is at the gym, can you take us there? We need to get to where Barrington is holding Jay. If not, it's totally OK. We'll get an Uber."

Calum barked a laugh. "Fara, you can't get an Uber with you guys dressed like ninjas. You'll be arrested immediately. I'll drive."

She hugged him again. "Thank you."

"On one condition . . . You can't go."

We all stopped and stared at Calum.

"What?" she asked quietly.

"Fara, Agent Hanlon risked his life to keep you safe. You barely escaped, and seeing how bad you're banged up, Barrington obviously has no problem hurting you to get what he wants. You can't put yourself in danger of getting captured again. You promised me that you would run away and never come back. But you came back. You broke your promise."

"I came back because a good man is dying, and I need to do something about it! I have backup! These guys are assassins and warriors—"

"Which is why you should let them go, and stay here."

"What do *you* want to do, Fara?" Ink said. She looked at him, startled, like it had never occurred to her that she had a choice.

"I want to go."

"Fara, you know that—"

"The lady says she wants to go, so she'll go," Ink said. "Now the only question is, are you going to pout and make us find another way to get there, or are you going to help?"

The two Inks glared at each other, the moments ticking away.

"This is ridiculous," I said. "Fara, is there any other way to get to where we need to go?"

She picked up a piece of equipment from the table. It looked somewhat like a palmbox, but smaller and sleeker.

"How did you get my phone?" she said as she started to interact with the device in a series of swiping motions.

"Adora got it to me. What are you doing?"

"Getting an Uber." That unfamiliar word again. Some kind of transportation?

Calum sighed, pulling her into yet another hug. Apparently, they were huggers here. "Fine. I'll drive you, but I'm going with you."

"Fine," I said, heading for the door. "But we have to go. Now."

⚡ ⚡ ⚡

I looked around warily as we walked to Calum's car, which was parked on the street in front of his apartment building. It was dusk here, just as it would be back home, the sun about to drift behind the horizon. I scanned for minions as I searched the area, then stopped. They wouldn't be here. Jurisdiction didn't control this world yet. From what I understood, it was still a democracy. I wasn't alone. Jack and Ink were doing the same thing, as Calum and Fara walked without so much as looking up.

I stopped looking for threats and started taking it all in. We were on a beautiful, fully paved street, lined with large, well-maintained houses of varying colors and giant, old trees. The artificial lights on the streets were just blinking on, casting a soft glow on the tranquil scene. I could smell lilacs on the air. What would it be like to live on a quiet street like this? Could I live here? The answer didn't matter. I didn't. I couldn't. Not yet.

Everyone was quiet as we drove through the streets of the city, and I watched as the towering buildings, markets, and restaurants streamed past us. I was struck by how *whole* the city felt. It felt vibrant. Alive. There were no gaping holes in the scenery where Jurisdiction's weapons had destroyed this building or that. There was no rubble in the street, or burned-out, ancient cars cluttering the sidewalks. Here, old buildings were interspersed with new. The longer I looked, the angrier I became at the unfairness of it all—how Jurisdiction continued to rob our world of this serenity, this physical beauty.

And not only of the beauty, but of the peace as well. Fara and Calum weren't constantly scanning roofs or looking over their shoulders for minions. I had no idea what that sort of security felt like. I hoped that I would experience that feeling when we took down Jurisdiction. But first, the mission.

We left the city behind, and I watched the fields and trees slowly get lost in the shadows of the setting sun. I took a deep breath to ready myself for this mission, feeling Ink and Jack doing the same thing. It was time to get our game faces on. If my memory of the High Governor's mansion was correct, we were almost there. Ink must have read my mind.

"If the grounds are like the High Governor's mansion, we can park in the trees and make our way in from there," he said. "It's where I hid during your mission, Blu."

"We'll start there, then."

Fara looked out of the window, her face pale but determined. "That's good, because we're here."

BLU 4

We turned down a dirt road into a small forest. The rising full moon cast shadow and light through the budding trees. After a few bumpy minutes, Ink indicated that Calum should park his car off to the side. I estimated we were about a quarter mile from the house. We couldn't risk getting any closer to the mansion, for fear of someone noticing us, and without Styx hacking into cameras, we would be going in blind. I hadn't realized how much I relied on Styx's upbeat voice chirping in my ear during missions. How did teams in this world deal with it?

I completed my final gear check, and saw Ink watching Fara, his brow wrinkled with concern. His face smoothed out into his perma-smirk when she caught him staring.

"We'll go in, get your boy, and bring him back here," he said. "Jack and Calum will stay with you. Can you open a portal from here?"

"Yes."

Calum watched us all warily and generally stayed close to Fara. "When she opens a portal," he said, "both the government and Barrington will know she's here. I don't know shit about rescue missions, but the faster you can do this, the better chance we have to get her out of here."

"Understood. OK, Jack. You know what to do."

Jack nodded. His job was to protect Fara with his life, so there wasn't much to explain.

Fara walked up and showed me her phone. "You can use this to communicate with us." She held the phone and put her thumb on a special place on the back of it. "You have to unlock it with your thumbprint . . . My thumbprint . . . Whatever. Anyway, then hold it to your mouth and say 'Call Calum' and it will contact his phone."

I smiled to myself, thinking about how Styx would be drooling over this tech, even though I personally would much prefer an ear comm. It was better than nothing, so I put the phone next to my palmbox. We were as ready to go as we could be.

"You guys," Fara said, looking between all of us, "I don't know how to thank you enough. Please, *please*, be careful. The big guy is a real asshole and likes hurting people, so watch out for him. I couldn't live with myself if any of you were hurt because of this. Because of me."

"My sweet Fara," Ink purred, "we will return, and I promise not to get the other you killed." He started a slow lope toward the building. "Come on, B. We need to rescue Fara's boy toy."

"Come back in one piece and try not to burn the place down," Jack said.

"I'm not making promises."

⚡ ⚡ ⚡

I caught up to Ink, who was crouching in the tree line on the edge of the mansion's lawn, surveying the huge open space that separated us from where we needed to be. Even though most of the interior of the mansion was dark, the grounds were flooded in security lighting, which was obviously a problem.

The other problem was the layout of the open space itself—it was a type of garden, filled with flower beds, sculpted shrubs, and brick walkways, but not one place to hide.

And then there were the guard patrols. Fara had told us that there were between two and five minutes between their rotations. Timing our mad dash to the mansion was going to be tricky.

We waited for the guards to pass one more time, then ran to the mansion, crouching low and staying as close to the hedges and shrubs as we could. When we reached the end of the garden, I sprinted to the door, Ink right behind me. He placed his palmbox next to the only camera in sight, initiating the disabling program. The camera made a popping sound and started to smoke. We wouldn't have much time at all before someone came to see why it wasn't working, but hopefully it would give us the opportunity to get in.

Ink kept watch while I unlocked the door with my palmbox and opened it a crack. I pulled a dagger from its sheath and we slid into the darkness. At the High Governor's mansion, this door led to an alcove just outside of the kitchen, but in this world the door could lead to just about anywhere. I was hoping that the weird coincidence universe thing was watching out for us and this was the right spot, but rescues tended to be shitshows.

My eyes adjusted to the dimness. We were standing in a small alcove like I had hoped, with an open door to a hallway. Ink reached up and disabled the camera with his palmbox as I inched forward and peered into the hall. The lights were low, as though the staff had already left for the day, and it made the place seem eerie. Maybe my feeling of dread was less from spooky lighting and more because the last time I was here, that crazy bitch Dagna almost captured me. I reminded myself that even though other horrible people were in this building (i.e., Barrington Park), her specific version of horrible wasn't. At least that was something.

Our boots were silent on the carpet as we crept down the hallway, looking for any sign of the agent. According to Fara, he was last seen in one of the rooms in this area. We just needed to find out which one. I peeked around the corner into the next hallway, and immediately knew where he was. The giant security guy who I recognized from the High Governor's party was standing in front of the door of the room where I'd stolen Jurisdiction's blueprints from. Of course it was him, and of course it was that room. I shook my head to focus. I didn't have time to marvel at the strangeness of it all. That this guy would be the same giant asshat security guard in both worlds was weirdly not that surprising. In a way, I was glad it was him. After the way he leered at my ass the last time I saw him, I was actually going to enjoy smacking him around. Quietly. With my boot.

The goon started talking to himself . . . but not actually talking to himself. He was talking into some sort of comm thing. I motioned to Ink that we had incoming, and he nodded to my palmbox, flattening himself against the wall. He would grab the goon and I'd disable him as we had done so many times before. Ink smiled and winked at me. Game time.

Ink grabbed the goon as he rounded the corner, and they struggled for a moment. I stood to the side, trying to find my opening to stun him, when there was a huge percussive noise and the wall next to my head exploded.

"Gun!"

Understanding flashed across Ink's face as he grabbed the goon's arm that was holding the gun in an attempt to disarm him. The world exploded again as they struggled, plaster from the ceiling raining down on my head. I had to disable this guy before he brought the whole house down on top of us. I didn't want to kill him, but it might come to that.

"Get him to stop shooting at me!"

"I'm trying . . . but maybe you could . . . stop standing there and . . . help."

I rolled my eyes at him as he forced the goon to drop the gun. The goon twisted around, putting his forearm around Ink's neck and squeezing. Ink struggled to get away, his face turning red in his effort to breathe. I was now officially pissed off at this stupid guy. He was trying to kill us, and if I read between the lines, he had given Fara her bruises. He was going down.

I had to get access to the goon's skin for the stun program to work, and since he was covered in a full suit and gloves, I'd have to settle for his neck. Unfortunately, this guy was at least a foot taller than I was, with barely any neck to be seen—a neanderthal in a jacket, more or less. I needed height to reach him, so I did what any other short girl would do in the same situation: I ran and jumped on his back with a whoop, wrapping my arms around his barely visible neck and squeezing. My attempt luckily had the desired effect. He paused as he tried to determine which of us was more of a threat—the guy he was strangling or the girl on his back. He mistakenly thought Ink was more dangerous and kept his attention on killing him, which gave me my opening to pull down the collar of his shirt and zap him with the palmbox.

Nothing happened. The brute was too big.

"Blu, I don't mean to whine, but can you get this damn guy off me?"

I grabbed the goon's shirt collar with my teeth and yanked, giving me more skin to work with, and pushed the palmbox against it, sending additional disabling juice into his system. At last, his arm loosened enough from around Ink's neck that he was able to twist free and grab me before I fell with the goon, who crumpled to the ground. We surveyed the carnage around us but couldn't dwell on it; the whole house had probably heard the commotion. So much for stealth.

"Thanks for the assist," Ink said wryly as he grabbed the gun.

"Anytime."

I opened the lock on the door with my palmbox and peered in, dagger drawn. I hoped there were no other guards. Through the dim light I saw something that was worse than guards. So much worse. Sitting in a chair behind the single table in the room was a man who had so many injuries that I couldn't catalog them all at once. He had been beaten and tortured within an inch of his life . . . if he was even still alive. His head hung limp and he didn't even look up when we entered. As I grabbed his wrist to check for a pulse, I sighed with relief, such as it was. He was alive, barely.

Ink kept a lookout, and I worked with my palmbox to unlock the shackles around his wrists. The fingers on his left hand stuck out at odd angles. They had been broken, maybe multiple times. I had to swallow the bile that raced up from my stomach—whether Dagna was in this world or not, this was the work of a monster.

I was kneeling down to remove the chains on his ankles when his eyes snapped open, locking onto me, cool and gray.

Even with his battered face, I would recognize those eyes anywhere.

"Fara? What are you doing here?" he croaked.

"Jyston?" I whispered.

"Only my mother calls me that," he said, his eyes never leaving mine. "How did you learn my name? And what happened to your hair?" He reached to touch my face and I let him, too stunned to move. My brain was unable to process what I was seeing. His face and body were battered, and his hair was shorter, but this was the Second Counselor. Fara's agent was Jyston. What . . . the . . . actual . . . fuck?

"It's a long story, my friend, but for another time," Ink said, hauling Jyston-not-Jyston to his feet. If Ink recognized Jyston, he didn't say anything.

"Calum? What the hell?" He got his feet under him and took a tentative step, wincing.

"Less talk, more running," I said. I strained to hear if anyone was coming. It wouldn't be long before we were trapped. "Can you walk?"

"Yeah."

I looked at him doubtfully, sure something in his leg or foot was broken. Ink handed him the gun, which he took in his non-mangled hand with a nod as he limped toward the door. The voices were getting closer.

"OK," he said. "I'll try to protect you both, but Fara, you cannot get caught. I didn't just go through all of this to have you back in this dickhead's clutches."

"I'm not Fara. And that's not Calum."

"What?"

"It's a really long story, but believe me when I say that we can take care of ourselves." I pulled the daggers from their sheaths and Ink took out his swords.

The agent looked surprised, at least as surprised as he could look with his face all banged up and puffy. "OK, then," he said. "Whoever you are, let's go."

We ran down the corridor. The agent kept up with us, barely. I wasn't sure how far he could get on his own. We ran past the kitchens and turned in to the alcove. I could hear shouting on the other side of the door, but I didn't think that the voices were close enough to catch us. Yet. I pushed open the door, looked both ways, and started to run toward the trees. I turned to see Ink helping the agent along.

"Get back to Fara!" Ink yelled. I glared at him. The mission was to get this agent guy back to our world, and I was going to see it through. I ran back and put the agent's other arm over my shoulder.

"Just leave me and go," the agent said through gritted teeth. His voice even sounded like Jyston's, deep and rumbling but without the teasing tone.

"No fucking way. I am not going to be the person to tell Fara we left you here."

"She's here?"

"Yes, and so is Calum, so let's get a move on."

"I told her not to come back for me," he said. "What was she thinking? I told her not to come back."

"Yeah, well, you're not the boss of her," I said. "Plus, if it weren't for her, you'd still be getting tortured. So shut up and run."

We had just made it to the edge of the garden when they started shooting at us.

We hit the dirt, covering our heads as the metal projectiles flew by, destroying the hedges and flowers around us.

"We need to make it to the trees," Ink said to the agent between gunfire bursts.

"There are two shooters," the agent said. "Stay still and let them come closer so I can take them out." He slowly rolled over. He was breathing heavy now, a bright red spot slowly spreading from his shoulder. He'd been shot. How the hell was this guy even still alive?

"When I say run, run," the agent said quietly.

"I'm not leaving you here, so stop the heroics," I said.

"You won't be, since I'll be running with you, but I can't have you behind me. I need a clear shot."

Over my shoulder, I could see two figures running in our direction. At least a half dozen others were pouring out of the house and heading our way. We had to go.

The seconds ticked by, and I started to worry that the agent had passed out. I took a furtive look at him. He was lying perfectly still, watching the men approach with the same sort of predatory calm Jyston had. Was this what the Second Counselor was like in a battle?

"Run!" he whispered. Ink and I sprang to our feet and sprinted for the trees. The agent flipped to his knees, and in one quick motion raised the gun and shot at the two goons closest to us. One of them dropped to the ground, part of his head missing, gore and blood exploding everywhere. The other had been shot somewhere, but it didn't even slow him down. He raised his gun and aimed it at the agent, who was desperately trying to get to his feet.

He wasn't going to make it.

Reacting purely on reflex, I flipped my dagger and threw it end over end right into the goon's eye, dropping him to the ground. His shots went wide and whizzed by us, close enough that I could hear them. Did I have time to retrieve my dagger? It was sticking like a flag out of the goon's eye socket. Probably not. I was going to miss that one. The agent stared at me, stunned.

"Who are you?" he asked.

I kept running. He'd find out soon enough, and I was still having a hard time processing who he was.

Ink ran back to help the agent, and the three of us made it to the tree line. I grabbed Fara's phone, did what she'd showed me, and the phone started making a ringing noise.

"Hello?" said Calum's voice. He was breathing hard, and I could hear commotion in the background.

"Fara needs to open the portal and you need to drive away. Goons incoming."

"Goons already here. Do you have Agent Hanlon?"

"Yes, but he's not going to make it unless we get him back to the infirmary at the Compound."

I heard more yelling. Then the phone went silent. The agent fell, and I ran back to him. Ink and I tried to get him back to his feet.

"You can't pass out now. We're so close. Fara's opening a portal right now to get us out of here."

"Can't . . . open portal . . . Will show . . . her location," he panted and tried to stand. Ink got him under one shoulder, and the agent winced.

"Well, we just need to get to her before they do," I said, putting my arm around his waist. "Once she's back in our world, we'll all be safe. Plus, you can't die now. She seems to have a thing for you, even though you're bossy."

"She calls me bossy too," he said with a grimace, and got back to his feet. Ink and I helped him hobble along, stumbling through the trees, and I sent a little request to the universe that the agent make it back to the rest of the group. We didn't come all this way just for this guy to die, but at the rate we were going, he might not make it. Then I heard a high-pitched scream.

Fara.

Ink dropped the agent so fast that I staggered under his weight. He raced toward the noise.

"Oh my god. Fara," the agent said. He tried to limp faster. "Leave me! Go help her."

"For fuck's sake! Can you please stop with the martyr act? It's annoying. My mission is to retrieve you alive and bring you back with me. I'm not leaving you, so save your breath and help me get to her faster."

"You sound . . . so much . . . like her."

We broke through the trees into a scene of utter chaos. I counted at least five bodies lying on the ground, blood everywhere. I quickly scanned them. None of the bodies were ours, although there were injuries. Both Jack and Calum had moved into defensive positions in front of Fara. Jack's cast was shredded on the ground and his arm hung limply by his side. Calum had a dagger in his hand, blood running down into his eyes. Not twenty feet away, Ink was wiping his daggers on his pants, while stepping toward Fara, two dead goons at his feet.

But what struck me was Fara. She was staring at Ink as he strode toward her and was shaking so violently that I was afraid she was going to collapse. At her feet, a body lay twitching, smoke rising from it. I could see the silver string from her head in the moonlight, which meant that there was a portal in front of her, but it was faint. She didn't even seem to notice that we were there as she stared at Ink.

"Fara, the portal!" I yelled, and she looked away from Ink, her eyes barely registering. Then she saw the agent limping along with me, and she ran to him, throwing her arms around him. He winced but hugged her back as best as he could.

"Oh my god, Jay. Oh my god. What did they do to you?" She started sobbing.

"Shhh . . . I'm OK, I'm OK," the agent said over and over while she sobbed into his chest.

Ink walked up to her and gently grabbed her shoulder. The agent stared at him warily, not letting her go.

"Fara, I don't mean to be a dick, but he needs to get to the infirmary, and we need to escape. Open the portal." Ink sounded almost apologetic. Well, at least apologetic for him.

"Sorry. OK," she hiccupped. I could hear the voices getting closer. The silver string got stronger.

"Calum," I said quietly, "you need to go now."

"I'm coming with you," he said.

"No. You can't. Not yet. It's a long story, but please believe me that we need you here. She needs you here."

"She's hurt!"

Fara was clutching her forearm, blood soaking a sweatshirt she hadn't been wearing before. Her face, however, was determined.

"We'll get her patched up when we get back. Please," I said, grabbing his hands in mine—it was what I did with Ink when I needed him to stop messing around and listen to me. He started, then looked down into my eyes. Up close I could see that his eyes were the same as Ink's, but softer somehow and lacking the impish mischief. "Please," I repeated. "We need you here, and you can't get caught. I'll take care of her. We all will. I promise."

The voices of the goons were getting louder. He searched my face for a second, nodded once, then started jogging toward his car.

"It's ready. Everyone, come behind me," Fara said. Her face was getting paler, but her jaw was clenched in determination.

Ink grabbed the agent, and I wrapped my arm around Jack's waist, being careful not to touch his broken wrist.

"Never a dull moment," he said through gritted teeth.

"What happened?" Whatever had gone down here had freaked everyone out.

"Let's get out of here, and then I'll tell you," he said.

We stepped behind Fara to see the Captain's office through the window, and one by one we walked through the portal. As I took one last look backward, I saw a face appear as the window shut—icy blue eyes full of rage and disbelief. We locked eyes when he tried to reach through, and I heard Fara gasp as the window closed with a hiss.

"That was Barrington Park" was all she said before wobbling and passing out.

FARA 5

Earlier

One minute Ink and Blue were there, and the next they had melted into the trees, toward the mansion. How did they even do that? How does a person train to be invisible? I had a lot to learn.

I snuck a glance at Calum. I couldn't even begin to explain how glad I was that he was here, although I was still pissed that he'd almost convinced me not to come. I knew that he was trying to protect me, and I appreciated it, but I needed to be here. He caught me looking at him, and came over to give me a hug.

"What are you thinking?" he said into my hair. I breathed him in and took strength from his warmth.

"It's complicated."

"Try me." I shrugged. He sighed. "I worried for my whole shift after Adora told me what happened. Which is why I punched Hewitt, by the way."

"I want to hear this," Jack said with a grin.

Calum didn't look amused. "He said something lewd about Fara staying with me. I just lost my shit and punched him."

"Good," I said and meant it.

"Douche threatened to fire me, but I got that fixed. And then I found a note from you saying you're all right. How did you even do that?"

"I had to let you know I was safe. I was so worried about you."

"About me? Shit, I'm fine. As long as you don't come back here again."

I pulled free of his arms, rolling my eyes. "I don't plan to." We weren't going to have this conversation again. "At least not until I get this ability under control. Especially now that Barrington knows I don't need a palmbox to open a portal."

"A palmbox?"

"It's what we've been calling the device. My mom figured out it came from a different universe. *Their* universe. Barrington created it."

"What? Barrington is from a different universe too?"

I told him everything that I had learned from the Captain, and Barrington himself. "And he . . ." I took a shuddering breath, not wanting to say the next words out loud. "He caused my parents' deaths, Calum."

"Are you sure?"

"He admitted it."

He put his arm around me and squeezed, his presence helping my frayed nerves. "I'm so sorry."

I couldn't respond without crying, so I didn't. The wind picked up in the trees, sending a chill down my arms. As grateful as I was for the clean clothes, they weren't warm. I stole a look at Jack, who didn't seem to be bothered by the cold. Was there training for that too? Or was it just that they were so used to wearing this gear that the cold didn't affect them?

Calum took off his hoodie and gave it to me.

"I'm OK."

"You're shivering."

"But you'll be cold if you don't have it."

Calum deflated right in front of me. The arm that was holding out the sweatshirt dropping limply to his side. He turned away.

"What? What's wrong?"

He was quiet for a moment. "I don't know how to help you."

"What are you talking about?"

"I don't know how to help you with this. All of this! I promised to keep you safe, and they still kidnapped you. Then you escaped to this magical other world where everyone dresses and talks like they're from some sort of *Mission Impossible* movie, without ever really explaining what's going on. You have a knife or dagger or whatever on your leg, for fuck's sake! Not to mention that there's now two of you and two of me and two of Hewitt. All I want is for you to be safe, but I don't know where to even begin, and you keep pushing away any attempts to help."

I took the sweatshirt and put it on. It was warm and smelled of him.

"Calum, I appreciate that you're trying to help me and protect me. I really do, but I had to come with them. I had to. Jay was captured because he tried to rescue me. It's all my fault."

"It's not your fault, Fara." I jumped. I had almost forgotten that Jack was there. He was so quiet, standing with almost preternatural stillness. His brown hair was blowing gently in the breeze, his dark eyes intensely watching the trees where Blu and Ink had gone. "It's not your fault," he repeated quietly. "Your agent friend made his own decision to come rescue you, and Barrington chose to capture him. You didn't choose to be kidnapped. It's not your fault."

I didn't respond, because I didn't agree, but I also didn't want to get into it with him right then. Even though he wasn't Hewitt, and even though he had been nothing but kind to me since I appeared, it was going to take a while not to recoil every time I saw him. To remind myself that he wasn't going to grab my ass or trap me in The Grill's break room, trying to stick his tongue down my throat. In their world, Jack was one of the good guys.

He gave me a sad smile.

"He's right," Calum said. "It's not your fault, Fara. But I'm still struggling to understand that there is this mythic bad guy who is stockpiling weapons from other worlds so that he can invade us here, in our world."

"He's not mythic," Jack said. "Ink watched as his parents were tortured. Blu was tortured. The Counselor is a horrible person."

Blu was tortured? That dislodged something in my memory, but as soon as it made its way to the surface, it was gone.

"Barrington is just as much of a horror," I said, remembering the sound of bones cracking as they smashed Jay's fingers with the hammer. "It sounds like a movie, Calum, but this is real."

Calum gently grabbed my face and looked into my eyes. "Then you can't stay there, either. It's not safe. You're my friend, and I can't stand the thought of you getting hurt."

"It's not about you, man," Jack said quietly.

"What was that?" Calum's voice was icy, but Jack didn't seem disturbed by it at all.

"I said, it's not about you. It's not about what you can stand or what you can take. Making her feel guilty for wanting what she wants is an asshole move."

"What would you know about it? You don't even know her!"

Jack just shrugged, continuing his watch of the forest beyond. I wrapped my arms around myself, trying to stop the thrum of dread that had made itself at home in my chest. Not that I didn't appreciate what Jack was trying to do—

because I did. And not that I didn't understand where Calum was coming from—because I did. But I hated this, all of this. Maybe Calum was right. I shouldn't be here.

⚡⚡⚡

We had been sitting in the clearing for what seemed like hours, even though logically I knew it hadn't been that long. The full moon cast deceptive shadows in the trees. The smell of pine and dirt floated on the cool breeze, and an owl called out in the distance. In any other circumstance, I would think this night was beautiful. But tonight I was filled with trepidation.

"How much long—"

Jackrabbit held up his hand, listening. I couldn't hear anything other than the wind through the tops of the trees.

He jumped to his feet. My heart started to race. Someone was coming, and it wasn't someone we wanted to see. I could feel myself starting to curl up like a ball, my arms wrapping around myself involuntarily. I wasn't ready for this.

Jackrabbit walked up to me. It looked like he was going to grab my arm, and I flinched, memories of Hewitt pushing their way forward. He dropped his hands to his sides. "Fara, take a deep breath. You can do this. Do what you have to, so you don't get caught. They won't hesitate, and neither should you."

I worked on calming my breathing as he'd suggested, wrestling the dagger out of my sheath. I tried to find my little fire deep in my gut, but I couldn't focus enough to feel it. It didn't matter. The baddies were coming whether I was ready or not.

Jackrabbit unstrapped a dagger one-handed and gave it to Calum. "Know how to use it?"

"Stick the pointy end in the bad guy?"

"Good enough for me. When they show up, do not hesitate. Kill them."

The dagger trembled in my hand. I would fight with everything that I had to not get captured. I would not let them take me. I would not let them use me to take over my world. I would do whatever it took to protect myself, and my friends. I told myself that over and over, clenching my fists until they started to tingle. I shook them out, afraid I would lose my grip on the dagger, but the tingling became more pronounced. Then the hair on my arms started to stand up, as though I was near electricity. Weird.

"Can anyone else feel that?" I asked.

"Feel what?" Calum asked.

"Like there's electricity around here somewhere."

They both shook their heads. Apparently it was just me. The feeling got stronger, uncomfortable rather than painful. I was only able to think about it for a second more before two men in suits came through the trees, holding guns in front of them. One was Agent Johnson, the chattier of the two goons who kidnapped me. Shit.

He turned to the other suit. "I'll get the girl, you kill the other two. Mr. Park wants her alive."

The other goon gave Agent Johnson a curt nod and raised his handgun, aiming at Jack. Agent Johnson walked toward me. My feet refused to move. I watched the chaos unfold around me, unable to run like Calum yelled for me to do, rooted to the spot in fear. Calum launched himself at Agent Johnson, who sidestepped him with ease, using Calum's own momentum to toss him into a tree. He hit the trunk with a sickening crunch. The look of pain on Calum's face was enough to start my feet moving—not away, but toward him.

Agent Johnson grabbed me as I tried to reach my friend. Panicking, I swung my dagger with all of my might, hoping that I would hit him somewhere squishy with the pointy end. He dropped his gun to catch my arm before I could stab him, and wrenched the dagger from me, slicing Calum's sweatshirt and my arm in the process. He dropped the dagger on the ground and tried to twist me around so that my back was held against his chest. I fought with everything I could, kicking and hitting. I barely registered that I was bleeding. I didn't know how deep the cut was on my arm. I didn't have time to care. I stomped on the insole of the goon's foot as hard as I could, but that didn't seem to slow him down. The panic was rising. My friends were going to die and it was all for nothing. Barrington Park was going to get me.

I heard the loud bang of a gunshot. Jackrabbit rolled out of the way, and the bullet hit his cast, which exploded into pieces that floated to the ground. Pain registered on Jackrabbit's face as his arm hung limp at his side, but he kept going, slicing down on the second goon's wrist with his dagger to force him to drop the gun. The goon looked up in surprise when Jack plunged his dagger into his stomach, dropping him to his knees. Jackrabbit pulled the dagger out and stabbed him again, this time in the heart. He kicked the gun away. The goon made gurgling noises as he bled to death on the ground. Jackrabbit scanned the area. In the middle of the mayhem, Calum's phone rang. It distracted Agent Johnson just enough for me to break free of his grip.

Calum groggily answered, said something, then hung up.

"Fara, you need to start the portal. They're on their way."

"How in the hell am I supposed to do that?" Johnson had caught me by the wrist. I pulled away with all my might.

Another goon in a suit came out of the trees. He began shooting at Jackrabbit. Agent Johnson used the moment to yank me toward him. He released my wrist, reaching to grab me in a bear hug again.

No.

I put both of my hands on Agent Johnson's chest. I was not going to let him get me. I would not work for them—I'd die instead. The crackling sensation in my hands intensified as I pushed him as hard as I could. Like a thousand shards of glass streaming through my skin, a bolt of electricity shot out through my hands, into his chest. I screamed.

Agent Johnson dropped to the ground, smoke and the smell of burnt hair and flesh rising from his body.

"What the fuck?" was all the third guy got out before Jackrabbit slit his throat, dropping the goon's body to the ground without a second look.

I looked at my hands in fear. The crackling sensation was gone, as was the pain. What the fuck? was right.

"You need to open the portal," Jackrabbit said. I forced myself to concentrate.

"Over here!" I heard someone yell. Jackrabbit and Calum stood in front of me, daggers raised.

More goons emerged from the trees. I heard some sort of commotion, but I couldn't see what it was. Then one goon dropped to the ground. The other looked around in a panic. "Show yourself!" he yelled.

"If you say so."

Focused on opening the portal, I couldn't see what happened, and I was glad to miss it. Then Ink was stepping over the goons' dead bodies and walking toward us, wiping his daggers on his pants. At that moment, with his hair tousled and blood-spattered, looking at me with an intensity that left me breathless, it firmly separated him from Calum in my mind. He was deadly. And he was on my side. He stalked toward me, cataloging every inch of me for injuries. Every nerve in my body was vibrating and felt exposed.

His eyes scanned me, then landed on Agent Johnson, still smoking at my feet. Ink raised one perfect eyebrow in question. I was about to explain when I saw Blu stumbling through the trees, half dragging someone with her.

Jay.

6 BLU

Ink was the first to reach Fara when she hit the floor of the Captain's office. He'd unceremoniously dropped the agent into a chair on the way, and the agent slumped onto the table, unconscious.

The Captain commed Styx as she got up from her desk. "We have an emergency. We need medics to my office immediately. One severely injured, two only slightly less so."

She made her way to the agent and checked his wrist for a pulse. "What happened?" she asked.

"To Fara? I don't know yet," I said. "But you can tell what happened to him. Jurisdiction happened."

She shook her head sadly. She took some scissors and started gently cutting the agent's shirt off. He didn't budge.

"He's in bad shape," I said. He wasn't the only one. Ink was talking softly to Fara, trying to wake her, while Jack leaned precariously in a chair, looking as if he were about to pass out too. We were all a mess.

"He wouldn't have lasted much longer if you hadn't rescued him." She paused her cutting and looked at me. "You are aware of who this is, I'm sure."

I was, although I didn't want to think about it. "What do you think it means?"

The Captain quietly snipped at the fabric. "I think it means that your gut instincts about Jyston may not be that far off. I know that they are not the same person, but they might have some overlapping qualities."

I wasn't sure what I was more afraid of—whether she was right, or whether she was wrong.

"Damnit!" Ink said. "She won't wake up."

"She did some pretty crazy stuff today," Jack said. "It might have worn her out."

The Captain's eyes met Jack's. "Tell me."

"I didn't see it all, but one of Barrington's assholes grabbed her. She screamed and it was like she electrocuted him by touching him. He started convulsing and dropped to the ground. That's in addition to opening multiple portals."

Everyone was quiet. What did that mean? Could Fara do things other than open a portal? I didn't have time to contemplate that question. Styx came rushing into the Captain's office with a bunch of medics trailing behind. I was surprised to see Sage enter last with a gurney, calm as ever. He was dressed as a medic instead of in his trainee gear. After Jurisdiction killed his husband, he had asked if he could leave the infirmary and train to be on the Team. He'd been training with us in the mornings, or more accurately, with the others in the mornings. I skipped most days.

"We're short-staffed tonight, so I'm filling in," he said.

"And we are grateful, Sage," the Captain said as the medic team reached her. Only Sage recoiled when he saw the agent's face. No one else seemed to recognize him.

"I cannot in good faith keep the Second Counselor in the infirmary at the Compound. It places the other patients, and our staff, in danger," he whispered.

"This is not who you think it is," the Captain replied. "I will explain later. For now, we'll say he's the Second Counselor's family member, and a defector. It's not that far from the truth."

Sage looked like he was about to argue but the Captain raised her hand. "This gentleman may be what we need to take Jurisdiction down. I will explain everything tonight, I promise. But we need him alive."

Sage looked skeptical, but he and another medic carefully grabbed Jyston-not-Jyston and loaded him onto the gurney as two other medics came in with another gurney.

"We'll need one more," the Captain said.

"We don't have any more," the medic replied. "They're all being used. Jurisdiction has been worse than usual today."

Jack started to get up. "I'll be fine." But he staggered.

"Put Jack on the gurney, even though he'll fight about it," Ink said. He gently scooped Fara up from the ground and headed out with her cradled in his arms.

I followed him up the path from the Captain's office, taking the shortcut through the Quad toward the infirmary. He was silent, staring straight ahead with the occasional glance down to the girl in his arms, and walking so fast that I had to jog to keep up with him. The Compound was quiet and dark, the full moon shining down from a cloudless sky. Ink marched on.

"Do you need help?"

He shook his head, his mouth pressed in worry. I was worried too. I'm no expert, but I imagine frying someone with your bare hands can't be that good for you. Plus, if the state of her sweatshirt was any indication, she'd lost a lot of blood.

The infirmary was in chaos. The medics hadn't been kidding about the above normal activity. Ink walked directly up to a medic who was in the middle of talking to someone else and interrupted her. She glared at him for a moment before registering who he was, and that he was carrying a person in his arms.

"This way." She led us back through the curtains to the surgery rooms. Ink gently put Fara on the bed the medic indicated, but didn't back away.

"She has a stab wound to her arm and other injuries unknown," he said to the medic, still crowding the bed.

"Ink?" He didn't respond to me. I grabbed his arm and pulled, but he shook me off, grabbing the medic instead.

"You will fix her, understand? She will not die."

The medic looked at Ink, worry on her face. Then she saw me and did a double-take. "But she. . . But you. . ."

I grabbed Ink again, this time not letting go. "They need to get near her to help her, Ink. You have to come with me."

He shook himself, then stalked out toward the waiting room as the medics took over.

7 FARA

I woke up in a strange room. It was dark, and there was a portal in front of my face, again. I recognized Calum's apartment through the portal, again. There was another swan note on the table. I reached through, gasping at the pain that shot through my arm. Man, that hurt like a bitch. And I was really light-headed. I tried to sit up.

Where was I? The last thing I remembered was seeing Barrington's face as I went through the portal. I felt my panic rise, and the portal got bigger. Grasping the note, I pulled my arm back and sank into bed, the portal closing with a hiss.

I stared at the note for a moment, not really seeing it, as I tried to figure out what had happened. I was dizzy and my arm throbbed. Those two things were new. I was in a hospital bed and wearing a hospital gown. I guess when they said "infirmary" I'd imagined those tiny Urgent Care clinics. I didn't realize that it was the real deal. How long had I been here?

I opened the note carefully. It only had one line on it.

"Please let me know you're OK. —C."

I looked around for something to write with. There was a pen next to my bed. I stretched to reach it, my arm throbbing. I turned the paper over and wrote on the back.

"I'm OK. Will write as soon as I know more. Stay safe. It seems inadequate to say it, but thank you."

I focused and reopened the portal. It was even easier to do it this time, maybe because my life was just that much more fucked than it had been—if that was even possible.

After I put the note back on the table and closed the portal, I lay there and let the events replay in my mind. Calum was hurt because of me. Jack too. I'd flambéed some goon—what the hell was that about? Ink and Blu had found Jay.

Jay.

I jolted upright and as the wave of dizziness hit me, I nearly threw up. I forced my bare feet to hit the floor. I had to make sure he was OK.

I stood on wobbly legs, holding onto the side of the bed. I took a second to steady myself, the breeze catching my backside . . . which was exposed. Ah yes, hospital gown.

"Although this has been thoroughly entertaining, I have to wonder where you're headed."

I yelped and almost tipped over. A strong arm grabbed my waist, and I took a deep breath, catching the faint smell of cologne. Ink was looking down at me, complete with a perma-smirk.

"Uh, hi?" I squeaked.

"Hi," he said. He didn't release my waist.

I took a step back, my legs catching on the edge of the bed, making me sit down with a plunk.

Ink backed up and sat down in a chair in the corner. He propped his ankle on his knee, watching me with that damn smirk on his face, his green eyes bright and tired. He looked exhausted.

"How long have I been in here?"

"Two days."

"Oh my god. What happened?"

"I was hoping you could tell me."

"Is everyone OK?"

"Relatively speaking."

I frowned at him. "What does that mean?"

He chuckled. "Jack's wrist is back in a cast after he rudely rebroke it by being shot. Blu is fine, but worried, although she'd never admit it."

"You're OK?"

"Do you care?"

"Of course I care! You risked your life to help me."

He ran his hand through his hair. "Well, then I'm fine."

We looked at each other, me wondering why he was here, and him . . . I honestly couldn't tell what he was thinking. Another moment ticked by, and I became acutely aware that I was still in a hospital gown. I wrapped my arms around myself.

"I need clothes."

"Where are you going?"

"I need to find Jay to see if he's—"

"He's all right, Fara. He was awake earlier and asked about you."

I stood up, then abruptly sat back down, not wanting to show Ink my goods.

"Can you tell me what happened?" he asked quietly. I looked around for something to wear. There were clothes neatly folded in the corner, which seemed to include Calum's sweatshirt. Ink rose and handed them to me.

I stood up and wobbled. Ink grabbed my waist again.

"Hang on there, speedy. You need to take it easy. Although, if you keep tipping over, that means I get to keep hanging on to you like this."

I tried to stand again.

"Well, if you're determined to hurt yourself, then I'm not going to stop you."

Although he was smirking while he held my waist, his eyes looked worried. I sat back down.

"How long have you been here?"

"Two days, give or take."

"You've been here the whole time?"

"Blu, Styx, and I took turns. Jack would have, but he's on bed rest too."

"You didn't have to do that."

He sat next to me on the bed. "So, what happened?"

"I don't know what happened," I whispered, afraid to talk about it out loud. "I felt this crackling sensation start right after Jack told us someone was coming. At first, I thought there was a storm because the hair on my arms was standing up, and it felt like the air does before lightning strikes. When the goon grabbed me to take me back with him, I pushed him and I felt this electric shock shoot through my hands. And it hurt really bad. And the next thing I knew, the goon was down and you were walking toward me . . . "

I put my head in my hands, not knowing where to look or what else to say. The portal ability was really weird, but my mom had that. This . . . What was this, even?

"Do you remember waking up?"

"Just now? Yeah. I accidentally opened a portal."

"You did that a bunch while you were out."

"What?"

He nodded. Well, shit.

"Sage saw one, so he knows who you really are. He also knows who the agent is, since he thought it was someone else. But I'll let Blu tell you about that."

The door to my room opened, and a medic in a white coat walked in.

"It seems that you're awake . . . and trying to get out of bed." He raised his eyebrows at Ink.

"I was trying to keep her from falling over."

"Of course you were. Time for you to go. I need to chat with my patient."

Ink looked at me as he turned to leave. The intensity of his gaze was uncomfortable, mostly because I couldn't tell what he was thinking the way I could with Calum. Then the memory of Ink stalking toward me in the forest came unbidden into my mind, blood and death surrounding him like some sort of avenging angel. I had to stop comparing him to my best friend—they were definitely not the same.

"I'm . . ." Ink ran his hand through his dark hair again. It made it stand up on end, like what Adora called "purposeful bedhead." "I'm just glad that you're OK."

"Thanks, Ink. Thanks for being here."

He left, shutting the door behind him.

"My word! That is the first time in my many years here that I have ever seen that playboy at a loss for words," the medic said as he took the clothes from my hands and put them back on the shelf. His face was serious, but his eyes were laughing.

I didn't know what to say about that.

"My name is Sage, and I'm a medic here," he said. His big brown eyes were kind and he looked serious, although the yellow headband that held back his short dreadlocks spoke of someone with a sense of humor. Maybe. He didn't look like he was in a kidding mood now. "How are you feeling?"

"I feel weird, to be honest. Dizzy, but awake?"

"And going somewhere?" Sage looked pointedly at the clothes.

"I really need to see if Jay's OK. Ink told me you know who he is."

"And who you are."

I wasn't sure what to add or how much I was supposed to say.

"Agent Hanlon should make a full recovery, but it'll take some time."

"I need to see him. Is he up for it?"

"Are you?"

I stood up, this time hanging onto the bed.

"I see you are as stubborn as the rest of the Team. We'll go see your friend, but on the condition you spend at least one more night here. Agreed?"

He helped me into my clothes, and a wheelchair, and pushed me out of the room and into a long hall with doors on either side. Some were open and empty. Others were closed, and I could hear people talking beyond. Nothing looked familiar.

"How did I get here?"

"Ink carried you from the Captain's office."

I was mortified all over again. I might be short, but I'm no waif. As my mom used to tell me, I'm "solid." He had picked me up and carried me? That was one more thing to feel awkward about, if tipping over in a hospital gown wasn't enough.

We made it to the end of the hall and Sage knocked on a door. I heard a familiar voice rumble, "Come in."

8 FARA

My voice caught on the sob that escaped my lips. "You're alive."

"I'll be back for you in a few minutes," Sage said and closed the door quietly.

Tears ran freely down my face as I stared at Jay in disbelief. He was real and he was alive. I didn't know what to say—I hadn't dared think about this moment before now, didn't ever hope that I'd be staring at him like this. He smiled at me again, although it looked like it hurt him. His face was a patchwork of bruises and cuts and he had a broken nose.

I drank him in, unable to get enough. His facial hair had grown and his dark blond hair was disheveled, but even with the bruises and the hair and everything, he was still so gorgeous and brave. He took my breath away.

I rolled my wheelchair nearer to him and grabbed the hand that was closest to me. The other one was in a cast up to the elbow. Visions of Barrington's goons torturing him came unbidden—the crack of his fingers under the hammer; the scream of pain that was the last thing I heard before I escaped. I sucked in a breath, trying not to fall into the memory.

"You saved me."

Another sob escaped. I needed to touch him, to hug him, to have him tell me it was all going to be OK. He pulled my hand gently, then scooted over in the bed with a grunt.

"Stop! What are you doing? Don't hurt yourself!"

"Can't stand to see you cry." He gave my hand a squeeze. "C'mere."

I gingerly climbed into his bed, trying to not touch him. He let go of my hand and lifted his arm, indicating I should put my head on his shoulder.

"It's OK. You won't hurt me. The bullet got the other side."

I shifted onto my side, gently placing my head on his chest, trying to move as little as possible. He put his arm around me. My tears wet his thin hospital gown. With his touch, I started to shake, letting the emotion of the past few days run through me. I didn't care if I opened another portal, or that I felt like I was losing control. At that moment, I let the realization of what could have happened wash over me, and the relief that it was over. He was here. We were safe. For now.

"Shhh . . . I'm all right."

"I never thought I'd see you again."

"You saved me, Fara."

"Actually, it was Blu and Ink—"

"It was you. You came back for me, even though you shouldn't have. It was you. Thank you."

I don't know how long we lay like that, him comforting me even though he was the one who probably needed the comforting more. I tried to breathe him in, to savor this moment that had been stolen, this moment that I didn't think I'd have again, but I couldn't.

"You almost died because of me," I whispered. "You almost died to save me."

"Fara, look at me." He put his good hand on my neck, pulling me up so that my forehead rested on his, and I could feel his breath on my face. "Don't you dare blame yourself for this," he said. "Don't you dare. Those assholes did this."

"But if it weren't—"

He pulled me in for a kiss. I was afraid I was going to hurt him, but he didn't seem to mind. He was as painfully gentle as before, and when he was done, he lingered on my lips, eyes closed, a faint smile tugging at the corner of his mouth.

"What was that for?" I breathed.

"I wasn't sure I'd ever be able to do that again, and I couldn't wait one more minute. Do you mind?"

"I'm afraid I'm hurting you."

He laughed, a deep, rolling sound. "Never."

"Then can we do it again?"

He raised a perfect eyebrow at me, and even in his battered and bruised state, I had eyebrow envy. "You don't need to ask me twice."

He pulled me in again with a smile. This time his arm snaked around me, pulling me against his chest . . . which felt as amazing as I had imagined. His tongue parted my lips and brushed against mine, sending a shiver down to my toes. My breath came heavier as I curled my hand around his hospital gown, half of me worried that I'd break him further, the other half kind of wanting to.

"Ahem." Sage was shaking his head. How long had he been standing there? "I'm pretty sure that's not what bed rest is supposed to look like."

I tried to sit up, but Jay held me to him. "Go away. We're busy," he grumbled.

"No can do. Fara needs to heal too."

He sighed as he released me, but I wanted to stay right where I was, reveling in the fact that he was alive, and I was alive. The moment I left, I would start to worry about everything that was happening. Right now, I was safe.

"Sage is right. You need your rest," Jay said into my hair. I sighed. "But don't worry. We will resume this soon. I promise."

"Besides, Fara, there's someone waiting in your room to talk to you," Sage said. "Actually, a few someones . . ."

Jay kissed my forehead. I hauled myself up and Sage helped me maneuver back into the wheelchair. As he turned me around, I glanced over my shoulder. Jay watched me go with those cool gray eyes and a small smile that made my heart flutter.

"You know," Sage said as he closed Jay's door and walked me back to my room, "I'm going to have to lock you in your room if you plan on sneaking back to see him."

"You wouldn't!" I whipped around to find Sage's eyes sparkling.

"No—I wouldn't. But don't get any ideas."

⚡ ⚡ ⚡

Styx and Blu were both sitting in my room when Sage and I arrived. Blu looked calm in a chair she had commandeered from somewhere, a faint smile on her lips, but Styx was grinning at me.

"You look just like the cat that ate the canary. I know that look all too well, don't I, Blu? You've only been up for a few minutes. What trouble could you possibly have gotten into?"

"Fara was helping Jay with his, ahem, *bed rest*," Sage said. He helped me out of the wheelchair and back into bed. I glared at him. "I'll leave you ladies to it. Remember, no sneaking off, Fara. I'll be back in a bit to check on you." He left, quietly shutting the door.

"Oooh girl! You need to spill it!" Styx said, bouncing in her seat. Her headband was a vibrant tie-dye today and she was smiling, but her eyes were tired. So were Blu's.

"I'm so sorry—"

"Nope!" Styx interrupted, waving me off. "We're not going there. Stay on topic. You were up to something fun with that hot agent man and I want the details."

"But you guys . . . You risked everything because I asked you to."

"Not just because you asked," Blu said. "Not to be rude, but this wasn't all about you."

"And believe me, Blu likes to make it all about her, so that's hard for her to say," Styx said.

Blu rolled her eyes at Styx. "The Team has been trained to do exactly what we did. We rescue people. We kill people. We—"

"—burn down houses," Styx said with a grin.

Blu rolled her eyes again. "Only when I need to." There was an inside joke between them that I didn't understand. How can you joke about burning down someone's house? "But it's never about us. Not really. It's about the mission: dismantling Jurisdiction and restoring democracy and protecting those who can't protect themselves. That's everything."

"It's more than everything," Styx said. "It's why we're here."

"Saving the agent was the right thing to do," Blu continued. "Not only because you asked us to, but because you said he's an expert on Barrington Park, and anything we can learn about what he's planning in your world is a bonus."

"Plus, he works for your government—so he'll hopefully be able to answer some questions the Captain has," Styx added. "And getting him out of Barrington's clutches before he gave up anything about you was smart."

"If it didn't further the mission," Blu went on, "we probably wouldn't have helped, whether we wanted to or not. So don't spend one second blaming yourself. Because that means you're missing the point."

"But—thanks anyway."

"No problem, girl!" Styx said. "So now that the agent is back, we're hoping that you are going to stick around for a while."

"I will. I mean, I have to, right? I guess I've been opening portals in my sleep, and Sage made me promise I'd spend another night here to further recuperate—"

"And make out?" Styx raised an eyebrow.

I blushed a deep crimson. "I wish. Sage threatened to lock me in here if I tried."

Styx laughed. "It'd be worth it, though! I can tell by how much you're blushing just thinking about that hot agent man's lips on your—"

"That's what Adora calls him." My face caught on fire. I couldn't help but laugh.

"Well, she's not wrong. Although you two do seem to have identical taste." Blu punched Styx in the arm. "Ouch! Don't get mad at me, chica. You're the one who's been kissing the second most deadly human in the world—and he doesn't seem to want to kill you. It sounds like he'd rather get into your—"

"Styx!" Blu said, clearly embarrassed.

"But," Styx said, undeterred, "don't you find it a little bit weird that the man Fara obviously has the hots for is the same man who kissed you recently? I mean, that's some next-level universe destiny shit."

"It probably doesn't mean anything," Blu said.

"Wait a minute!" I was late to the party, as usual, but slowly catching up. "Blu, are you telling me that Jay's counterpart here is part of Jurisdiction, and he . . . kissed you?"

"Yep!" said Styx cheerily. "And that's not even the best part. The Second Counselor has been helping our friend Blu here keep from getting caught during her missions. He has saved her ass almost as often as I have."

That was some coincidence. How was it even possible that the two of us, from different worlds, were *kissing* the same guy? Sort of. But that wasn't even all of it. There was the coincidence that the governor's mansion was the same layout as wherever Blu went to steal the blueprints. And that Blu's best friends (minus Jackrabbit) were the same as mine. In all of the possible universes, how could it be that so many things were . . . parallel?

FARA 9

"Can I come in?" the Captain asked, holding a tray with a file under her arm.

I sat up, waiting for the dizziness that never came. At least that was over . . . whatever that was. I waved her in and flinched. My arm still hurt, but that was to be expected.

She closed the door with her foot, set the tray on my bed, and turned on the lamp—each move precise and efficient. Even though the curtains were closed, by the increasing dimness, I could tell that night had fallen. I must have fallen asleep after Blu and Styx left.

"I thought you might be hungry, and Ink was headed this way with food, so I intercepted him. In other words, blame Ink for whatever is on the menu."

I turned my attention to the tray and smiled when I opened the box. The mashed potatoes seemed to smile back at me. There was also a donut and what looked like steak. The drink was coffee. I was in heaven.

"He must have chosen correctly."

I took a bite, my eyes slightly rolling to the back of my head with mashed potato pleasure. "Thank you," I mumbled between bites. I realized, belatedly, that I had no idea how to pay for this food, or the hospital stay. It sent another shot of worry through me. Too late now, but I'd ask when I had the opportunity. Maybe they'd put me to work to pay for it all?

"You don't have to stay," I said. "I know you have a million things to do."

"Nothing pressing. The Team is in my office debriefing Blu and Ink's last mission, and hopefully planning the next one. They can handle that themselves. I already got the gist of what happened, and I don't mind having a break from them. They can be a bit much sometimes." The corners of her mouth curved up, an act very reminiscent of Millie, the Captain's kickboxing doppelganger. "Fara, the Team told me about what happened during the agent's rescue. But I'd like to hear it from you."

"I'm assuming you're talking about what I did to the goon? I honestly don't know what to tell you."

"Just try to explain as best you can."

I didn't know exactly what happened, or why this extra ability appeared during the rescue. I certainly didn't know why it hadn't happened before. I definitely would have remembered electrocuting someone. I had no context for it at all, other than I was afraid of what I did. It wasn't like the guy was a good guy. He tried to kidnap me, again, and had given the order to kill Jackrabbit and Calum. But I killed him. I did that. My stomach started to roil. I put my food aside.

Then I forced myself to tell her everything that happened during our rescue.

"Did my mom ever mention being able to fry someone like I did?"

She thought about it. "No. The only thing I knew she could do was open the portals. She never mentioned that she could do what you did, nor that she suspected you could."

"Great."

"But after the Team told me what happened, I thought that maybe she wrote about it in her notes. Since Sage won't release you until tomorrow, you might have some time tonight to read them, if you aren't too tired."

"I will. Thank you."

"You are most welcome. I do have one more thing I need to ask before I go. We previously spoke about you staying here and helping the Team, at least until you have your abilities under control. But after this last mission, I don't want to assume that you still want to stay. Though I certainly hope you do, I would understand if you didn't."

She was letting me out of my promise to help them. I could go home.

I wanted to. I really wanted to, to try to pretend that all of this was a nightmare, and go back to waiting tables and having beers with Calum and live normally again. But that was a pipe dream and I knew it. I couldn't go back until I was able to suppress my abilities—now plural. That's what Jay had meant when he told me to run, when we were captives at Barrington's. To jump through the portal to hide until I could go home safely.

"I would like to stay, if you'll have me."

"I was hoping you'd say that. While you've been in here, I took the liberty of making some arrangements for you. One more night in the infirmary will let me put the finishing touches on your apartment. It's in the same building as the rest of the Team. I hope that is all right with you."

I blinked. "That is way too kind."

"Not at all. You can stay for as long as you want. We're glad to have you."

"But I can't pay for—"

She waved me off before I could finish that sentence. "It's the least I can do for the daughter of a friend. Figure out your abilities. Read your mom's notes. Come to Team meetings to help as you can. Train when you feel up to it. But take time to recover. There is no hurry. You are welcome here."

She stood to leave, giving me a small smile. "Come to my office when you're released tomorrow, and we'll figure it out from there."

Once she had left, I sank back into my bed, torn between being thrilled at the prospect of having a safe place to stay, and missing my friends and my life. But what life? With my ex-boyfriend Beck gone, my apartment trashed, and Calum more than likely mad at me, I didn't have much to go back to. It made my heart hurt.

But I still needed to get my abilities under control so that I didn't accidentally fry someone or open a portal during dinner rush at The Grill, or during my date with Jay. I looked at the folder sitting on the table, caught between wanting answers and being afraid of what I would find. Was knowing worse than not knowing? Or, was it worse that the answers might not be there? Regardless, I was avoiding the inevitable.

As I opened the folder, an envelope slipped into my lap. It was addressed to me, in my mother's writing. My breath caught, and I forced myself to open it.

My Dearest Fara,

I'm not sure how to begin. As I sit here watching you do your homework, eyebrows furrowed in concentration, it is hard for me to imagine that this note is even necessary. My hope is that you never need to read this, but if the past years have proven anything to me, it is that the impossible is certainly possible.

I have so many things I want to tell you, my special, beautiful girl. But I am afraid that I might be out of time. Some baddies have threatened us, and I need to hide these notes so no one can find them. I cannot allow them to use this knowledge. To use us.

But first things first. Since you are reading this, you have already managed to travel through a portal to another universe, which in and of itself is amazing. I hope you were not afraid the first time you opened the portal. The first time I opened a portal, it was by accident. I had no idea what it was, even though my expertise is the multiverse. It was embarrassing, really—I finally have proof that my theories are correct, and I don't recognize them? But now I do, and you do too.

The universe was kind in where it deposited me when I came through the portal. It was the Captain's office (whom you have probably met). I have a theory about why I ended up in her world (in my notes), but I don't know why it was her office. Maybe that is a mystery the universe won't divulge so easily. Hopefully, that is where you landed, but it might not have been. From what the Captain and I can tell, your portals open to wherever Blu is at the time you open a portal.

I worry that she could be doing something dangerous when you decide to come through. Maybe not. Hopefully not. All I can do is trust that should it come down to it, you will be safe.

I'm sure that you have a thousand questions about everything, and hopefully these notes will help you. I'm learning new things every day, and I have recorded what I have learned. I just wish I had more time. So much is still unknown. I am sorry for that—once again. But if I know anything at all, it is that you are smart and will succeed where I have failed. I have faith that you will figure all of this out, no matter how inadequate my notes. My legacy.

I hope you believe me when I say that I always intended to tell you of these things in person, but I put it off.

How do you tell your most cherished person that you screwed up? How do I explain to my daughter that in my greed for knowledge, I set off a chain of events that could have cataclysmic consequences? I am a coward for not telling you, and I recognize that it's too late and too dangerous now. So I continue to hide your abilities to keep you safe, not only from others, but from yourself. I know that my methods will have long-lasting negative effects, but unfortunately it is the price you must pay to keep safe. And for that I am sorry. So, so sorry.

I am sure you must be angry with me for not preparing you for all of this, and for what is to come. And I accept that. I have an ocean full of regrets. But no matter what you read here, or what conclusions you come to on your own, know that I love you more than anything in all of the universes combined, and everything I have ever done has come from a place of love.

You are so special, Fara. Not because of what you can do, but because of who you are becoming. You are kind and gentle. You are empathetic and wise. I hope that you will someday realize that you are stronger and braver than you have ever been allowed to be; than I have ever allowed you to be.

My beautiful daughter, the membrane between our worlds is thinning, which means that something has happened to disturb the order of things. You will need to be strong for whatever is to come. Trust the Captain: she is a friend and very wise. Also, trust Blu. She is quite the handful, but you could probably use someone like that in your life right now. Do not trust

Barrington Park, should he approach you. Do not trust anyone I work with, or our own government. They do not have our best interests at heart. I know in my heart of hearts, you will fight for what is right. I am so, so proud of you. I will miss you every day. Stay safe. And remember, I love you more than donuts.

 M

A tear dripped onto the paper, which I was clutching like a lifeline. My mom had written this. Her hand had touched these pages. I felt my heart crack open, the grief of losing her renewing itself and mingling with all of the other horrible things that had happened since her death. Not just the past few days, which were frightening, but everything. How much I was struggling to find my way without her guidance. How tired I was of just surviving and not ever really living. Of being so afraid all of the time.

I put the file under my pillow and swung my feet over the edge of the bed. I couldn't stay here alone. The mental breakdown that I had been putting off until we rescued Jay was bubbling toward the surface. I was about to shatter.

I slowly stood up, waiting to see if I was dizzy. When dizziness didn't come, I slipped out of my room and down the hall, my socked feet making no noise on the tiled floor. I needed Jay to hold me, to help me keep the pieces of myself together. I needed him to protect me, even from myself. Through the dim light of the hall, I could see him lying in bed, his face turned toward the door. He opened his eyes.

"Fara?"

I couldn't answer, my shaking increasing. My mom had deliberately kept this from me. And she was dead now, with no way to tell me herself. Dead and never coming back. Dead because of Barrington Park. But I couldn't get my mouth to work.

"Fara, tell me. What happened?"

He moved over to give me space, holding the covers up so I could slide in next to him. He wrapped his arms around me, careful not to hurt me with his cast, even though I was probably hurting him just by getting in the bed. He held me and let me soak his hospital gown with my tears. Eventually I cried myself out, the torrent subsiding.

"I'm sorry—"

"Don't apologize."

"But—"

"Do you want to talk about it?"

"No. Not yet."

He stroked my hair.

"Am I . . . am I hurting you?" I tried not to move.

I could feel more than hear his chuckle. "Even if you were, I'd never tell."

"But I don't want to hurt you."

"Fara, everything hurts, but you make me forget that."

My breath hitched at the sweetness of that statement. I didn't want to move. I wanted to stay right here, hiding from myself for a while. "Can I stay?"

"You can stay here forever. But I might be tempted to kiss you again."

"I'd like that."

He stopped stroking my hair, lifting his head so he could look me in the eye. "Are you sure? I don't want to take advantage of—"

"—me losing my shit? It's OK."

"Only if you say so."

"I say so."

In the dark, I could barely make out his features, but his eyes caught the light outlining the door and almost glowed. They were fixed on me. It reminded me of the first time I saw him standing by my car with such a predatory calm. It had made my heart skip a beat. Now my heart was skipping because he was staring at me with the same intensity, but for a different reason.

He gently pulled me in for a slow, sweet kiss, then looked into my eyes. "OK?"

"Again."

He rumbled a laugh and pulled me in for another kiss. I let my fingers trace up and down his spine . . . which I realized was bare. Ah yes, hospital gown. The thought of his beautiful body next to mine with nothing but a thin layer of fabric between us made my heart race faster. Holy shit, was he sexy. I hitched my leg over his hip to get closer, and he let out a groan—not in the good way. I had hurt him. Great. Nothing says sexy like reinjuring someone.

"Are you all right? I am so sorry!" And I was sorry. And embarrassed. And awkward.

"Fara, please do not apologize."

"But I hurt you!"

"I'm already hurt, and I wouldn't miss this opportunity for anything. I have wanted to do this, all of this, since the first time I met you."

He rolled onto his back with a small moan and pulled me onto his chest.

"So," I ventured, "you're not mad that I came in here, freaking out, then hurt you more?"

He chuckled. "No, I'm the opposite of mad. Contrary to how I might appear at this moment, I am happy."

"Are you sure?"

"Yes, Fara, I am sure. If it hadn't been for my job, I would have asked you on a date as soon as you told me that you broke up with your boyfriend."

Ugh. Beck.

"Actually," he went on, "while we cleaned out your apartment, I contemplated having your boyfriend arrested so that I could ask you out sooner, but I figured you might be angry about that. Plus, I'm sort of a rule-follower, if you didn't know."

I snorted.

"I'm serious, Fara. You are so beautiful. You don't even realize how beautiful you are. When you laugh, when you call me bossy, when you tease me. When you talk to your car and your stomach. All of those things make me want you."

He wanted me.

My chest squeezed. This beautiful, brave man wanted me, even as we sat in a hospital bed in a different universe. Even though my life was a shitshow. Even though I wasn't as beautiful as he said I was, or as he was. Even though he'd almost died because of me. He wanted me in spite of all of it. I couldn't help but smile into his chest.

"Feel better?"

"Getting there."

"Good."

He stroked my hair for a while as we lay there in not-quite-uncomfortable silence. Eventually his hand went still. He had fallen back asleep. I looked up at him, memorizing the lines of his face. I wasn't sure when we would have a chance to do this again, and I wanted to savor it, but he also needed to get better. As gently as I could, I moved his arm so I could get up.

"Stay."

He hadn't opened his eyes, but the corner of his mouth was curved up.

"OK, Bossy McBosserson."

His lips tugged up into a real smile, and he opened one eye. "Stay. Please?"

"Better. But you need your rest."

"I don't care."

I giggled. "Sage will be pissed."

"Don't care. Please stay."

I smiled and lay back down, my head on his chest. And that's where Sage found us the next morning.

BLU 10

Last night was busier than I had expected, and I had collapsed into my bed. Dawn and training came too early. I was wiped. Maybe because we had hardly slept while Fara was in the infirmary, or maybe because we were still trying to figure out how to infiltrate Dagna's building, and the stress of that was wearing on me. Or maybe it was because one of Ink's groupies had cornered me last night, peppering me with a thousand questions about him, until I shut my door in her face.

Regardless, I was in a foul mood this morning, and even bashing Ink around during training didn't make me feel better. Hopefully, we'd find something useful at Dagna's building today. We needed some good news.

Jurisdiction's anti-tech security kicked in as Ink and I approached Dagna's building, our comms and palmboxes now useless. Styx and her tech team had been working to dismantle the anti-tech. All we knew was that its self-destruct capabilities had almost taken Styx's head off. Hopefully, its being from another universe wouldn't stop our resident tech genius from figuring out how to dismantle it, but it obviously made it harder. I mean, how often do you run across technology from another universe? Apparently, more often than we thought.

When Ink and I were here a few days ago, the Second Counselor suggested that we explore the trail he used to sneak up on us. I still didn't understand why he was helping me, and I was hoping that the information he provided that day was accurate. Was he leading us into a trap? While Jyston had technically saved my ass on more than one occasion, as Styx said, it didn't mean I trusted him, and I certainly didn't trust our surroundings. From our other reconnaissance trips, we knew that there was a crazy amount of security surrounding the building. It also confirmed the Captain's suspicions that more than kids were inside. Jurisdiction wouldn't put up such a fuss for humans. There had to be weapons in there.

I pulled the truck under a tree to give us some cover and shut off the engine. Ink checked his gear and slowly opened the door.

"Here goes nothing," he said, sliding down and landing silently on the ground. He wasn't immediately impaled by spikes—a good sign. He looked around for cameras, then shook his head. He didn't see anything.

I breathed a sigh of relief when I wasn't impaled either. That wouldn't be my preferred method of dying; actually, it might be close to my last.

"Are you coming, or are you going to hang out and wait for your boyfriend?" Ink whispered.

I glared at him and indicated with my middle finger that he should move merrily along up the trail. We set out through the trees, checking every few feet for traps or cameras. The trail Jyston had directed us to was little more than a deer path. It was big enough for a person to walk but not much else. Since we were going to have to eventually rescue kids, I wasn't sure how practical using this trail would be for our mission, but it seemed perfect for snooping. It appeared that Jyston's intelligence was good, so far.

The trail wound over a small ridge and when we crested it, I could see we were at the tree line above the building—as close as we had ever been. From where we stood, I could make out the entire building in detail, from the entrance at the front of the building off to our left, to what looked like a loading dock on the right. In front of us, tucked into the corner of the building, was a door that was completely hidden from both of the roads and entrances. While I wasn't sure what it was used for or where it led, I did know that it could be a useful entrance or exit for sneaking around.

Ink pointed to the main road on our left. A large van was making its way up the long drive. It parked in front of the building. Minions came out and opened the van doors, pulling people out like sacks of potatoes. Not just people: kids. The oldest looked to be just a bit younger than me, and he was clutching a little boy who couldn't have been older than five or six. They were dirty, thin, and shaking, with blood on their clothes. I had to fight the bile that raced up my throat. How? How could humans do this to other humans?

From the look on Ink's face, I knew he was doing exactly what I was doing—calculating how to save those kids. The two of us could probably do it, and my brain started to work out a way that we could, but then I stopped. If we did that now, then what of the other kids who were already in there? What of the weapons? My stomach knotted again. We couldn't help now, but we would be back. We would get them out.

"I'm glad to see you took my advice."

Ink and I spun around, daggers in our hands. Jyston leaned against a tree, his hands up. He was making no move to grab a weapon, though he wore a lethal smile. We all stood staring at each other for a moment, until Jyston broke the silence.

"Well, this is quite awkward. I was hoping to catch you alone so that we could continue our chat and . . . other things. It appears that your bodyguard has tagged along."

"Asshole," Ink spat. "You obviously don't know Blu very well if you think she needs a bodyguard. Just because she hasn't kicked your sorry ass yet doesn't mean that she can't."

"No. I suppose she doesn't need one. Which makes her all the more intriguing."

I sighed, exasperated. "Second Counselor, how did you know we were here? Are we being watched?"

"Not by anyone else but me."

"What is that supposed to mean?"

Jyston ignored Ink's question. "Ink, I think you might find that going down the trail toward the building might be interesting."

"Why would it be interesting?"

Jyston looked bored.

"You're trying to get rid of me," Ink said.

"Yes," Jyston said simply. "And it is easier to send you to get information that you'd find useful than to kill you outright. I have a feeling that Blu would be angry with me if I harmed you, and I work very hard not to have her angry at me."

"I will kill you if you touch him."

"I'm pretty sure you'd try, Blu, and then what fun would that be? But before we dissolve into violence, I really do believe going down the trail would be beneficial to your cause."

"Why should I trust you?" Ink asked.

"You shouldn't," Jyston replied, never taking his eyes off me. "But then again, I really don't care if you take my advice or not."

Ink looked at me in question. Jyston had not led us astray. Yet. And he had not actively tried to kill me. Yet. So it was worth the risk. I gave Ink a nod, and he headed in the direction Jyston had indicated.

"Where was I? Oh yes, why I came out into the woods in the first place, other than to have scintillating conversation with your friend, there. Have you ever attended the Powerbike Inground Tournament?"

I couldn't have heard him right. "You came here to ask me if I've attended the PITs? You came all this way to ask me that?"

"I do so enjoy our conversations, even if they are about mundane topics. Have you been?"

I had no idea where this was going, but I'd play along, for now. "Obviously not." The PITs were a Jurisdiction elite event, invitation only.

"I'd ask you to go with me as an honored guest, but I believe that would not be in your best interests. Or mine, really. Anyway, what do you know about the PITs, as you call it?"

He came closer to me as he asked, hands still up. I involuntarily took a step back. He shook his head with a chuckle.

"Beautiful Blu, have we not already established that I do not want to kill you?"

"I still don't understand why."

His face broke out in a grin. "You're so unappreciative. Isn't it enough that I prefer you alive?"

I couldn't help the matching grin that spread across my face.

"So, what do you know about the PITs?" he prompted.

"They're a brutal competition where Jurisdiction sets their prisoners against each other for the entertainment of the elite. I'm glad I'm not invited. I don't appreciate people using human beings as entertainment."

"Yes, yes. You probably would want to burn the place down. It is quite unsavory. But did you know that it's not only prisoners who compete in the PITs? Mercenaries, gang members, and others are allowed to enter some of the competitions. In fact, many of the more unpleasant characters who work for Jurisdiction compete in the PITs. Including the driver you see below."

"So? I'm sure Jurisdiction has plenty of assholes on its payroll."

He took another step toward me. I could see his muscles straining against his black combat gear. My heart pounded. Was it because I was afraid, or because I was hoping he would come closer? I needed to focus.

Jyston arched his eyebrow. "Blu? It's not like you to daydream. I hate to ask, but are you feeling all right?"

Shit. "Just got distracted for a second."

Jyston chuckled, the sound reverberating in my chest.

"That's a first. What I was saying was, these mercenaries are usually quite chatty among themselves in the holding room before the PITs start, talking about all sorts of jobs that they contract for."

"Are you saying that we should enter the PITs? Are you nuts?"

"Some might say so."

I thought about what he was saying, and what he wasn't saying. If we could get into that room somehow and listen, we could get all sorts of information regarding the comings and goings, or even bribe someone for one of the driving jobs. That might be our way in. I'd have to bring it to the Team. But it was possible that someone from the Compound could compete in the PITs. That person would have to be crazy, but it could work.

I forced myself to look back at the people below, to remind myself why I was here. To remind myself that I would do anything I could, including entering the PITs, if it meant that this building was destroyed and all of the prisoners freed.

The kids had been brought inside already, but there were a few others huddled together—two young women, a handful of Jurisdiction minions, and the driver. I watched as the driver leered at one of the women. He made a grab for her, and she stepped back to avoid him. In doing so, she ran into one of the minions; I knew what was going to happen before it did.

The minion she'd run into grabbed her by her hair with a sneer, turning her around to face him as his other hand roamed freely over her body, groping her through her thin clothes. The second woman started screaming and shoving at the minion, trying to free her companion from his clutches. I didn't have to hear their words; their faces said everything. These poor women. Even if the Team didn't enter the PITs, I would still find that driver, and the rest of the minions, and kill them all.

I turned away to face Jyston, my rage causing the edges of my vision to blur. It was his people doing these horrific things. No matter his motives or that he was helping me—he still belonged to these assholes. Without giving it much thought, I lunged toward him. My dagger was at his heart. He didn't try to stop me.

"Look at her! Look at how those people, *your* people, are treating them! How can you be OK with this? You come here asking about the PITs, while a woman is being assaulted. Is this just a game to you?"

"It is not a game."

I pushed the dagger against his chest, creating a hole in his shirt and drawing a tiny speck of blood.

"I should just kill you right now. Save the world the trouble."

He looked down at me but didn't move. "Blu, I know you don't believe it, but if you kill me, someone worse will take my place. I understand why you hate me, and you have every right to, but . . . I'm your best chance."

"My best chance at what? If you're my best chance, then do something! You're the leader of these shitheads. If you don't do anything, then you're just as bad as they are!"

"Everything is not always as it seems."

"What the fuck does that even mean? What is happening down there is *exactly* what it seems!"

There was a loud crack and a sharp cry, and we both turned. A minion was standing over the young woman who had tried to save her friend. She was sprawled on the ground. The back of her shirt was torn, and blood was beginning to ooze through what remained of the material. The other minion still held the friend but had turned her around, forcing her to watch the display, as if to say "This is what happens when you stand up for yourself."

The minion was holding a whip.

I drew in a sharp breath, pushing the panic down. I turned away from the beating. It wouldn't do to have a full-blown panic attack when I was already in danger. I could handle almost anything, but this . . . I wasn't sure I could handle this. Jyston met my gaze, and for a split second I saw genuine concern in his eyes.

"That was you, once," he said, mirroring my own thoughts. He gently pushed my dagger-hand away from his heart. "Do you remember much of that time? You were young when they took you—"

"I remember enough. Your people took *everything* from me! Everything! And I have spent the past fourteen years trying to get it back!"

I stepped away from him, unable to catch my breath, forcing the sob that was trying to escape back down into the pit of my stomach. It felt like a giant hand was clenching my heart, but I refused to cry. I refused to let him see the fear that chased me every minute of every day. I had locked up those memories, shoving them down so far that I could pretend they hadn't happened. Because I knew, deep down, that Jurisdiction had broken some essential part of me . . . when I was their prisoner.

Maybe I had been like Fara once—kind and sweet. But they took that away from me when they tortured me. Thinking about what I lost . . . I had been forged into a brutal killer, honing my skills to make sure that no one ever had to go through what I went through. Despite our flirtatious banter, Jyston was the enemy and I should end him now. But something in my gut stopped me.

"Do you remember how you escaped your cell?"

My voice was barely above a whisper. "Why do you care? Why are you even here, Jyston?"

He rubbed his hands over his face, his hair falling over his forehead. It was the most normal thing I had ever seen him do, and it scared me more than anything had so far. It made him almost human. "Just humor me. Do you remember how you escaped?"

My heart thumped so hard in my chest that I thought it was going to explode, but my brain had already started thinking about his question. I couldn't remember the specifics of my escape, only that the Captain had found me just outside of the Compound's entrance, barely alive. What I did remember, in vivid detail, was being stolen by two minions when I was running an errand for a Team member in the city center. I was brought to Jurisdiction's headquarters. I remembered the whippings and the beatings and the constant interrogations. I remembered wanting to die. Why was it happening to me? How could people do this to another human being? Did they think I had sensitive information about the Compound?

For a year, after I escaped, I'd slept in Ink's room with all of the lights on, because I couldn't stand the dark or being alone.

I remembered someone coming into my cell, wrapping a rough blanket around me, and carrying me out of the building as I was barely hanging on to consciousness. I'd always assumed that it was a Team member who rescued me. But I never talked to the Captain about my captivity—every time I tried, it triggered a panic attack. Even now. I remembered the person who carried me was gentle. I was going in and out of consciousness. I looked up at his face, but he had a hood pulled down. His face was in shadow. I strained, trying to remember anything about the person who rescued me. And there it was. The bright gray eyes that looked back at me from under the hood. Eyes like a wolf.

"It was you. But why?"

He gently grabbed my face and stared into my eyes. So much emotion was there, and it was so jumbled up that I couldn't tell what he was feeling.

"Because someone had to."

He looked up, like he heard something, then bent low so that his lips grazed my jaw, right below my ear. "We'll finish this conversation later," he rumbled.

I could barely breathe, as much from the revelation as from his proximity. His hands were lightly resting on my arms, his warm breath on my cheek. I could feel everything, and it was too much. I couldn't tell if I wanted to kill him or kiss him.

He stepped away as Ink came back through the trees. Jyston looked back down at the minion with the whip, disdain on his face, along with his usual mask of boredom. For that's what it was, I realized—a mask.

"I must say, scenes such as that make me dislike Dagna even more, if that is at all possible. Torture and whatnot is so medieval. Quite honestly, it's beneath me. However, try as I might, I cannot seem to convince the Counselor that she is a pariah and this building could be put to better use."

"What are they using it for now, other than torturing kids?" Ink snapped.

"Oh, the torture isn't the end game. Dagna is just not very creative when it comes to getting people to do what she wants them to do. Those ones in the van are being brought in for cheap labor, to work on her *special projects*."

"What special projects?" Ink said.

"What fun would it be if you had all of the information? No fun for me at all, I should say. Anyway, Ink, I hope you found something worth your time. I must be going." He raised his hand in a flourishing, haughty wave. "Blu, as always, it was a pleasure. We will meet again, soon. Oh, and tell your *cousin* hello for me."

11 FARA

Sage had woken us up with a lot of tutting, but underneath his displeasure his eyes were smiling.

"How are you both supposed to heal if you're rolling around in bed?" he said as he stood over us.

"We weren't 'rolling,'" I said weakly. Jay chuckled beside me.

I felt like I should be more embarrassed, but refreshingly, I wasn't. I had slept fairly well, even though I was concerned about hurting Jay if I moved too much. But every time I had tried to go back to my room, his arm tightened around me, and I snuggled back down into his warmth. With him, I didn't have to think about my mom's notes or electrocuting people, or opening portals, or living in a different universe. With him, I was safe. I felt like he would take care of me.

"All right, you two. No more snuggle time. Fara needs to get up so I can treat you both and get to training."

I sighed and Jay squeezed my shoulder. "We'll do more of this later," he said with a smile. I grinned at him, and gingerly sat up.

"You'll have all of the time in the world to 'not roll around' once you get out of the infirmary," Sage said with the shadow of a smirk. "But until then, you need to heal. And sleep. Someone from the Team is going to want to talk to you, Jay, once you're up for it. I'll have food brought in for both of you in a bit."

"Who's the Team?" Jay asked.

"They are the ones who came with me to rescue you," I said. Jay nodded at me, his eyes slowly closing. He needed to rest. I leaned down and kissed him gently, then followed Sage to my own room.

"How are you feeling?" he asked after he closed the door. When I didn't respond, he sat down in the chair in the corner of the room and indicated I should sit on the bed. "Fara, you are smart to be reserved around new people, especially given what I know now. Believe me when I tell you that you can trust me."

I smiled at him—I couldn't help it. With his short dreadlocks and kind eyes, he reminded me of a young Bob Marley—but as a doctor and not a legend. Then again, was Bob Marley a legend here? Was he alive still? Was he singing in this world, or did he choose a different path? Was the song "Three Little Birds" still a thing? My dad, if he had still been alive, would have been devastated if it wasn't. There were many things I would probably never know about this world.

Sage waited patiently for me to turn my attention back to him. "The first time I saw you open a portal, I have to admit, I was a little freaked out, but luckily Ink was in here and explained what it was. He also threatened me within an inch of my life if I told anybody who you are." He paused. His eyes crinkled on the sides, the only indication he was teasing me. "Ink seems pretty taken with you."

"From what I understand, Ink is pretty taken with everyone."

Sage laughed, and I had a feeling that sound was a rare treat. I grinned at him.

"That's true, to an extent. So, are you feeling up to leaving here? I'd suggest another day for observation, but I have a feeling that neither you nor our other guest would get much sleep."

I blushed at the thought of Jay's lips on mine, then felt guilty. He was obviously really injured, and I had injured him further with my shenanigans.

"Is he going to be all right?"

"It was touch and go for a bit," Sage said, "but he's tough. If you hadn't saved him when you did, he probably wouldn't have made it. But since you did, he'll make a full recovery. He might need some help getting his hand working again, but he should be up and walking with crutches before too long."

"How long until he can leave the infirmary?"

"A couple of weeks, at least."

Well, at least I knew that he wouldn't be going back for a while, but what that meant to me—to us—I didn't know.

"The Captain said I need to go see her in her office after I'm released."

"After I get back from training, I'll walk you there. Sound like a plan?"

⚡⚡⚡

True to his word, Sage came and got me after I had eaten my fill of some sort of egg thing that I couldn't recognize. It tasted OK. It wasn't a donut, but honestly not much else was. Considering the Captain was feeding me out of the goodness of her heart, I was not about to complain.

Sage was quiet as we left the infirmary, but it didn't feel uncomfortable or unnatural. Maybe he was just as quiet and awkward as I was when he wasn't in his comfort zone. Or maybe knowing where I came from and what I could do was too much for him. I hoped that wasn't the case. I felt more comfortable around him than anyone else so far, which wasn't saying much, but it was something. I was so deep in thought about Sage and the rest of this bizarre set of circumstances as we walked down the path, I had to do a double-take. *No way.*

Sage stopped too. "What? What is it? Are you all right?"

"This path. I've seen it before."

"What? How?"

"In one of my dreams—my portals—I saw this walkway and the trees. It's like it was taken directly from my head."

I walked up to an old tree that was growing right along the path and gently took one of its blossoming leaves into my hand. "I opened a portal when I was asleep, when this all started. I was staying with my friend Calum. He's Ink. It's weird. Anyway, when the portal opened, Calum reached through it and grabbed a few of the leaves from the tree we could see. These leaves. That's when I realized I wasn't hallucinating, and that there really was a window. Before then, I thought I was losing my mind."

"Being stuck here, you might wish you had been delusional. I wonder why you saw this spot right here."

"Do you know about my mom's notes?"

"The Captain felt like I needed to know everything about you to make sure you got the best care. Plus, it was hard to hide the fact that you kept opening portals in your sleep. She told me that if you didn't wake up by today, I'd need to read your mom's notes to see if there was something in there to help. But I never had to."

"My mom's notes say that when I'm home, it appears that my portals open to wherever Blu is. So I'm guessing that she was here when I was sleeping."

"This is a fairly busy path. It leads to the Captain's office and the mess, among other places."

"That's so weird. It really feels like I've been here."

"In a way, you have."

⚡ ⚡ ⚡

The Captain was sitting behind her desk and signaled that I should take a chair across from her.

The office was more spacious than I remembered from my unceremonious arrival. It took up the entire first floor of the building. It was worn down, but unlike my equally dilapidated ex-apartment, this space didn't feel sad. It felt lived in and well loved, like the Velveteen Rabbit of offices. The wooden floors were worn to the nails, and though the giant table in the center of the space was battered, it somehow added to the charm.

"Thank you for meeting with me, Fara. How are you feeling?"

"Better, thank you. Sage gave me some herbs to take the edge off the pain in my arm, but I have to say I miss the stronger stuff back in my world."

I had contemplated opening a portal and asking Calum to send back some ibuprofen, although it seemed like a pretty ridiculous use of my abilities. Plus, he was more than likely mad at me for everything that had happened.

"I'm sure you'll find you miss many things. How are you feeling otherwise?"

"OK, I guess. Still a little weirded out by everything."

"You will probably feel that way for a while. Just know that we are all here to help you. I know the Team has already taken a liking to you—"

"Because I'm Blu—"

"I don't think so, Fara. You proved yourself to them while rescuing the agent, and they admire that. Anyway, as I told you last night, I have taken the liberty of having one of the apartments in the Team's building fixed up and furnished for you. It might not be as nice as what you're used to, but it's yours for as long as you want."

"That's so amazing. Thank you."

"Wait to thank me when you see it. It's not much."

"My apartment was crap even before it was trashed by Barrington's goons, so I'm sure this one's perfect. I don't know how to repay you."

The Captain waved me off. "No need. I'll take you there now, if you want."

We left the Captain's office, and I followed her up the broken brick path. The sun had fully risen, casting its golden glow through the early spring leaves of the trees. The breeze was already warm on my face. The path was mostly deserted. I tried to take it all in, but the walk to the apartment was short, and we were standing in front of the building in no time. It was red brick, like the Captain's building, but it didn't have vines growing all over it, or the creepy Gothic vibe—not that I would have minded.

The door opened onto a long hallway with doors on either side. The Captain led me through a door on the right to a staircase.

"You are going to be on the second floor, next to Ink and down the hall from Blu. Even though I think you need your own place, I thought you might want to be near people you know, or are beginning to know."

She stopped in front of a plain brown door and opened it, handing me a key in the process. "The Compound is safe, so whether you decide to lock your door is up to you. Blu doesn't lock hers unless she's trying to keep someone from waking her up in the morning. Although they mostly pick her lock, anyway. From what I understand, Ink locks his door. But that only started after he came back from a mission to find an overzealous trainee in his bed—uninvited."

I barked out a laugh, and the Captain smiled conspiratorially at me. What the hell? That was like next-level celebrity stalker stuff. There was a part of me that couldn't believe someone had had the audacity to do that, and another part of me that wondered what Ink did with the girl after he found her.

The Captain held open the door and let me walk into the apartment first. I couldn't help the grin that spread across my face.

It was perfect.

The wall to my left was made up entirely of windows that looked over some green space with trees. The worn cream curtains were tied back, letting in beautiful shafts of light from the midmorning sun that danced along the hardwood floors. On the opposite wall, there was a double bed with several pillows and a thick comforter. Next to the window were a couple of faded, giant, overstuffed chairs and a side table, and the small kitchen had a plain table with a couple of hard-backed chairs. Off the kitchen was the bathroom, with a small window over the tub that streamed in more light. It was stocked with soap, deodorant, shampoo, and conditioner, or at least that's what I assumed they were. I'd have to take a closer look at them later.

The Captain had thought of everything. The entire place was warm and bright, and even though it was older and in worse repair than my old apartment, it didn't feel sad. It felt . . . good. I threw my arms around the Captain, and she patted me awkwardly. Apparently, they weren't big huggers here.

"It's perfect. I don't know how to thank you."

She waved me off, again. "Some poor trainee washed Blu's laundry for her, so she's loaned you clothes until the armory can get you a few sets of your own. The kitchen has some staples, but most of your food will come from the mess hall. If there is anything you need, please let me know. I'm sure we can scrounge it from someplace or other."

"Again, it's perfect. Thank you. What can I do to repay you?"

"For now, read your mom's notes. The more we know, the more we can work with you. Also, I want you to start coming to principal Team meetings. I think your perspective will be useful. Blu and Ink are on a mission as we speak, so if you could come to the debriefing after they return, I'd appreciate it. I'll send someone to come get you."

Attending some meeting while others were out there risking their lives seemed like the least I could do.

After the Captain left, I walked around my apartment, not really believing what I was seeing. This place was wonderful, and it was mine, for now. After touching every surface and opening every drawer and cabinet in my apartment (my apartment!), I spread my mom's notes out on the bed, hopeful that I could make it through more than one sheet of paper before I dissolved into a blubbering mess. My arm was still throbbing something fierce. I guess getting sliced by a dagger and having multiple stitches was not something that just went away overnight. Bummer. I could use some better pain meds.

There was a pad of paper and a pen on the bedside table. Time to bite the bullet.

Dear C,

Where to even start? Probably with an apology, since I'm pretty sure you're angry with me—with all of this. I'm so sorry. Truly. I am so sorry that you got hurt rescuing Jay. But mostly I am so sorry that you got sucked into this whole mess. I don't know what I would do without you. Please don't stay mad at me for long.

Now that you've forgiven me (see what I did there?), I have to say that writing you a note from another universe is a bit crazy. Honestly, if I can't talk to you in person, this might be my new favorite kind of communication. It sort of reminds me of junior high. Except that I'm not going to ask you, if you like me, to check 'yes' or 'no.' At this point you'd probably check 'no,' and I wouldn't blame you. Once again, sorry.

I'm also sorry that I didn't respond to you sooner, but apparently whatever electroshock thing I did to the bad guy overloaded my system, so I passed out for two days and they put me in the infirmary (their version of a hospital). Don't worry, I'm fine. I promise. I'm going to read my mom's notes to see if there are any answers about that crazy thing that happened. I really don't want another ability, though. Especially since I can't seem to control the first one.

I'm doing OK. My arm still hurts like a bitch, and they don't have heavy-duty painkillers here. Speaking of that, I know it's a super weird request, but is there any way you could leave me a bottle of ibuprofen? I could really use something to help with the throbbing. Also, if you think of it, can you leave me some of my clothes too? Blu is letting me borrow her stuff until I can get my own—but I think I'd feel better with something from home.

How's Adora? Does she know anything? Have you been safe? Have Barrington and the government left you alone? I think about you and worry about you so much. I wish you could be here, but I hope to be home soon.

Write when you can.

Love,

F

I put the pen down and opened a portal, folding the note as Calum's apartment came into view. I looked arcund as much as I could to see if I could catch a glimpse of my best friend, but I couldn't. I let the portal close with a hiss.

I sagged back onto my pillows and went over the events of the past couple of weeks. Had it really only been that long since Jay showed up at my gym and accused me of having a weapon in my shithole apartment? There was no way I could have ever guessed then that I would be sending letters by portal-mail from an apartment in another universe. Life was so weird.

12 FARA

I awoke to the feeling of my bed moving, even though I wasn't.

"I'm used to throwing things at Blu to wake her up, but your place is so clean there's nothing to throw."

Ink was lying next to me, head propped up on his hand, a smirk on his face as he stared at me.

I shot up in bed, disoriented, with my heart pounding. Where was I? Was I sleeping? What was happening? Why was Ink in my bed?

Ink's smirk turned into a grin. "And now is the time you tell me to fuck off and get out of your room."

It registered, then. I was in my new apartment, and Ink was trying to wake me in a way that only he could pull off. I must have fallen asleep after sending Calum the note.

"Fuck off and get out of my room?"

He chuckled and hopped up, his green eyes full of mischief. "That's better. If you're going to live here, you need to start telling us off."

"I'll work on that."

"Believe me, Fara, you will have ample opportunity to tell us to fuck off. Especially me. I'll make sure of it."

I wiped the sleep from my eyes. Ink was walking around my room, looking in my closet and opening up my drawers. It was like he had so much energy that he didn't know how to sit still, and so he just investigated things. I watched him from my bed, half mortified that he was looking through my meager stuff, and half entertained by the process. The light, pleasant smell of his cologne clung to my comforter. How long had he been in my room? In my bed? I couldn't think about that now, especially since I was staring at him. He looked over his shoulder with a sly grin and I blushed. Bastard.

"You do that on purpose," I said as I hoisted myself up.

"Hmmm?"

"You pose so that girls can ogle you."

I walked into the bathroom to wash my face and try to do something with the blush that was a permanent resident on my cheeks when Ink was around. He was a flirt with everyone, I told myself sternly. It wasn't personal. It was just him.

"It's for their benefit."

I splashed water on my face and searched for a hair tie. "Right. Because every girl has a hidden desire to stare at you?"

"Yours is not so hidden, Fara."

Not personal. "I stare at you because you look like my best friend."

"Sure you do."

My head whipped around. He was leaning on the doorway of the bathroom, eyebrow raised. How had he sneaked up on me?

"Do you not have *any* boundaries? For real! Out!"

I grabbed the hand towel I had just used to dry my face and chucked it at him. He caught it and walked away, laughing.

"I'm here to retrieve you, neighbor, for lunch. Then to debrief in the Captain's office."

I pulled my hair up in a bun that would never have passed The Grill's manager, Douche's, requirements. Luckily for me, I didn't have worry about him right now. I had brushed my teeth, and since there was no makeup to be found anywhere, I was as ready as I could be. I wished I had makeup, especially since the bruise on my face, while fading, was still a lovely shade of purple and green. I sighed at my reflection. How was it that someone who looked exactly like me could look so much better without any makeup than me? Weren't we the same person?

Ink peeked around the doorway again, rolling his eyes at the sight of me staring at myself in the mirror.

"Come on, sweetness, we need to go."

I rolled my eyes at him, hoping it was as annoying as the reverse, but he laughed, so I doubted it. I went to leave, but he stopped me.

"Rule one: never leave your room unarmed. Even though the Compound is safe and has been for years, you don't want to get caught unaware."

"I'm not sure I have anything."

"The Captain wouldn't have stocked your room without at least a dagger."

I looked around my room, trying to locate something that had a sharp, pointy end. Ink had already walked over to my bedside table and lifted a sheath with a dagger inside.

"Keep this on you, unless you are sleeping. Then it goes by your bed."

He handed me the sheath and I tried to remember how to attach it to my clothes. I was waiting for him to tease me, but he didn't.

"What? No comment?"

"Not this time. It's important that you learn how to protect yourself, and I'm going to help you learn. We all will."

I started struggling with the contraption, biting my lip in frustration, but I refused to be deterred. I mean, I figured out how to live on my own at seventeen with no family or money—I could figure out how to put on a fricking dagger.

"That's it. Now you need to buckle the sheath around your thigh, then make sure it's attached to your belt." I buckled the thigh thing and attached it to the belt and buckled that. He obviously read the discomfort on my face. "You'll get the feel for it, and then you can decide what you want the armory to make for you."

The dagger was already in its sheath, so I raised my eyebrows at Ink in question. He grinned at me. "That's more like it."

I pointed out that I'd seen several Team members walking around without weapons, and he laughed. "We can also kill most anyone with our bare hands. But you'll get there. Until then, carry a dagger."

⚡ ⚡ ⚡

The mess was really just a large cafeteria, with long tables, a buffet line, and a kitchen hidden in the back. Food steamed under heat lamps at the front.

"I don't know what kind of food you have where you're from, but take whatever looks familiar," Ink said.

It looked exactly like the sort of food I was used to, much to my relief. There were a couple of things I couldn't identify, but that might have been my lack of experience rather than an alternate universe thing. I was about to help myself to some fries when I stopped and put the empty plate down. Ink looked at me, puzzled.

"I have no way to pay for this." I didn't even know what kind of currency they used. I was in debt here already: the food, my apartment, the infirmary bill, clothes. So much debt.

"Fara, it's all free."

"Free?"

"Yes, free. Food, a place to stay, and education are free at the Compound. Captain's orders." He added a huge steak to his plate.

I couldn't believe it. The fact that I could have as many cheeseburgers as I wanted without breaking the bank was heaven to my ears. When was the last time I hadn't had to worry about money? Oh. It was before my parents died. I clamped down on the sorrow that was threatening to rise. The lunch line was probably not the best place to open a portal.

Picking up the plate, I headed down the line, asking Ink questions when I didn't know what something was. Eventually I settled on a cheeseburger and fries, with a giant coffee.

When Ink saw my tray, he chuckled.

"What?"

"If there was a donut on that tray, you would have picked out all of Blu's favorite foods."

"Theoretically, we are genetically the same."

"True. But does that mean you should both love cheeseburgers?"

"Cheeseburgers are universally delicious."

We headed to a table away from everyone else. As Ink led the way, every person in the room, without exception, watched him. They were either trying to be discreet and failing, or they were unabashedly gaping at him, as if he were a rock star. No wonder he locked the door to his room. He raised his chin in greeting at a few people, but to my amazement he didn't pay the others much attention. He was focused solely on me.

While I enjoyed my cheeseburger, Ink didn't say much. It seemed out of character for him. Mid-bite, I looked up to find that he was studying me. I blushed—I couldn't help it. He noticed that *I* noticed and grinned sheepishly.

I swallowed. "What?"

"It's a bit weird, sitting here with you in the same spot."

"This is Blu's spot? I'm sure it is weird."

He took my staring as a sign he could really study me, which was a tad disconcerting. "Even though you are almost identical, your mannerisms are so different, even down to the way you sit and eat, that I catch myself seeing you as a different person."

"I *am* a different person."

"You know what I mean." He threw a wadded-up napkin at me. It hit me in the face. He almost looked chagrined. "Sorry. I'm used to people dodging what I throw."

I laughed and threw it back. "I'm not from around here, remember?" He caught it without taking his eyes off me.

"Hey, Ink. I was just heading to the Captain's office. I think I found some stuff."

The voice was super familiar. I looked up and almost choked on my cheeseburger. Beck was standing there, looking at me with a puzzled expression. No, not Beck, just his version over here. I took a drink of my coffee, trying to cover up my reaction.

Beck-not-Beck stared at me and stared at Ink, and Ink stared quizzically at me.

"Fara, this is Dev. He's part of the team that works with Styx." Dev gawked at me as I mumbled "nice to meet you" into my coffee cup. Holy shit. It never occurred to me that Beck would be here. Was he a mooching asshat like he was in my own world? Ugh. Beck.

"What was that about?" Ink asked, laughing as Dev walked away.

"Sorry."

"Seriously, stop apologizing for everything. You didn't do anything wrong; you just freaked out when you saw our resident tech nerd, and I was wondering why."

I took a deep breath. "That's my ex-boyfriend."

"What?"

"That guy, in my world, is my ex-boyfriend. Very recent ex-boyfriend. Like, a couple of days ago."

"Him? Really? He doesn't strike me as your type. Is he a techie sort of guy in your world?"

"Not really. In my world, he's a mooching asshat sort of guy."

Ink snorted. "Is that why you broke up with him? Or was it something else?"

"Bad sex," I quipped, then turned forty-five shades of red. That was something I would have said to Calum. But this wasn't Calum—and I wanted to crawl under the table. Ink's eyebrows reached his hair; then he threw back his head and laughed, not at all bothered by my joke.

"Well, that's as good a reason as any. Better, probably. But I thought the guy we rescued was your boyfriend? You naughty little thing, dating them both at once!"

"Ugh—no! I can't even walk and chew gum at the same time."

"So what happened?"

"Why do you want to know?"

He ran a finger around the rim of his coffee cup as he watched me. His eyes had a hint of mischief in them that I had never noticed with Calum, but I found myself smiling. "Maybe it will soothe my curiosity about you," he said. "Fair?"

"Fair. Only if I get to ask about you next."

"Deal."

As much as I really didn't want to think about Beck, I told Ink about my relationship with him anyway, such as it was. The long hours I worked to support him, the partying, the general selfishness. Saying it out loud made his decision to break up with me almost seem like a blessing. Not quite, but almost.

"What an asshole. No wonder you looked at Dev like that."

"Yeah, and I feel bad. It's not Dev's fault that my ex is a total asshat."

"True, but I'm going to give him monumental shit about it from now on."

I was mortified at the thought. "Please don't! That poor guy can't control looking like my selfish ex!"

Ink's eyes told me that he was definitely going to give Dev shit. Great. Now I was going to have to hide from him.

He nodded toward the infirmary. "The other guy's from your government, right? How did that even start? I mean, I understand why he wants you."

I decided to ignore that last part. Ink was being himself, and it didn't mean anything. "Once he realized that his superiors were going to interrogate me in a less than awesome way for information about the palmbox, he decided to help me. One thing led to another. But nothing is happening until all of this crap is over."

"So you haven't been together that long?"

"We're not really *together*. I mean, he kissed me, then I got kidnapped and he tried to rescue me, then we rescued him." I shrugged. "There hasn't been a lot of time to talk about our long-term relationship goals."

Ink laughed at that. "Just a kiss?"

"Yes! Although that is none of your business."

"Fine. And you and the other me?"

"Calum and I are best friends. I've known him since I was little."

"And you guys never . . .?"

"Seriously, none of your business! Although the answer is no. He doesn't see me that way."

"I doubt that."

"Whatever. He doesn't. Believe me. Why are you asking me about my love life? And why am I telling you all of this?"

He grinned at me, popping part of a cookie in his mouth. "Because I asked and I'm awesome."

"Right. OK, enough about me. What about you? Girlfriend? I hear you have quite the reputation with the ladies, and that you lock your door because of overly excited groupies."

"Did Blu tell you that? Well, that only happened once. Wait . . . twice."

"They just can't get enough?"

"Or something."

"So you don't have a girlfriend?"

"Why have a girlfriend when I can pick and choose?"

"Like a girl buffet?"

He snorted. "Really, Fara, you make it sound worse than it is! I like women and they seem to like me. Why not have some fun?"

"Why not settle down?"

He paused, and although he was still smiling, the glint in his eyes dimmed. "What's the point? I won't live to grow old with someone anyway."

Oh.

The matter-of-fact way he approached dying young made my heart hurt. I found myself wanting to hug him, but I refrained. We weren't quite friends yet.

"For what it's worth," I said instead, "I think that you're less of an asshole than you pretend to be."

He gave me a genuine smile. "I'll take it."

BLU 13

The Captain waited for us to get into our seats before beginning the debrief. "Good afternoon. I think introductions are in order. Silver, Dev, this is Fara."

I had been watching Ink and Fara since they walked into the room together. Fara seemed to be more relaxed, if only just a bit. Ink was giving her loads of shit about something, but instead of folding in on herself, she managed to tease him back a little. Hopefully, his antics were helping her feel comfortable with all of us, as opposed to making her want to gouge his eyes out. It was always a near thing with him.

I wasn't the only one watching Fara and Ink. When the Captain said her name, it took Silver a couple of heartbeats before she realized that Fara and I shared a face. Her reaction was subdued, but I could still see her figuring out how Fara fit into her chances with Ink. Poor girl. Eventually she'd give up her harmless crush and move on.

Dev, on the other hand, didn't have quite the same reaction. Had Fara already been introduced to him? Was that why she was currently—and unsuccessfully—trying to hide from him?

Once the Captain concluded the routine business, it was my turn to relay what had happened at Dagna's building. I decided to start with the biggest revelation: Jyston's appearance.

"He knows Fara is here. He called her my 'cousin,' but something tells me that he knows more about it than he let on." I looked around the table. "And I don't know how much the rest of Jurisdiction knows either."

"How in the hell does he know about her?" Styx asked. "Very few people have actually seen her. She's mostly been in the infirmary."

"I don't know, but that concerns me," the Captain answered. "We need someone to stick with Fara until we can plug this leak. Fara, it's not that we want to be intrusive . . ."

"I know that I can't take care of myself like you guys can, so if you think that I need to take precautions, I'll do that."

"Then that's settled," the Captain said. "You'll be safe at the Compound, but probably no more missions for you until we have more information. Team, let's figure out a way to unobtrusively keep an eye on our guest." She shuffled some papers, then moved on to the next order of business. "Ink, why don't you go ahead with your report?"

Ink sketched out a rough map of the area. "The Second Counselor sent me down the trail, and while it pissed me off at the time, it actually led to some good scouting. The trail leads down behind the building, just outside of the fence." He scribbled a dark patch on the map. "There is a small, unmanned gate in the fence just at the end of the trail, next to a pit, here. A mass grave." Fara gasped. The rest of us were used to Jurisdiction's atrocities; it was no surprise.

"Between the building and the trees, the gate is hidden from sight from pretty much every angle but the trail, unless you are directly in front of it."

"Is it electric?" Styx asked.

"I threw a stick at it and it didn't fry, so I don't think so. I think the Second Counselor led us to the only way in—or out—of the building without being seen."

"Is it big enough to get the prisoners out?" Styx asked.

"It's a long shot. The trail isn't guarded, but the area leading to the trail is. Once Jurisdiction figures out what's happening, they could catch a big group on our way back to the getaway vehicles. But a couple of people could get in to raise some hell."

"That sounds promising. And there were no spikes of death or anything?" Styx asked.

"No," Ink replied. "It's such a small area that I'm sure Jurisdiction doesn't consider it a security risk. I hate to give the asshole credit, but if it weren't for Jyston, we wouldn't have found it."

The Team discussed how we could best use that information, determining that it might make sense to go back again for more reconnaissance.

"And we might have another way," I said, after the conversation started winding down. "Jyston also suggested we enter the PITs."

There was a brief, stunned silence, and then the room exploded as everyone started talking at once. The Captain raised a hand.

"Before this devolves into more chaos, why don't we give Blu the opportunity to explain what she means?"

Jack was shaking his head by the time I was done. "Is Jyston out of his mind? There's no way we can enter the PITs without getting spotted or killed trying to get in, or killed during the competition, or captured, or any other terrible thing." He crossed his arms. "My spies can't even get close to the stadium because it's so heavily guarded. It's one of the areas of the city center we just ignore. There's no way at all we can do that!"

"With Jyston's help—"

Ink snorted. "Screw that guy. I bet he won't risk his ass to get us in."

It wasn't like I hadn't thought about all of the things the Team was bringing up, but my gut was telling me Jyston was trying to help. I needed to find a way to make this work.

"What are the pits?" Fara asked quietly, which stopped our bickering—albeit briefly.

The Captain explained, "It's an acronym—"

"It's a fucking nightmare," Jack said.

I opened my mouth to argue, but the Captain cut in before it became an all-out brawl. "It stands for Powerbike Inground Tournament. Jurisdiction calls it a game, although it's anything but for the prisoners who are forced to participate."

"From what I understand," Ink said, "it's like a brutal version of 'capture the flag.' The prisoners are forced to ride giant motorized dirt bikes in pairs in an arena of sorts. It's usually played to the death."

"That's terrible," Fara said.

"It is," the Captain replied, "which is why I'm wondering what Jyston thinks we can hope to get out of entering them."

"Information about a way to get close to the building, probably," I said.

The Captain steepled her fingers, deep in thought. "Blu, not that I don't trust your instincts," she said, "but before I risk any of the Team in the PITs, we need more information, and I have someone who can provide it. For a price."

"Who?" I asked.

"I believe you and Silver have already met him. You called him 'the Pirate.' Fairly appropriate, actually. Although when he lived at the Compound, we called him 'Warhorse.'"

"You do know him!"

"I've known Warhorse a long, long time," the Captain said. "He was one of the founding members of the Compound. He was a great warrior. It was a huge loss to the Team when he left."

"So why would this Warhorse guy help us?"

"We'd bribe him, of course. Once I realized he was still alive, I had Jack gather intel on him and his camp." She gave a little smile. "It turns out that he has participated in the PITs before. Several times, in fact."

"How much would it cost?"

"Maybe not as much as you think. Recently, some of his people were taken by Dagna. He might be willing to help if it means getting them back."

"Silver and I can talk to him," I said, my wheels already spinning.

"That might be a good start."

14 FARA

The Captain had us break until after lunch tomorrow, giving Blu and Silver time to meet Warhorse. She asked if I was up for training in the morning, and after a moment's hesitation, I knew I was, even if my arm hurt like a bitch. I needed to do something to get these emotions under control, at least until I read enough of my mom's notes to see if there was an alternative way of controlling my portal ability. But any sort of physical exertion would help for now. That was my working theory, anyway.

As we walked out of the Captain's building, Styx threaded her arm through mine, like Adora had done a thousand times. I couldn't help but smile.

"Where are you off to?"

"I was thinking about bringing food to Jay, then heading to my apartment to read my mom's notes."

Jack stopped mid-step. "I'm going that way. Want company?"

It was his polite way of babysitting me, but I didn't mind, especially since I still had no idea where anything was.

"Here," Styx said, pulling a piece of equipment out of her pocket that looked like a cross between a hearing aid and one of those goofy Bluetooth earpiece things.

"This is a comm." She showed me how to put it in my ear and use it. "It'll connect you to the control room, and they'll send someone to walk you back to the apartment. Although" she whispered, "you might not need it if you're spending the night with the hot agent man . . ." She waggled her eyebrows at me.

Before I could protest, Ink said, "Fara, I wouldn't expend all of your energy tonight. You have training tomorrow morning. Unless, of course, you want to come next door when you get back to your place?"

"Ugh! Seriously?" Blu smacked him as he chuckled.

"You know the offer is open for you as well."

"You know that I can feel unsatisfied all on my own."

"Ouch, B! I promise that you would feel . . ."

I didn't hear the rest of it, as Jack caught my eye and I followed him up the path to the mess.

"We'd be there all day if we waited for them to get done squabbling."

I walked through the line at the mess, putting random food in a container, not really sure what Jay liked to eat. It was a weird thought. The fact that I wanted to strip him naked and had slept in the same bed as him but didn't know if he liked green beans seemed strange to me. Maybe a year of lackluster bedroom antics with Beck had amplified my libido? Or maybe having a near-death experience with someone made the question "Do you prefer baked or mashed potatoes?" rather superfluous.

The medics nodded to Jack as we walked through the infirmary, then did a double-take when they saw me. It hadn't occurred to me that they wouldn't know who I was, since I'd spent a full two days here. However, from their reactions it appeared that Sage and the Team had kept most of the other staff away from me. I mean, I couldn't blame them, since I was opening portals willy-nilly while I was passed out, and that kind of thing doesn't need a massive audience.

Jack walked through the maze of corridors like he knew where he was going.

"You certainly know your way around here," I said.

"I've spent a lot of time here, either as a patient or visiting. This world isn't easy to live in sometimes."

I could only nod. I knew it was dangerous. I also knew I didn't know even half of it.

He took a right at the end of the corridor, and I recognized the hall where I had been recovering. My stomach did a nervous little flip—I was almost to Jay's room. I hadn't been nervous the past couple of times I saw him, with everything that had been happening. But now I was. I gripped the food container a little tighter than necessary and took a deep breath.

Jack was already heading to the door opposite Jay's.

"If she's up for it, I'll bring Willow by to say hello."

"Friend of yours?"

"She took a sword to the stomach in the last mission, when I broke my wrist. Well, the first time I broke my wrist, anyway. I think you'll like her."

He knocked once on her door and went in. I was left standing in the hall with food, wondering why I was nervous.

FARA 15

"Come in."

I slowly opened the door and peered into his room. The light was off, although there was the soft glow of a night-light coming from somewhere. Jay was lying back in bed, his hair disheveled, and his face still a mess.

"Did I wake you? I'm so sorry—"

"Is that food I smell?"

My feet were still unwilling to move farther in. All teasing aside, I wasn't kidding when I told Ink that Jay and I hadn't really discussed our relationship, such as it was. He had admitted that he wanted me, and I knew that I liked him. Why was I overthinking this?

"They didn't have spring rolls, so I got the next best thing."

"What's that?"

"A donut."

His laugh rolled through the room, breaking the spell that had me glued to the ground.

"Are you even hungry?" I hadn't bothered to ask. I just assumed—

"I can always eat," he said, struggling to sit up.

"Wait! Hang on, let me help you before you hurt yourself."

I raised the bed so he was more or less sitting up, turned on the bedside lamp, and for the first time I could see in the light, and in great detail, how terribly injured he was. I schooled my face so that I wasn't wincing, remembering that he had forbidden me from blaming myself for his injuries. I couldn't help it, though.

"Fara, you looking at me like that is hurting my feelings." The corner of his mouth tugged up.

"It's just . . ."

"I look like shit?"

"Sorry. This is the first time I've seen you in the light since you've been here."

"My ego is never going to recover from this conversation."

"No! I mean, I still think you're like, ridiculously good-looking. But in a more—"

"—beat-up sort of way?" he finished, his fork halfway to his mouth and an eyebrow raised, and I couldn't stifle the giggle that escaped. He met my gaze, his eyes flickering with a touch of humor. "You find me ridiculously good-looking?"

I blushed. "You know you are. Don't deny it."

"It never really mattered to me."

"Only a ridiculously good-looking person can say that. Those of us with mere mortal genes might find it matters a bit more."

"I wouldn't call your genes 'mere mortal.'"

Right. "How is your treatment going? How are they here?"

"It's . . . different. Strange. Some things are exactly like they are at home. And others are like forty years behind. And," he said with a wince, "their painkillers aren't worth shit."

"I know! Oh, that reminds me. Hang on." I started the process of opening a portal.

"Fara, what—"

The portal opened, showing Calum's coffee table like always. On it were some of my clothes, a giant bottle of ibuprofen, and a note. This time it was folded to look like a hummingbird. I reached through, grabbed my stuff, and closed the portal, only to find Jay looking at me warily.

"What was that?"

"A parallel universe care package. I thought you might want to share in my bounty."

"You mean, you're using your ability to pass notes and get ibuprofen?"

"Sure."

"More than once?"

"Yes. Jay, what is it?"

"Fara, I thought the idea of staying here was to figure out how to control your ability so you could come home. What you're doing seems irresponsible."

His reaction caught me off guard. "They can't track me here, Jay. Everyone here has palmboxes—"

"Palm what?"

"Devices. And not once has one of them beeped when I open a portal. The only two that seem to track my portal abilities are the original one that your department has, and the one Barrington created, neither of which are in this universe." He looked skeptical. "Plus," I added defensively, "I need practice. I'm working on using my powers to better understand them."

"You shouldn't be using them at all. It's dangerous."

"It's not dangerous to use them here! Look, right after I leave the infirmary, I'm going back to my apartment to read more of my mom's notes. I need to stop opening portals in my sleep, and I'm hoping she'll tell me how to do that."

He didn't argue with me any further, although his eyes were clouded with worry. I understood what he was saying—the whole reason I was staying here was to get my powers under control so that I could go home.

"So, do you want the ibuprofen, or are you going to make a point and not have any?"

Even beneath the bruising, I could see his jaw twitching. He was trying to keep a straight face. I grinned at him as I handed him the pills.

"See? Interdimensional grocery shopping isn't so bad."

"I'm serious, Fara. Please be careful."

"I am, Jay. I'm going to work on suppressing my abilities. I promise."

"Abilities. As in plural?"

Oops.

"Yeah, so . . . I accidentally electrocuted one of the baddies when we rescued you."

"Accidentally *electrocuted*?"

"I don't understand it either. It was like an electric shock that came out of my hands when one of the goons tried to grab me. I don't know where it came from, but I'm hoping my mom's notes explain it. I can't pass out for two days again."

"No, probably not," he said with a sigh. "Just be careful, OK? I really would like to eventually take you on a real date."

"One that doesn't include running for our lives?"

"Preferably," he said as he cupped my cheek with his good hand, rubbing my cheekbone with his thumb, which sent little happy vibes down to my feet. I leaned over and gently kissed him.

"I'd ask you to stay, but Sage would have a coronary," he said, my forehead resting on his.

"You need to get better, and you can't do that if I'm all up in your stuff."

"All up in my stuff?" The corner of his mouth curved up.

"Uh huh. So, I'll come visit you tomorrow, if that's all right with you."

"I look forward to it."

I stood up, but before I could leave, he grabbed my arm.

"Fara, I'm not sure of everything that is going on here, but the fact that you have a dagger strapped to your thigh isn't a good sign." His brow was furrowed with concern. "Can you promise me not to use your abilities here? It's not safe."

"I can't promise that, Jay. But I promise to read my mom's notes to see how to control them better." I didn't want to fight with him about this, and I understood where he was coming from. Sort of.

"Please don't do anything reckless, all right?"

I kissed him on the lips again, lingering a bit longer to savor the moment. I knew what he was asking me to do—to stay in my room, to not use my powers, to work so that I could go back home, to be safe. It was what we had planned before Barrington kidnapped me. It was what he asked of me when I escaped. It was what I'd told the Captain I wanted, what I'd told myself I wanted. It was the safest thing to do, for me. For us.

But listening to the Team talk about how they wanted to make this world better, and would risk everything to do it, or how Ink didn't think he'd live long enough to make a relationship matter, got me thinking. Was there any way, small that it might be, that I could help them? What if I could train with my abilities? What if I stayed?

16 FARA

I was proud of myself for having figured out the comm and telling the voice on the other end that I was supposed to have someone come get me. Whoever answered didn't ask any questions; he just told me that someone was on their way and to wait there.

The smell of antiseptic in the infirmary was starting to make my head hurt, so I stepped outside into the cool night air. I looked up at the stars and recognized the Big Dipper. It was comforting, somehow, to see the same stars.

"You must be Blu's cousin," a sultry voice said from behind me, startling me. I hadn't seen or heard anyone approach.

A tall, dark-haired beauty was smiling down at me. Her hair was piled effortlessly on top of her head, perfect tendrils framing her heart-shaped face. Her skin glowed in the moonlight, as did her eyes. I had never seen her before, in this world or mine.

"Hi?"

She stuck out her hand. "I'm Iris. Sorry to startle you. I've seen you hanging around Ink and I thought that I should introduce myself."

"Nice to meet you, Iris."

"I'm sure Ink's told you about me."

"Uh, not really. Sorry?"

She looked genuinely perplexed by my lack of knowledge of her. Did he say something to me? Had I just forgotten?

"Well, it's no matter. I hear you're going to be staying at the Compound for a while?"

Something about the way she asked made me uncomfortable.

"For a while, yeah. I guess."

She took a step closer to me, almost into my personal space, and I realized that she towered over me. Like most people.

"Where are you staying?"

"I'm not sure. Everything is up in the air." It wasn't like she'd said or done anything other than make conversation, but something was off about her.

"Do you live in the apartments?" I ventured.

"No, I live in the dorms, although you'll probably be seeing me around. I spend my days working at the armory. And my nights with Ink."

Oh! She was one of Ink's groupies. That's why she was asking all of the questions. She was seeing if I was a threat. The feeling I was getting was "crazy girlfriend." I certainly didn't care if she was sleeping with Ink, so her jealousy was misplaced. She was hot; I couldn't blame him.

"That's great," I replied, and my shoulders sagged in relief when I saw Blu walking up the path. I didn't want to be talking to crazy girlfriend anymore.

"Iris, I see you've met my cousin," Blu said in a tone that had an edge to it. It held none of the dry humor or mock irritation I associated with her. I'd never heard her use it before. Maybe I wasn't the only one who didn't want to deal with crazy girlfriend.

"Wow, the resemblance is strong in your family! You guys could be twins."

"We get that a lot," Blu replied. "Where were you off to?"

"I was just getting some night air. Hoping to catch Ink wandering around. Any idea where he might be?"

Blu sighed, a sound that was both irritated and resigned. With Ink's antics, I'm sure more than one girl had irritated Blu on his account.

"He's already in bed, Iris. We have early training tomorrow."

Her lips formed a perfect pout, making her all the more gorgeous. "Oh, so stopping by his apartment wouldn't be a good idea?"

"Probably not."

"OK, then. Just tell him hi."

Blu made a noise that was noncommittal. "Fara, you ready?"

We began down the path toward our apartments, as Iris headed in the other direction, toward the big white buildings.

"Who was that?" I ventured once we were out of earshot.

"Someone Ink needs to have a conversation with. Even though he always tells them that he doesn't want a relationship, some of the more persistent ones don't get the hint."

"I feel sort of bad for them."

She looked truly surprised. "Why? He's honest with them from the start. It's not his problem that they don't want to believe what he's telling them."

"True."

"Anyway, how was your hot agent man? Did he give you presents already?" She was eyeballing my stash of clothes.

I laughed. "I got these from one of my dumb ideas." I explained what had happened. "Jay wasn't happy about it."

"Fara, why would you think that was dumb? That is an ingenious use of your ability! Think of all the awesome things you can bring here. Why was Jay mad about that?"

"He said that the whole reason I'm here is to learn how to suppress my abilities so that I can go home. He said using them is dangerous."

"I say that's bullshit, but whatever."

I had expected her to tell me that using my powers was putting myself and the Team at unnecessary risk, and that I should work on suppressing them. But she surprised me. She thought Jay was wrong. I'd have to think about it more, but not now. Now, I needed some sleep.

As we passed by Ink's apartment on our way to mine, his door swung open. He was standing in his doorway, shirtless, and I couldn't help but stare at him—at his washboard abs, to be precise. He caught me staring, and I quickly looked away, but not before he raised an eyebrow. He knew he looked good.

"For god's sake, Ink, put on a shirt. You're not the lead in a romance novel." I could almost hear Blu rolling her eyes, though I was intently studying the ground by my feet.

"And cover this up? Why would I do that?" I looked up to find him winking at me. Bastard. "If the Captain didn't require clothes, I'd walk around naked so I could show off my more *impressive* attributes."

"From what I remember, it wasn't that impressive."

"Ouch, B!" He made a grab for her, but she skirted out of the way, swatting at his hand.

"Stop thinking with your dick for a sec, and I won't insult your brain," she said. I laughed at the look on his face, which was a mixture of mischief and pout. I had forgotten that they had dated once. Although, "dated" might be an exaggeration. If they had feelings other than friendship for each other now, it wasn't apparent.

"Was there a reason you were standing out here, or was it just to show off?"

"I was just making sure that my new neighbor was settling in OK."

He was checking on me? "I'm fine. Thanks."

"You're welcome. I want to be a good neighbor, you know. So, if you need anything like sugar, toilet paper, a massage . . . "

I didn't know how to respond, so I didn't. It wasn't that it still made me uncomfortable, but I wasn't good at banter like they were. Maybe with enough time here I would be. Blu sighed, the sound of the long suffering.

"By the way," she said, "Iris cornered Fara and all but pissed on your door to mark her territory. You either need to declare your love for her and stop screwing around, or you need to have a chat with her. It's getting out of hand."

"What did she say?" he asked me.

"She was asking me a bunch of questions and seemed upset that you didn't mention her to me. She creeped me out a bit, but it's really no big deal."

Ink sighed. "Sorry about that. I'll take care of it."

"There is nothing to apologize for, honestly."

Once they had left, I walked into my apartment, exhausted. I needed to read my mom's notes, and the note from Calum, but first I needed to take a zillion ibuprofen. My arm was throbbing in time with my heartbeat.

I put away my small pile of clothes, realizing how pathetically few belongings I still had. A pair of my sleep shorts had survived the Great Apartment Massacre, so I changed into those and one of my cheap T-shirts, and got into bed to start reading. Before I could even unfold the hummingbird, my eyes dropped closed. I reached over to turn off my lamp. My last thought before sleep took me was that I was excited about training tomorrow. I couldn't remember the last time I had been excited about anything.

FARA 17

It was way too early in the morning when Blu came and got me for training. She wasn't a morning person either, so we clutched our coffees and donuts and silently made our way down the broken brick path to an open green space—the Quad. People were already standing around in small groups, talking. Jack was there, along with Ink and Silver. Dev was also there, and I ducked behind Styx as he looked at me. Ink caught me trying to hide and laughed. Jerk.

There were others who I didn't recognize, standing around with a sort of nervous energy. They kept sending furtive glances over at Blu, Styx, Ink, and Jack, and whispering like those four were A-list celebrities or something. But once their eyes landed on me, the whispering doubled in intensity. I put my head down, trying to ignore the attention. I had been here a couple of days and thought the newness would have worn off already, so I hadn't expected this.

"I've never been comfortable with the attention either," Blu said with a ghost of a smile. The Captain hadn't been exaggerating about Blu's status here. Just by looking like her, I was already a superstar, even if I didn't feel like one. At all.

The Captain gave a couple of announcements and got the training started for the others, then turned her attention to me. "I'm not going to go any easier on you than I would a new trainee. Today you'll be working on hand-to-hand combat. Is this your first time?"

While kickboxing had combat elements to it, I had never sparred with anything more than a punching bag. But I was excited about learning how to kick some ass. Maybe it'd help me the next time Hewitt decided to get handsy. Maybe if Barrington's goons decided to grab me again, I wouldn't feel so helpless.

Sage was the only other trainee in my group. Had the Captain done that on purpose, to take some of the pressure off me from the gawking? For whatever reason, I was grateful that it was just Sage with me.

"Feeling better?" he asked.

"Much, thank you."

"I didn't see you in Jay's room this morning, so either you snuck out early or . . . "

"I didn't stay there."

"Smart."

Over Sage's shoulder, I saw Ink and Blu had started what looked like Matrix-level kung fu. The other trainees had stopped to watch them, and I couldn't blame them. It was impressive.

"Need I remind you," the Captain said in their general direction, "that the last time you both took things too far, Ink ended up in the infirmary? We need to teach these two the basics."

Blu stopped a roundhouse kick inches away from Ink's chest, then slowly lowered her leg to the ground. The technique and control that one move took, not to mention the other things I saw them doing—for fun!—made my heart beat faster. I was going to learn to do that. I was as excited as I was freaked out.

The Captain explained the training process, then had Blu and Ink teach us basic defensive moves, like how to escape if we were grabbed. Each of them took turns being the captor and the captive, and they slowed the motions down to show us what they were doing.

I watched Blu carefully, since she was at least a foot shorter than Ink. She didn't even seem to notice it. It was something that I was going to have to learn to do, since we were the same size. It gave me hope.

After a couple of repetitions of the same maneuver, I saw Ink's grin widen a split second before he made a grab for Blu that didn't look anything like they were teaching us. Before I could warn her, she'd spun out of the way without so much as a look of surprise. With the same motion, she hit him in the head with the back of her fist, and kicked his legs out from under him. Her moves were so fast they looked fake. As he fell with a grunt to the ground, a grin spread across her face—it matched his.

"I thought we were just practicing," Ink said as he got up, rubbing the back of his head.

"That was not a basic hold you attempted, asshole. You're showing off for your groupies. So I did what I'd do to a minion who tried it. Wanna try—"

But before Blu could get the last word out, Ink made a grab for her again. She dodged it, and the game was apparently on. The two of them weaved in and out of each other's grasp, their movements so precise and lightning fast that I was afraid someone was going to end up back at the infirmary again. The goofing around they had been doing earlier was nothing compared to this. However, the looks on their faces were anything but angry. They were beaming like they were having the best time ever. Maybe they were.

Finally, Ink was able to grab Blu, who twisted and took his legs out from under him again, dropping onto his chest as he fell to the ground. She gave him a kiss on his cheek and was starting to get up when he rolled her over and pinned her, his face triumphant.

"Get off me! I won." She laughed.

"I wasn't done yet."

"Doesn't matter. I won."

"Can you two please stop so we can train the people who actually need training?" the Captain said, exasperated. Ink ruffled Blu's hair, got up, then pulled her to her feet. While she was trying to look angry, she was smiling.

"OK. Ink, you're with Fara, so Blu, you're with Sage. I'll be around to help in a bit, but I'm going to check on Jackrabbit to make sure he doesn't reinjure himself."

Ink brushed himself off and sauntered over to me. "Are you ready?" His manner was easygoing, like he was trying to make me feel comfortable.

My stomach gave a little flip. What had I gotten myself into?

"All right," he said. "So, have you had any training at all?"

"Not really. A little kickboxing."

"I'm assuming that has something to do with kicking and boxing?"

I laughed in spite of myself. "Something like that."

"Well then, you have a little bit of experience."

"Not like you guys."

Ink's face softened. "No. Not like us. But then again, you didn't grow up having to fight for your life every second. Fara, be grateful that you don't know much of what we do."

I knew he was right, but then again, I had the exact opposite problem. I had never learned how to defend myself, and instead had been taught to push down my feelings and not make a scene. I understood why my parents did it—to protect me from opening portals right and left—but that didn't change the fact that it happened.

Ink was studying me. It was still weird that someone who looked like Calum was unable to read what I was thinking. It was like he was trying to figure me out.

"What?"

"It's weird," he said, echoing my exact thoughts. "I'm still expecting you to call me an asshole and punch me in the face."

"And I'm expecting you to tell me to be safe and careful."

"Why would I tell you that?"

"Because I could get hurt."

"But you're an adult, right? Telling you not to do something just in case you get hurt seems dumb to me. Ready?" He walked behind me and gripped my shoulders, hard enough that I couldn't easily escape, but it didn't hurt. "Now we get to the fun stuff," he said, and we started training in earnest.

An hour later, I had (almost) successfully demonstrated how to escape two different holds. Training was hard work, but I found myself really enjoying it, especially given that Ink was a great teacher, and not at all what I expected him to be like. He was still charming, but he displayed none of the breathy sexpot thing. Maybe it was because he took his job seriously, and right now his job was to train me. Or maybe he had gotten over flirting with me. And while he was careful not to reinjure my arm, he didn't go easy on me. At least, it didn't feel like he did.

"Not bad," he said when we were finally finished.

"Not bad yourself." I gently nudged him with my shoulder. "Seriously, thank you."

"My pleasure—and we get to do it all again tomorrow."

"My muscles are going to hate me."

"I have a remedy for that." He gave me a wink as he sauntered away. I guess he wasn't quite done with the flirting, and I guess I didn't really mind.

18 BLU

Once training was over and I had thoroughly kicked Ink's ass (and trained Sage, which was just as important), the Captain stopped to tell me the last known location of Warhorse. I found Silver in the mess, and we got ready to head off. Ink and Jack both offered to go with us, but I didn't want to add any more volatility to the situation. Warhorse knew us, and hopefully we could use that to our advantage. At this point, we could use all the advantages that we could get, slight though they might be.

As I walked past Ink's apartment on my way to get my gear, I heard a raised voice—Iris. I guess she wasn't happy with what Ink was telling her, but as long as she didn't try to murder him in his sleep, this little fuss wasn't my concern. Truthfully, it wasn't the first time I'd heard a woman yelling at Ink. It probably wouldn't be the last.

I put on my new armor, having recently paid a trainee to do my laundry at the Captain's request. Fara needed clothes until she could get her own, and I had an abundance—they just hadn't happened to be clean. I put my daggers in their sheaths and decided to leave the sword here.

I looked at myself in the mirror as I brushed my teeth. The shaved side of my head was starting to grow out, so at some point I'd need to decide what I wanted to do about it. I was still pissed at Ink for lopping off one of my pigtails with a sword, which is what forced me to shave that side of my head in the first place. Improbably, Ink's shenanigans had started a trend. Some of the younger Team members and trainees had shaved the side of their heads too. Styx said I should take it as a compliment, but it still weirded me out—I wasn't a fan of the hero thing. If they knew how many times a day I screwed up, they would probably change their minds (and their hair). However, if it made them feel better to look up to me, then who was I to get mad about it?

Iris stepped out into the hall, wiping her eyes. She stopped when she saw me.

"You tried to warn me," she said with a delicate sniffle. "You told me he didn't date, but I thought I could change that. That I was enough to change him."

I sighed. "Not that it's any of my business, Iris, but it's not about you being enough. Ink doesn't want to be tied down with anyone. Don't take it personally."

"But I've never been told no," she said, with such a look of wide-eyed incredulity that I almost laughed.

"I guess there's a first time for everything."

She didn't seem to notice I was talking, so I started walking toward the exit.

"Blu?"

I turned around, suppressing a sigh. I needed to go, and her drama was not my problem.

"Yeah?"

"Do you think if I tried out for the Team, he'd change his mind?"

"No. The Team doesn't have any open spots right now, anyway."

"But your cousin is on the Team."

"That was a special circumstance."

"Do you think I should ask the Captain?"

"Iris, if you want to join the Team, then ask the Captain. But don't do it for Ink. It won't change his mind. Trust me on that."

19 BLU

I drove my car slowly through the ruins of the streets toward the city center as Silver kept a lookout for minions who might follow us or generally get in our way. The streets would be in better repair once we got closer to Jurisdiction's headquarters, and at that point we could pick up speed. Until then, I wanted to keep the axle of my car in one piece, and so we drove at a crawl.

"It hasn't changed," Silver said as she looked out of the car window.

"What?"

"The city. It hasn't changed in the past year, since I came to the Compound. Nothing has been fixed. It's all still shit."

"Except, conveniently, the city center."

"Right—except there. Assholes."

The city center was the heart of our metropolis, such as it was after the war. The center was filled with the city's businesses that had managed to stay operational, and houses or apartments also owned by the elite. They were the only ones who could afford it. The few profited over the many, and the perks of being in Jurisdiction's pocket were good roads and new buildings.

This far out, however, it was a different world. As I avoided a pothole roughly the size of my car, I turned on my comm to check in with Styx.

"Hey, friend, you there?"

"Yep!"

"Do you have eyes on the alley?"

"No. And I don't have a good feeling about this, B. There are no cameras working in that alley or on that entire block. It's like they've been disabled or something."

"That might be why Warhorse chose the location."

"Or it could be a malfunction. Without eyes, I can't tell you what you're walking into. The periphery is clear, at least. Just some office buildings and what looks like a sandwich shop. Mind stopping and getting me lunch? It looks delicious."

"I would love nothing more — but I'm sure we're not invited."

"You're such a party pooper. OK, I'll keep my eyes on the periphery, and will check back in forty-five minutes. If you don't answer, Ink's on standby."

"Thanks, although we won't need it."

"Famous last words."

Once we were close enough to walk, I parked my car out of the way. This close to the city center, most of the destroyed buildings had been removed and replaced by sparkling high-rises and beautiful houses. Around here, with the lovely landscaping and new construction, it was easy for those living this life to convince themselves that Jurisdiction wasn't that bad and there was nothing wrong with how things were. It was an oasis in an otherwise decimated city. Why would they care that the rest of the city was in ruins and children had to beg for meals? Why would they care when they couldn't see the husks of houses many were still left to live in? If they couldn't see it, and it didn't directly affect them, the problems didn't exist, right? Coin and power have a strange way of changing a person's perspective. And once you have them, you'll do anything to keep them. It's just human nature, even if it sucks.

I wasn't the only one who seemed to be more contemplative than usual. "Silver, you're being unusually quiet."

"Sorry."

"Nothing to apologize for, but last time we visited these folks, Jyston held a dagger to your throat, so I was just making sure you're OK."

"Yeah. It's not that." We headed down an alley, avoiding the trash scattered on the ground. "If we manage to get into the PITs, then I want to be part of the team that competes. I want to drive the bike."

That wasn't what I was expecting at all. "Why?"

"It's a long story."

"I'm listening."

"It's just . . . I know how to ride. My brother taught me. I'm actually really good."

"Your brother?"

"Yeah—he was the best. He used to race motorcycles and dirt bikes in street races. It was dangerous and stupid, but we needed coin. My dad struggled to take care of us after my mom died."

"I understand that."

"He got a reputation for being the one to beat, and some of the Jurisdiction minions thought that they should teach him a lesson. A minion entered one of the races and lost to him."

I peered around the corner of a building to make sure we weren't being followed. "I'm assuming the minion didn't take the loss well?"

"That's an understatement. When my brother told him to pay up, the minion started beating him, calling him a cheat and all sorts of stuff." We hopped over a retaining wall and hid behind a dumpster. "My dad was there and stepped in to protect my brother, but when the minion hit my dad, my brother went ballistic. The other entrants and my brother rioted and beat the minion to death. It was all caught on Jurisdiction's surveillance. They arrested everyone."

"I think I heard about that riot."

"Of course the minions came for my family. When they did, my brother hid me in the crawlspace above the kitchen in our house."

She told me how she'd watched between the floorboards as her brother and father were brutalized before being hauled off to prison. The minions burned the house when they left, and she'd almost died.

I stopped as we approached the alley where we would meet up with Warhorse. "Holy shit. How'd you end up with us?"

"It was Sage, actually. My neighbor found me in the garden behind our house as it was still burning. I had burns and had inhaled so much smoke. I was a mess." She rubbed her arm through her sleeve.

"And she helped you?"

"Ha. Far from it. She asked me what happened, and I told her, asking her to get help. But she didn't. She went about her day. She went shopping."

"What a bitch."

Silver clenched her fists at her sides, then let them go slowly. "She did manage to tell everyone who would listen in the market what had happened, but somehow forgot to ask anyone to help me. Sage was in the market when he heard the story. He forced the woman to tell him where I was, and came and got me. I would have died in the garden had it not been for him."

She pulled the sleeve of her shirt up over her elbow to show me the scars. My rage rose, not only because of the minions and what they did, but because of that woman. I wouldn't mind paying her a visit. "Does she have a name?"

"I'm keeping it to myself. She's mine."

I could understand that. "Did you ever compete in the street races?"

"A few times."

"Did you win?"

"Yes."

She was quiet as we made one last sweep of the area. I could ride anything on two wheels, as could the rest of the Team, but to have someone who was trained in the sort of close-quarters competitive racing like she was? That would be a huge asset.

"OK. Let's see what we find out. But I promise I'll bring your request to the Captain if we enter the PITs."

"Thank you. I know I haven't proven myself yet, but I can do this."

"Well, before we get to that—let's go pay our friend a visit."

⚡ ⚡ ⚡

When we entered the alley, we were greeted by a half-dozen people coming toward us with makeshift weapons, looking very much like an angry mob.

"The last time you bitches were here, Dagna took two of us and killed two more. I think we ought to kill you both now to save us the time."

"You really don't want to do that," I said, tapping my daggers. "We need to talk to Warhorse."

"I don't go by that anymore," said a voice from directly behind us. It wasn't often that someone got the jump on me, and I was impressed. "Considering the trouble you stirred up last time, I should let them have a go at you."

"Naw. I don't think I'll let that happen today." I palmed my daggers and met his gaze. I wouldn't be intimidated by this lot, and we needed information. Finally, he broke my gaze and started walking.

"This must be something of grave importance, or you wouldn't have bothered coming down here again. Would you like to step into my new office? Although this one isn't quite so luxurious."

We followed him through the crowd, who were glaring at us with open hostility.

"Why does everyone want to kill us?"

"They blame you for what happened with Dagna."

"That was Jyston. We had nothing to do with that."

He walked to a part of the alley that had blankets on a pallet and a couple of packing crates. The walls were gone, or at least hadn't been erected yet. It looked like they had just claimed this spot and were still making camp.

"You did have something to do with it, even if you don't want to admit it."

"How?"

"Jyston only came down to see us because of you."

"You think Jyston wouldn't have bothered checking on a group of people spying on him? I know you're not that dumb."

"That's what they think."

"What do you think?"

"I think that it sounds like the Compound has a spy, and that spy led Jyston to you, who then led him to me. So, pardon me if I'm inclined to agree with my people."

There was nothing I could do about their feelings now, even if their anger was misplaced. I threw a pouch of coins down on his pallet.

"All right," he said. "What do you want to know?"

"I hear you know things about the PITs."

"Maybe."

"Tell me about them."

"Why?"

"Doesn't matter."

"It does to me."

I took a moment to study him. His tangled beard hung down his chest, his cheeks were ruddy, and his mass of red hair was tied back with a string. He still sported the eyepatch.

Had he lost his eye while on a mission for the Team? I'd ask the Captain later. His plain brown shirt was a patchwork of rips and mends, and his pants were held up by a belt.

"Why do you want to know about the PITs?"

I sighed. We weren't getting anywhere with him like this.

"We're thinking about entering."

"Why the hell would you want to do that?"

"That's our business. Plus if we win, we'd have the chance to name a couple of prisoners to be released."

I looked him directly in the eye. It didn't take him long to get my meaning.

"I will tell you as much as I can, but I need you to secure the release of my two people if you win. I can't be associated with your entry."

"We can't secure the release of your people if we aren't even entered in the game."

"Final offer. After what happened last time you were here, I can't risk having my name associated with yours, even if it blows my only shot of rescuing my folks. Dagna will keep taking and killing my people just to prove she can. Talking to you right now is as much of a risk as I'm willing to take."

It was better than nothing. And if we couldn't secure entry into the PITs another way, then we could always come back.

"Deal. Tell me what you know."

Warhorse spent the better part of thirty minutes telling us about the PITs. The more he told us, the worse it sounded—and it had sounded pretty atrocious even before we talked to him. He said that only the really desperate or crazy entered willingly. I realized I might be a little of both.

After Warhorse decided he had given us as much information as he wanted to, he unceremoniously kicked us out of the alley. As Silver and I turned the corner to where we had hidden my car, I had my daggers in my hand before my brain could process what I was seeing. Jyston was leaning against the hood of my car, looking as if he had all the time in the world to loiter. Silver looked at me in question, her daggers out as well. Did we need to run?

"Your car is a bit small for my taste, but it suits you."

"What are you doing here?"

"Can't I just stop by to say hello from time to time?"

"Not really, no."

"Pity. I do so enjoy our conversations."

He pushed himself off my car and took a step toward us, a smile tugging at the corner of his mouth.

"I would have joined you while you were having your chat with Warhorse," he said, "but I thought I might save you the aggravation."

"That's kind of you, Second Counselor. What do you want?"

"I thought we had moved past formal titles."

"Fine. Jyston, what do you want?"

My comm buzzed and Styx chirped in our ears. "Your forty-five minutes are up! You aren't running for your lives, are you?"

Jyston raised his eyebrow. "You might want to answer her, or she'll send in your bodyguard."

I rolled my eyes at him before I realized I had. How would the second most powerful person in the world react to my accidental insolence? If it bothered him, he didn't show it. He actually chuckled at me.

"We're just having a little chat with the Second Counselor. I'll let you know how it goes—"

"Oh my god. You're talking to your boyfriend right now? Does he look sexy?"

"Styx, he can hear you."

I wasn't prone to blushing, but I felt the heat rise in my cheeks as Jyston's eyes lit up with laughter. Silver was standing perfectly still, seemingly caught between wanting to run and wanting to laugh. I couldn't blame her, since I felt exactly the same way.

"Well, that was a nice little tidbit. I hadn't realized I had the pleasure of being your—what did she call me? Oh yes. Your boyfriend." He smirked. "I feel that I have been remiss in my duties, then. I haven't even sent you flowers or taken you on a date—"

"It's . . . it's not that I think you are. It's just that . . . that's what Styx calls you. I wouldn't ever . . . " I was stammering. That was new.

"Oh no, you aren't getting out of this conversation that quickly," he said as he stalked toward me, eyes full of mischief. When he looked at me that way, all reason went out the fucking window. I looked away.

"I am honored to even be considered worthy of that title," he said, "and will do my very best to remain so, though it may not be entirely accurate. I'll have to think of a better term for what it is I am to you."

He stopped right in front of me and gently took my chin, forcing me to look at him. I still was hanging onto my daggers for dear life, afraid that if my hands were free, I would touch him, or kill him. Or both. It was a near thing.

He leaned down to whisper in my ear. "Don't worry, beautiful Blu. Your secret is safe with me."

"What secret?"

"That I'm your boyfriend."

"You're not!" I took a step back, giving myself some breathing space. I had to stop this conversation and focus.

"It's too late now. What would be a gift appropriate for the occasion?"

"Me not killing you?"

He laughed, a full-throated, deep sound that made my toes tingle and the blush on my cheeks spread. I was absolutely mortified.

"That's a start, although that was never on my agenda. I think I have just the thing."

"Uh, Blu?" Silver said tentatively. I had almost forgotten she was there. "I think we have a tail."

Someone in Warhorse's camp was staring at me. When we noticed him, he ran away.

"Shit!"

Jyston, at least, looked chagrinned as he watched Warhorse's lacky run between the buildings. "Ah, yes. Well, it appears that my best intentions of keeping you out of hot water with that lot were thwarted by my desire to spend more time with you. Sorry about that."

"Jyston, not that this hasn't been interesting, but can you please get to the part where you tell me what you want?"

"So assertive! Good thing I like warrior women, or we might need to reconsider our relationship."

I groaned. "We don't *have* a relationship! You're the leader of the shitheads, and I want to kill all of your people! That's it!"

He shrugged, but he was grinning. What had Styx gotten me into?

"Ah, yes. What I need. I'm assuming you came to see Warhorse to get information about the PITs. I'm also assuming that he wouldn't even consider telling you how to enter the competition. I can help with that."

"What? Why? Do you want us killed that desperately?"

"Not really. At some point, you'll need to trust me on that. Unfortunately, I have to take my leave. I'm sure Dagna has discovered by now that the cameras in this area are offline. I will get you the entry information when I am able, but I promise it will be before the PITs."

He grabbed my hand and kissed it, this time palm up. A little shiver ran up my spine. "Blu, it is and always will be a pleasure. Silver, it was nice not having to threaten you."

He turned and disappeared around the corner of the building, but I wasn't quite done with the Second Counselor. I sprinted after him.

"Jyston!"

He turned, his eyebrow raised.

"How did you know about my cousin?"

"Now you're asking me the right questions. There is one among you who reports to me. Don't worry, this person reports *only* to me, and the information stays with me. I would rather not share you with anyone else at Jurisdiction."

"A mole?"

"How else would I know where to locate you for these friendly chats?"

I seethed. The mole had been working for him all along!

"Wait. I know that look on your face. Before you get on your moral high horse, this person is providing me information under duress, and is having quite the quandary about it." He grinned. He was enjoying this!

"Who is it?"

"You'll figure it out. There might be another among you who reports to Dagna, but as you can probably imagine, she doesn't share her deepest secrets with me."

He sketched a bow and began to leave.

I watched him walk away, questions within questions circling me along with feelings that I couldn't identify, and couldn't afford to have. None of it made sense, and the only person who could explain was him.

"Wait! Please, Jyston. I have to know. Why are you doing this? Why did you save me? And why are you helping me now?" I said, grasping for some reason, any reason, that he would be helping me. "It can't just be that Dagna finds me annoying. I mean, that might be part of it—but there's something else. There has to be."

He held my gaze, his mask of boredom and cruelty gone. Something was happening between us. Something had shifted with that question. Or maybe it had already shifted, and I was just catching up. It was as if he was letting me see *him*—not who the rest of the world saw, but who he really was. He looked tired and a little sad, and a hundred percent human. I held my breath.

"There are things that are happening, Blu. Things I cannot tell you, even though I wish I could. Hopefully someday I will have the opportunity."

"You can tell me. You can trust me." I don't know why I said it, but after I did, I realized I meant it.

"I believe I can, beautiful Blu." He smiled sadly. "Then the answer is this: it is time for me to start proving I can be trusted too."

20 FARA

I drew a bath hot enough to almost melt me, grabbed my mom's folder and Calum's note, and sank into heaven. I might miss showers at some point, but now was not that point.

I started with Calum's hummingbird note, smiling as I unfolded the delicate paper. His handwriting was elegant script, and it brought back memories of his teasing me when he'd read my notes for class. He always said that my handwriting was only legible enough for interpretation, not for actual reading.

Dearest F,

First, I'm not mad at you. Not even a little. Not even at all. I am, however, trying to figure out how our lives changed from avoiding Douche at The Grill to writing letters between parallel universes, but we'll adapt. I will say it brightens my day to have one magically appear on my table, even when they ask me for things like ibuprofen. Speaking of that, I'm not sure about the rules for inter-universe pharmaceutical sharing, but fuck 'em. Hopefully, this ibuprofen helps with the arm, and with any lingering problems you have with the shockwave thing.

On that note, it appears you might need a new title, since Master of the Universes may not include that newfound ability. Bringer of Lightning and Chaos? Interdimensional Traveler and Human Stun Gun? All joking aside, please be careful. I worry about you—

being able to do what you do is not normal. Not that anyone would ever accuse either of us of normality.

My head is fine. It was just a scrape. And do not apologize for it. You know I would take that, and more, if it meant keeping you safe. And know that if the other Hewitt ends up being an asshat, then I'll punch him for you too. At least I know I'm good at that.

Adora is freaking out. I'm not trying to make you feel bad (because I know you will and shouldn't) but she doesn't know where you are or what happened, and she's working crazy hours to cover your shifts. Douche has threatened to fire you more than once, but she staged a walkout of the entire staff until he changed his mind. She's a good friend, and I'm not one to tell you who to confide in, but you might want to consider letting her in on your secret.

As for me, things have been interesting. The goons stop by every day but haven't approached me—yet. I also got a call from the Department of Weapons Technology. I haven't called them back, but I have a feeling it's just a matter of time before they show up on my doorstep, or at The Grill. Can you ask Jay what he recommends doing? Is he coming back soon? If he is, maybe he can just deal with them.

And of course I'd check "yes" if you asked if I liked you—you're inherently likable, even if you are Master of the Universes plus some. Please stop flogging yourself about what's going on. It's not your fault, all right? I'm helping because you're my family and you'd do the same for me. More, probably.

Let me know you're OK and if you need anything, like donuts or whiskey or a beer or three. If you can find any cool art supplies, feel free to send them my way. There might be benefits to parallel universe shopping. Stay safe.

—C

Although the letter was purposely lighthearted, I could tell he was worried about Adora. I decided that I would ask Calum to tell her. It was the least I could do, and considering Barrington was taking more drastic measures to find me (like staking out Calum's place), it was only a matter of time before they approached her. She needed to be prepared. I'd also stop by the infirmary to see what Jay thought about his department reaching out to Calum. With everything else that had happened, I realized Jay and I hadn't really talked about all of the things I had learned; or what had happened at the department before he came to rescue me. I knew my mom's former assistant had Barrington's palmbox, but I didn't know what that meant to me, and to everyone else. It was probably a conversation that needed to happen today, if Jay was up for it.

My bath was getting cold, so I got out and rummaged for some clean clothes. Luckily, some of my underwear (or *underthings* as Jay had called them) had survived my Great Apartment Massacre, so I had that going for me, which was nice. Beggars couldn't be choosers, and while I really was grateful Blu was sharing her clothes with me, underwear was another thing entirely. I pulled on some leggings, another black tank top, and Calum's sweatshirt and considered myself ready. If only Douche allowed this sort of appearance at The Grill—I would get at least thirty minutes more sleep if I didn't have to do hair or makeup. I might even start liking myself this way. Maybe.

I found what looked like a coffeepot in my small kitchen, and ground coffee too. In the cupboards, I located something that resembled creamer, sugar, and a giant coffee mug; the

Captain really did think of everything. After a few failed attempts at figuring out how the contraption worked, and with enough swearing, eventually I was holding a cup of coffee. Fortified, I sat down to read my mom's notes.

It appeared that the notes had been organized in the meticulous way of a scientist (a trait I unfortunately did not inherit from my mother). The papers were separated by folder dividers, each bundle labeled and secured by a black binder clip. The first bundle was titled *History and Theory*. I scanned through the other bundles: *Portals*, *Miscellaneous* . . . and my breath caught. *Other Abilities*. With any luck, it would provide some insight into how I'd electroshocked the goon, and why I passed out after doing so. Maybe, hopefully, there were answers in here.

I started at the beginning with *History and Theory*. However, as soon as I took off the binder clip and looked at the first page, my hopes were dashed. Pages upon pages of complicated mathematical equations with shorthand notes in the margins, or notes that made no sense without context such as "attempt created spark," whatever that meant. If all the notes were like this, I was royally hosed. Maybe the Captain knew someone who could decipher this? I hated to ask for help, since I'd already asked for so much, but there wasn't anything I could do with this without someone who understood the mathematical equations of . . . whatever this was.

After more sifting, I found some pages that were more words than numbers, and I started to read what I could. While the notes were in my mother's beautiful handwriting, their tone was clinical, which meant that I could read them without dissolving into a puddle of tears.

She confirmed much of what I already knew: how we had been infected with what she called "toxic light," and how the portals were triggered by strong emotions. Her theory was that the stronger the membrane was between the worlds, the less likely it was for me to open a portal. She detailed how she had taught me to suppress my emotions, but also that it was impossible to control my emotions when I was asleep, though physical activity helped.

Well, that answered that question. Would I always open portals when I slept? Maybe. Or maybe they would just randomly stop, like they did for the four years after my parents died. Had they actually stopped, or did the palmboxes just not pick up on them then? I had no idea.

This portion of the notes ended with a lengthy memo explaining her decision to keep her findings from the government.

"I will continue to run experiments to see if I can determine the nature of our emerging abilities," she wrote. She spent a good portion of this missive frustrated with her inability to determine the nature of the abilities. "I know it is not scientifically possible; that there is no scientific basis for how the light transferred into us and gave us this power. It is more science fiction than science, and I am determined to use scientific means to prove how it happened."

I could just imagine my mother fretting over this seemingly impossible ability. More than by the ability itself or the fact that the device came from a parallel universe, she was bothered that the ability wasn't based in something she could dissect or explain by mathematical equations or any known scientific theory. Sure, she could explain the multiverse. That was (from what I barely understood) just theoretical physics. But how did the ability to travel between worlds get into our DNA? Was that even what had happened?

I chuckled at myself—at my complete lack of care for the science behind it. When the Captain explained that I was infected with toxic palmbox light, and that was what caused my ability, I sort of mentally shrugged and went "all right." But then again, I was raised on a healthy diet of *The Avengers* and wasn't a gifted scientist like my mother. If the Hulk could become beefy through gamma rays, then I guess I couldn't be bothered to question if I could become Master of the Universes through palmbox light.

I got to the end of the section and gently placed the notes beside me on the bed. While not as heart-wrenching as her letter to me, reading them was still an emotional experience. I missed my parents. But more than that, I desperately wished with all of my heart that my mom was here with me, talking me through these issues in her calm, matter-of-fact way. But she wasn't here and there wasn't anything I could do about it. It was up to me now to figure this out, and I was determined that I would. But right now, I needed a break. I set off for the infirmary and Jay, a welcome distraction, and then some.

ϟ ϟ ϟ

The Team member who walked me to the infirmary would have been in high school if she'd been in my world. Instead, she had a sword and the nervous energy I associated with all of the Team members. I had no doubt that she was deadly, and once again I felt how much of a disadvantage I was at here. At her age, I was worrying about my social studies final, not how to take down an evil empire. But, then again, at her age I was also forced to figure out how to live on my own after my parents died. I guess we both were required to do what we had to do to survive. My survival just happened to require learning how to squeeze every drop out of a paycheck; hers, learning fifty ways to kill a minion.

Jay was being wheeled into his room. I stood back as the medic helped Jay back into his bed, then left us to talk privately.

"You were staring at my ass, weren't you?" He was suppressing a grin.

"It's hard not to, with you in that hospital gown. And it's . . . really nice."

"Thank you?"

He grabbed my hand and pulled me down into a kiss. His lips were soft, and he was as gentle and sexy as before. I placed my hand on his shoulder, felt the thick pad. Ah yes, bullet.

"My injuries are getting in the way of what I want to do," he said into my mouth.

"Then get better."

He absently—sweetly—rubbed his thumb back and forth over my knuckles. His face was still a patchwork of bruises, and the skin around his eyes was black and blue from his recently reset broken nose. But his eyes were clearer than yesterday. He studied me with a smile.

"You look happy," he said.

"I'm hanging out with you."

He shook his head. "To what do I owe this pleasure?"

"Can't I just come see you?"

"You could, but that's not why you're here."

"I'm just here to see you and ask how you're feeling. And stare at your butt."

"Fara, it's OK that you came to talk to me about something. I'm not offended."

"It's not that I don't want to—"

"Fara, please just get on with it so I can get back to kissing those beautiful lips of yours before you have to go. It's bad enough that my body can't keep up with my libido—"

"OK, OK, fine." I grinned. "But I maintain that I came to stare at your butt."

He rolled his eyes, an act that didn't seem quite natural on him.

"Two things. First, I started reading my mom's notes."

His face lost the grin, and his mouth set into what I was starting to think of as his "business face."

"Did they tell you how to suppress your ability?"

I shouldn't have been surprised that it was the first question he asked, but yet I was.

"I only read some of them. I'm going to read the rest tonight or tomorrow."

I told him what I'd read, along with everything else I'd learned since the last time we caught up—what Barrington and the Captain had told me. Everything. It was a lot of information.

He sat for a long time after I finished, looking out of the window. I held his hand and waited.

"I have to get home," he said finally. "That sheds light on some of the intel I gathered about Barrington and his business, Specter COMS. I need to warn the department so we can start to plan for a possible hostile takeover." He looked at me gravely. "And you need to get your abilities under control so that you can come with me. If all this Counselor needs is to capture you to fulfill his plan, you can't stay here."

A thousand emotions were warring within me, concern over his well-being winning out. "Jay, you need to heal before you go back. The Counselor hasn't been able to figure out how to get to our world yet, and even if he has, it will take time for him to implement his plan. And who knows what Barrington has told your department. He might have already convinced them that he's the good guy and I'm the bad guy. He might be behind the reason your department wanted to question me in the first place."

"Then that's all the more reason I need to go home. I have to stop them."

"How? I don't mean to be rude, but you can't even walk right now." I agreed that he needed to go back, but I hated the thought of it. "Please, at least talk to Sage about a realistic timeline."

His thumb had stopped its lazy pattern on my knuckles.

"Fine, but don't think I didn't notice you ignored the part about you coming home. Fara, it's not safe here. You need to get your powers under control."

"Jay, I'm safer here than at home, at least for now. The Compound is safe. I'm surrounded by these crazy deadly people, and they have all sworn to protect me."

"*I* can't protect you if you're here and I'm home."

"I hate to break it to you, bossy, but you can't protect me right now at all. Get better, OK? I want to be able to spend more time looking at your butt."

I reached down and kissed him, both of us understanding that I was avoiding the issue. He wasn't going to fight about it with me right now, but I knew he wouldn't let it drop. And I didn't know why I was hesitant about going home.

"So—the second thing . . . I read my note from Calum—"

"You opened another portal?"

"No, I just finally got around to reading the note that came with the ibuprofen . . . which I brought you more of by the way. Anyway, he said that your department has reached out to talk to him."

"Damnit! I knew telling him about everything was going to be a liability!" He angrily tossed the ibuprofen bottle onto the bed. "Tell him to avoid them if he can. I don't know how far Barrington's influence reaches. We can't risk him letting them know about you or any of this."

"He won't tell them, Jay. Even if they bring him in, he won't tell them."

"They have ways—"

"You didn't tell Barrington about me, even after they tortured you, right?"

"No. But Fara, I have training."

"Doesn't matter. He won't tell."

"All right, but he might need to hide until I can get home. He might have to come here."

BLU 21

I sat in the car, my hands resting on the steering wheel. Some part of my brain knew we had to get moving, but I couldn't get my feet to work. I couldn't get my brain to work. My mind kept going back to the revelation that we were right about the spy, and whoever it was, they reported directly to Jyston. That there might be more than one spy at the Compound. But the part that scared me the most was that I had feelings for the Second Counselor. I couldn't. I shouldn't. But I did.

I couldn't afford the distraction.

"Blu?" Silver said tentatively. "Are you OK?"

I started to drive. "Yeah. I'm fine."

"Jyston seems to have an interest in you."

"It seems so."

"What were you talking about at the end? I followed but couldn't hear you."

"Silver, it's not that I don't trust you, but he told me something that I need to bring to the Captain first."

She didn't argue, although I could tell she wanted to. I changed the subject.

"Did Warhorse's intel match what you know about the PITs?"

"Yeah. I'm not sure how we're going to pull this off."

"I know. It's all sorts of fucked up. Hopefully Jyston is true to his word and can get us in."

"I don't like relying on him for something like this. He could royally screw us."

"He could have captured us today and didn't. I don't know what he's up to, but it seems like his hate for Dagna has gained us an ally. At least, a temporary one."

⚡ ⚡ ⚡

I walked into the Captain's office to find Fara sitting at her desk. I hesitated, not wanting to interrupt, but the Captain waved me in. Fara smiled at me as I walked in, and I couldn't help but smile back.

"Fara was just asking me about having someone review some of her mother's notes," the Captain said, indicating the seat next to Fara.

"Yeah, a lot of what's in here is all sorts of mathematical equations that I don't understand. I was hoping someone here might."

"Styx?" I asked the Captain.

"Or Dev. Just bring it to one of them and let them know what you need."

At the mention of Dev, Fara's demeanor changed subtly, and not in a good way.

"I will. Thank you."

She got up to leave, but the Captain motioned for her to stay.

"Captain, it's about the mole . . . " I let my sentence trail off just in case she wanted to change her mind about Fara sticking around. She motioned for me to go on.

"Jyston showed up today, again, and confirmed that there is a spy here, although he asserts that this spy reports only to him."

"What Jyston says is true."

"You know?"

"Yes. It's Jackrabbit."

The air seemed to leave the room. I slumped back in my chair, stunned. How could Jack be the spy? How could he do that to us? I trusted Jack with my life!

"Does he know you know?"

"He does. We've already had a little chat."

"How? I don't understand . . . "

"It happened during the Hastings mission."

My world stopped. Other than being Jurisdiction's prisoner as a child, nothing had come close to the horror of the Hastings mission, or had as big of an impact on the Team.

"What—how?"

"For those two weeks when he was Dagna's prisoner."

Jack. Our Jack. Our head spymaster was a double agent.

"I hate to ask," Fara said, "but I've heard you all mention Hastings a bunch. What is it?"

I met the Captain's eyes across the desk. Fara didn't know what she was asking. She didn't know that telling her about it would force us to relive one of the worst days of our lives.

"Blu, since you were there—are you up for telling Fara?"

"You don't have to—"

"No," I said. "If you are even considering staying here and helping the Team, you need to know the worst of what happens here. You need to know what you're up against." I took a deep breath. "Hastings happened about a year ago."

The Captain rubbed her wedding ring. This story was certainly hard to tell, but I was sure it was harder for her to hear.

"It was supposed to be a regular mission, nothing too crazy, although the location made it more difficult. Hastings is a small town about an hour's drive from the city center. The entire town was ruled by some petty lord, and he was a first-rate tyrannical asshat. However, what we cared about was that he was in charge of the prison Jurisdiction had built on his land."

The Captain walked over to the coffeepot and turned it on.

"We had received verifiable intelligence that Jurisdiction was sending Compound prisoners to that prison. Jurisdiction isn't stupid. They move Compound prisoners regularly so that we can never find them to stage a prison break. However, they were planning on housing over twenty Compound prisoners in Hastings, at least for a bit."

"Who were the Compound prisoners?"

"Mostly Jack's spies or other Team members who were caught on missions. Dagna likes to keep them alive so she can entertain herself with them under the guise of getting information."

"That's awful."

"It is, which is why when we found out that Jurisdiction was moving a large portion of the Compound prisoners to Hastings, we planned to break them out, or at least planned as well as we could. We didn't know where the prisoners were coming from, so we couldn't intercept them en route. Our best bet was to spring them after the transfer."

The Captain handed each of us a mug of coffee, and I wrapped my hands around it, trying to keep them from shaking.

"The Captain's wife, Robin, led the whole principal Team on this mission," I continued. "We hoped to save our people and maybe some other prisoners along the way. We had to keep the Team small for logistic reasons. The more of us we brought, the fewer people we could bring home."

I took a deep breath, steeling myself for what came next. I could almost smell the blood and bile racing up my throat. I felt panic rising but reached down to that place of fire and lightning. This wasn't happening right now. This was a memory. And if the Captain could live through it, so could I.

"Unfortunately, the entire mission was a trap. Dagna was there herself, and we were ambushed by minions that outnumbered us five to one. The prisoners were sick, starving, beaten, and unarmed. It was a massacre." I took a long sip of my coffee, letting it burn my throat, which hurt less than remembering this.

"When the Team had finally escaped to the extraction point, we realized that Robin and Jack were missing. Ink went back to the prison to look for them. He found Robin's head on a pike in the prison yard, but there was no sign of Jack. We waited for as long as we could, until more minions found us. But we had to leave. We figured that Jack had either been captured or killed. We would have to try to rescue him later." The air caught in my throat. I swallowed.

"Go on." The Captain's own hands trembled as she held her coffee mug.

"Two weeks later, we still had no idea where Jack was, and we were about to start raiding known Jurisdiction strongholds when he somehow stumbled into the market, beaten almost beyond recognition. Someone at the market alerted the Captain, and Ink and I went to get him. A fruit vendor administered first aid as best as she could. He couldn't speak. His vocal cords were damaged from screaming. I won't go into his injuries, but he was in the infirmary for over a month, and he didn't speak for the entire time he was there. He never told us how he escaped, and I never asked."

Tears streamed down Fara's face. She reached for my hand and squeezed.

"All told, we lost twenty-four people that day. Every prisoner was slaughtered. And Robin died trying to save them."

The Captain's eyes were lined with silver as well, but no tears fell.

"Ink and I went back and retrieved Robin's remains. She is buried in the Compound's graveyard. Ink also killed the petty lord while I burned down his manor."

Reliving Hastings on top of the Jyston thing had left me emotionally shattered. The revelation about Jack. How was I ever going to trust him again?

The Captain seemed to read my mind. "Blu, I know you want to confront Jackrabbit, and I won't stop you. Before you do, I want you to hear this: Jackrabbit wasn't the only one Dagna captured at Hastings. She caught another prisoner named Shade."

"They had Shade?" I knew that she was one of Jack's spies before getting caught during a mission. They had been friends, possibly more. Jack was never one to blab about his personal life.

"When he was in captivity, Dagna tortured Shade in front of him," the Captain said. "Finally, Dagna told him that they would keep Shade alive only to torture her over and over until he gave in and gave Jurisdiction the information that they wanted. He told her some things that we could recover from, but then offered to spy for her if they let Shade go."

"He offered? What the fu—"

The Captain held up her hand. "He felt, as our head spymaster, he could outsmart her and feed her misinformation while keeping Shade safe. It was risky, but he didn't think he had a choice. His plan backfired. Dagna let Jackrabbit go, but she kept Shade with the threat that should he fail, they would do unspeakable things to her, and then kill her."

I could only imagine what Jack and Shade had endured. Fara squeezed my hand again.

"Jack spent months sending Dagna around in circles, feeding her enough information to keep her interested but never giving away anything truly important. Eventually Dagna caught on to his ruse."

"How do you know she figured it out?" Fara was gripping my hand so tight that it was tingling.

"She put one of Shade's fingers in a box and had someone give it to Jackrabbit while he was in the market one day."

"It was meant as a message," I said, my stomach clenching in anger. "She'd dismember Shade one piece at a time until Jack was useful to her."

"Yes."

"Is that how she knew when I was waiting for Jyston to leave for the party?"

"Unfortunately, yes. Jackrabbit had to tell Dagna about the mission, Blu, for fear of what would be done to Shade. That's why Dagna showed up that day."

"But that was the only day she showed up. It's been Jyston ever since . . . "

"Jackrabbit isn't sure how or when it happened, but Jyston wrested control over him away from Dagna. According to Jackrabbit, he hasn't seen Dagna since, and only has dealings with the Second Counselor. Jyston has kept Dagna away from Jackrabbit, and by proximity, us."

"Jyston was telling the truth."

"He was. Since Jyston took over, the only thing that he asked Jackrabbit to tell him was when you left the Compound and where you were going, which explains how he is always where you are."

"Why me?"

"Jackrabbit doesn't know. All he knows is those were his orders."

"How long have you known?"

"After he and Willow found Dagna's building, I started to suspect Jackrabbit was in trouble. He never would have found it without inside information. However, after Jyston let on he knew Fara was here, I confronted him. He admitted to what had happened and offered to throw himself out of the Compound. I refused. I told him to continue reporting to Jyston, since it appeared that the Second Counselor was trying to help us in his own convoluted way."

"Does Jyston know you know?"

"Yes. Jackrabbit, of his own volition, told Jyston he was outed and expected to be killed for it. Instead, Jyston asked that he be kept informed of your whereabouts, but in exchange he would warn you, Blu, if Dagna's minions were endangering your missions. We agreed to his proposal, and he has kept up his end of the bargain. Jyston also released Shade. She is in the infirmary."

I don't know if I would have made the same choices Jack made, but I wasn't the one in his position. What Jyston said was true: Jack probably was having a horrible moral quandary about what he was doing. And then my rage rose, not at Jack, but at this world. How could we live in such a place where things like this were allowed to happen? Where someone like Jack had to make such terrible choices?

"OK, I won't kill him," I said. Fara looked relieved. The Captain knew, better than anyone, that once I understood Jack's circumstances, I couldn't stay mad at him for long. I was going to ream his ass, but I'd get over it.

"Are you going to tell the Team?"

"I think that they deserve to know the whole truth."

"We have another problem, though," I said. "Jyston told me that there might be another spy here—one who reports to Dagna."

The Captain nodded thoughtfully. "I was afraid of that. Jackrabbit thinks so too, although neither of us has a clue as to who it might be. I'm hoping Jackrabbit's spies can uncover the leak. Did Jyston provide any clues?"

"Unfortunately, no. He indicated that he and Dagna weren't on the best terms."

"Maybe she's figured out Jyston is up to something and is trying to use it to her advantage."

"Let's hope not. He's becoming a good asset."

The Captain raised her eyebrows in a look that told me she thought I was full of shit.

"Are you sure that's it, Blu?"

I wasn't having this conversation yet. I wouldn't know what to say if I did.

"Well, it's not my place to pry," the Captain said. "Just make sure that you have a clear head. Jackrabbit is already distracted by all of this, which is how Willow got hurt. I can't have my whole team lost in the clouds."

⚡ ⚡ ⚡

I knocked on Jack's door, hoping he was inside. I was still angry at him, and probably would be for a while.

He opened the door, brown hair tousled as if he'd just woken from a nap. I punched him in the face.

"What the fuck?" he said. I helped him up from the ground. I'd made sure not to break his jaw or nose, but he'd have a nasty shiner for a while.

I pulled him into a fierce hug, and he tentatively hugged me back, rightly confused by my behavior.

"I know—" My voice hitched. Damnit. I didn't want to cry. I wasn't good at crying.

"I'm so sorry," he said, his voice wobbling.

I pulled back and took his face in my hands. His brown eyes were lined with tears, but I wanted him to hear every word I was going to say. It was important.

"You are my family, Jack. Do you understand? Family. That means that when shit goes down, you do not handle it alone. You come to me, and we solve it together, whatever it is.

I am beyond hurt that you didn't think I would help you, that you didn't think you could trust me to keep my mouth shut. You, Ink, Styx, the Captain? You mean everything to me. If we go down, we go down together, OK?"

I hugged him again, and we both cried.

"I'm so sorry," he said over and over.

Finally, I pulled away and smirked at him. He looked at me warily.

"I forgive you," I said, "*but* you are going to do something for me. Especially since Jyston used you to get to me."

"I'm almost afraid to ask."

"You should be. When is the next time you're supposed to meet Jyston?"

"Tomorrow night—"

"I'm going in your place."

He froze. "That's the worst idea ever."

"No it isn't. It's not even the worst idea *this week*, Jack. Anyway, if he wants to know where I am, I'm just going to make it easier for him."

"Blu, this isn't a game. He could kill you."

"You don't believe that any more than I do. Plus, I have some questions for him."

"Blu—"

"Jack, he has been playing this game of cat and mouse with me since this whole thing started. I think it's time to show him who the cat actually is."

"Just don't be mad at me when you're dead."

"I'll come back to haunt your ass."

FARA 22

As Blu left the Captain's office, I wiped the tears from my eyes. I could tell that Blu felt betrayed, but I understood what Jack did more than I ever wanted to. I had almost given myself to Barrington for the same reason—so that he'd stop torturing Jay. I couldn't believe Jack had held out that long. He'd been there for two weeks. I had barely endured it for minutes.

The Captain gave me some more coffee, and I settled at the big table. I had a little time to kill before the Team came in like a hurricane.

"Captain, may I borrow a pen and paper?"

"Sure."

She didn't ask what I needed them for, although she was going to see it anyway.

C,

Yes! Please tell Adora everything. I would tell her myself, but I'm afraid of putting it all in writing because I've become that level of paranoid—which should probably bother me more than it does. And please tell her not to worry about saving my job, although I really appreciate the thought. I can find another waitress job somewhere else if have to.

Jay says you should avoid his department until he returns. He is planning on coming back sooner than he should with his injuries, but he's hell-bent on being honorable. If you needed to hide, you could always come here. Seriously. I'll come get you. I know, I know, you don't want me there because it's dangerous and I'd alert them that I'm back, but it's a risk I'm willing to take if it means keeping you safe. You might not mind it here, although there are parts that are super strange. Like they don't have telephones or the Internet but they have a master armorer? I'm still figuring it out.

I started reading my mom's notes, and we were right about so much, which is awesome, but it doesn't make any of this less weird. I haven't read the part about the extra ability yet. I'm hoping to do that tonight or tomorrow.

Since this new power will help me with world domination, I think I can stay Master of the Universes. Or maybe I can use it to toast bread? Either way, it's something new.

I miss you, my friend. Let me know if those department assholes start pestering you, or if the goons stop being polite and you want to come see the leaves for yourself.

xo F

I started the process of opening the portal. It didn't take long at all, especially after listening to what happened during the Hastings mission. Eventually the window grew big enough to see Calum's coffee table, and I reached in to leave the note. My makeup bag was on the table—Calum must have found it in his bathroom. I grabbed it and closed the window with a thought.

"I'll never get used to seeing that," the Captain said.

"Jay thinks it's a dangerous and irresponsible way to use my abilities."

"What do you think?"

"I don't know yet."

"Well, you obviously disagree with at least part of what the agent is saying, or you wouldn't have done what you just did."

That was true. I didn't see the harm in opening up portals to write letters to my best friend. He was overreacting.

"What else does Jay think about your abilities?"

"He wants me to work on suppressing them so I can go back home when he does. To hide."

"And is that what you want?"

"What would you do if you were me?"

She smiled. "I'm not you, Fara."

"You know what I mean."

"I don't think you're ready for that conversation yet."

Before I could think more on it, I heard laughter and voices outside of the door. How the Team managed to be so upbeat and happy, when they dealt with so many horrible things, was a testament to their resilience. Especially after Hastings. They seemed to thrive under pressure, whereas I usually just shut down. Adora and Calum had that ability too. Was it something they were born with? Was it just that I was born with awkward, scaredy-cat genes? But Blu wasn't awkward, and she was definitely not a scaredy-cat. Maybe genetics had nothing to do with it.

Styx walked in first with Ink not far behind, his eyes alighting on me, perma-smirk in full effect. He walked behind my chair as he made his way to his own seat and leaned down to murmur in my ear, "You are always beautiful, Fara, but you look particularly lovely today."

His breath was hot and made me tingle, and I told myself that this was just Ink in his "breathy sexpot" mode and that, once again, he wasn't serious. I swatted him away and he grinned.

Blu and Jack walked in a moment later. Their eyes were rimmed with red, but both were laughing. Styx and Ink looked at them askance, but didn't say anything. It struck me as weird. I couldn't be the only one wondering why Jack looked like he'd been punched in the face.

The Captain called the meeting and asked Blu and Silver to report on what they learned from Warhorse.

Blu began. "From what he told us, one of the monthly PITs competitions is solely for mercenaries. No prisoners compete. Apparently, whoever wins is granted their choice of lucrative Jurisdiction jobs, or the release of prisoners. This draws quite a few participants from the underground crime lords and gangs. Jurisdiction invites only those they believe would be the best qualified to handle whatever jobs are up for grabs."

"Why would we care about that? It's not like we want Jurisdiction jobs," Ink said.

"Don't we?"

"What are you talking about?"

"Our way in might be getting one of the jobs driving the vans to the building."

"How the hell would we pull that off?" Jack asked.

"Look, I know it sounds crazy, but these thugs conduct business deals while they're waiting for the PITs to start, trading information or jobs that they know the other participants need and would pay coin for. It's like a monthly criminal business meeting. Because most of the jobs surrounding the building are *unsavory*, those are usually the jobs that are up for grabs at the PITs. We can buy the job off the mercenaries."

"It sounds like we could just bust their party and buy the job without having to enter the PITs," Ink said.

Silver spoke up. "You can't get into the room without an invitation. The security surrounding the PITs is pretty hard-core. And they won't let anyone out of the room until it's time to compete. Otherwise, the mercenaries would get the invitation, conclude their business, then sneak out to avoid the horrors of the PITs."

"So we need to get an invitation, which I'm assuming Warhorse is helping us with?" Jack asked.

"No. But Jyston is."

There was a collective intake of breath from the Team. I guess they weren't all that pleased that the second baddest guy in the world was going to enter them into the PITs.

The Captain was the first to speak. "How and when is Jyston supposed to give you the information?" she asked.

"He'll be in touch before the PITs, which is in three weeks."

"OK, then we have time to decide if this is something that is worth pursuing. I still believe that we need to have another reconnaissance mission to further study the small trail at the building. Ink, take Styx and go check that out tomorrow after training."

She clapped her hands, bringing the meeting to a close. "OK, I think that's all we can do for now. Ink, can you stick around for a minute?"

23 FARA

After the meeting, as we ate at the mess, I handed over some of my mom's notes to Styx, who was absolutely gleeful at the prospect of deciphering her formulas.

"You know what this means, right?" she asked. I knew exactly squat about what it meant. "It means that I might be able to replicate your mom's experiments."

"Styx, you don't want to infect anyone else with the . . . ability, do you?" I asked.

She laughed. "No. Although I wouldn't mind it if it were me. How amazing is it to be able to travel between worlds? But what I mean is that with the formulas, I might be able to turn a palmbox into a portal opener, like the original one. I can't wait to try it out!"

Blu and Styx dropped me off at the apartment building. With nothing else to do, I'd go back to my room to read some of my mom's notes. I needed to start taking that seriously.

Deep in thought as I walked by Ink's room, I jumped when a crash came from inside. I stopped, wondering what I should do, when I heard him yell. There was another crash.

I opened the unlocked door. Ink spun around, his daggers in his hands. His green eyes looked right at me, but it was like he wasn't really seeing me. He flipped his dagger like he was going to throw it.

"Ink?"

He threw his daggers—one, two—and they embedded themselves in the wall above his bed, which was twice the size of mine and completely disheveled. In fact, his entire apartment was in upheaval.

"Ink?" I tried again.

He let out a snarl as he picked up a side table and threw it across the room like it was nothing. It landed with a crash against the closet. He stalked over to the wall, kicking a chair out of the way, then yanked out his daggers. He turned back and threw the daggers again with such speed I hadn't seen them leave his hands. He stalked back over to the wall, grabbed them, and slammed one into his bedside table. Whatever had happened, he was in the midst of some sort of trauma and was going to hurt himself.

He turned to throw his dagger again, slicing his hand in the process. He yelled, frustrated, then punched a hole in the wall right next to my head. Blood dripped onto the floor, smearing on everything he touched. The whole scene was violence and chaos.

I didn't know what to do or how to help him, so I did the only thing I could think of. I took a step to close the distance between us and touched his arm to try to bring him back here from . . . wherever he was. I could feel the corded muscles under my hand tighten, ready to throw.

"Ink, please. Wait."

Breathing hard, he let the remaining dagger clatter to the floor as he looked at his hands, at the blood that was now smeared all over the floor and the wall, at the gash on his palm. He dropped to his knees without looking at me, and I followed, trying to catch his eyes, to let him know that I was here for him, for whatever he needed. But he didn't see me. He was stuck in some sort of nightmare that wouldn't end. I wanted to hold him, to help him, to do something, but what? A single sob escaped his tightly clenched jaw. He finally looked into my eyes, pleading for something, some relief I couldn't provide him. My heart broke for him.

"All I can see is Robin's head on that pike," he whispered as he sank down onto his heels. "All I can see is the blood dried on her cheek, and the piles of bodies on the ground. Over and over. I've been reliving it, over and over, for a year. And then you almost died. I couldn't save you either. And now, fucking Jack! Why did he have to get captured? Why did he have to be the spy? I've failed. I am failing. Why are our lives so fucked up?"

He put his head in his hands. His body shook. I tentatively wrapped my arms around his neck in as gentle a hug as I could manage. At first, he didn't respond at all. He kept his face in his hands, racking sobs breaking through. At some point, he rested his forehead on my chest. I kissed the top of his head. I didn't know what else to do.

"What can I do to help?" I whispered.

"You're doing it."

We knelt there as he cried himself out. I don't know how long we stayed like that, but eventually he looked up at me, his face blotchy and smeared with blood, his lips still trembling. His hands had moved to my hips while we knelt there, his fists clenched tight into the material of my tank top, like he was afraid I'd slip out of his grasp. His face was so close to mine I could see that his eyelashes were wet with tears. As he stared into my eyes, there was no hint of mischief, or laughter, or sex, or fun, or even an assassin kneeling before me. At that moment I really *saw* him. He was allowing me to see him as he truly was, not how he wanted to be seen.

He took a shuddering breath. "Why did you stay?"

"Because you needed me to."

"I could have hurt you, Fara."

"You wouldn't have."

"I wasn't exactly myself. I'm still not."

"I trust you, Ink. You're my friend, or at least I hope you are. You wouldn't hurt me."

"I'm not so sure about that."

"I am."

And I was.

I could feel his warm breath on my face. My arms were still wrapped around his neck. Neither of us said anything, and I knew that I needed to let him go. I couldn't get myself to. He shuddered slightly, releasing my waist, and I lowered my arms, wiping an errant tear from his cheek.

"Better?"

The silence stretched on. We might not be touching, but neither of us made any move to get up. It was so quiet that I could hear his breathing, and my own pounding heart. His eyes were bright and so unguarded that I couldn't look away, even if it felt too close—too intimate. After what seemed like forever, but not nearly long enough, he closed his eyes and let out a deep breath. When he opened them, he stood up and walked to the kitchen, opening cupboards in search for something or other. He still looked like he wasn't quite himself. My gut was telling me that for someone like him, someone who'd prowled around opening my closet and inspecting my bathroom drawers, who went on missions and did combat training for fun, sitting around talking about his feelings wasn't the answer to helping him. But I thought I might try something else.

"I want you to teach me to throw daggers like that."

He stopped what he was doing and walked over to stand right in front of me, brushing a hair out of my face.

"Do you really want to train with me after . . . all of this?"

"I'm not scared off that easily."

24 FARA

The sun was still out as we walked to the Quad, the dappled light straining to get through the trees and dancing on the path. I would have stopped and taken a moment to enjoy it, but Ink was still unusually quiet.

"Want to talk about it?" I ventured.

He turned to me with a look I couldn't quite place.

"What?"

"That's what Blu and I say to each other," he said. "It's just weird that you said it."

"It's a pretty normal thing to say after someone . . . Well, it's a pretty normal thing to say."

"I guess. Well, the Captain told me about Jack. She said that you and Blu already know. I went to confront him, and apparently hit him in the same eye as Blu did." He let out a humorless laugh. "It's just . . . I'm so mad at him for betraying us. So mad that he put Blu's life in danger."

He stopped and his breathing hitched. I grabbed both of his hands and pulled him off the path to give him some privacy, the act feeling natural somehow. We were standing in the woods in almost the exact spot I had seen in one of my dreams, the sun coming through the trees and dancing off his dark hair. He looked down where our hands were entwined and kept speaking.

"But mostly I'm mad at myself. I should have saved them. That's my fucking job! I'm the best there is so that I can save them all. And I failed. How can I keep doing this if I can't save them? Can't save you?"

"No matter what you think, it's not your fault. The baddies did this, not you. It's not. Your. Fault." I squeezed his hands.

"Why am I telling you all of this? You don't need to deal with my bullshit."

"Because I'm your friend, Ink. Or at least, I hope I'm becoming one, and I want to help you through this. I might not be a badass like the rest of you, and what you all go through is something I've only had a taste of, so I can only imagine how you feel. But I'll help however I can because I care."

He kept looking at our hands. "Fara, promise me that no matter what happens, you will stay this sweet. Don't let me, the Team, the rest of the world—any of us fuckers—harden you."

Now was not the time to have this conversation. Sweet didn't save me from Hewitt or Barrington, or keep Jay from getting tortured. Sweet didn't save my parents from being killed. Sweet had done exactly zilch for me.

As if reading my mind, he took a step closer, so I had to look up at him. His cologne was mingled with sweat, the bandage on his hand rough against my skin. He finally looked at me. "You can be sweet and stand up for yourself, Fara. You can do both. Don't forget that, OK?"

He took a breath, shook himself a bit, and the perma-smirk returned. His entire demeanor changed in the blink of an eye. It was disconcerting. I guess when you lived like the Team did, you had to pull yourself up by your proverbial bootstraps quickly or you could be dead. That was a sobering thought.

"You know your secret is safe with me."

He looked surprised. "What secret?"

"That you're not really an asshole."

⚡⚡⚡

I'm not sure how long we trained. Ink had been serious and exacting during training, but I was grateful. I was starting to feel more comfortable holding a dagger. It was well after dark when my stomach growled so loudly that even Ink couldn't ignore it anymore. He turned from the shed on the corner of the Quad where he'd been putting the training supplies away and raised an eyebrow.

"Hungry?"

"I'm used to it."

"You don't ever have to be hungry here, OK? Eat every cheeseburger if you want. Although Blu might fight you for the last one."

"Then, are we going to dinner right now? Otherwise, I need to comm someone."

"Sure. I just didn't want to assume. I mean, weren't you going to take your boy toy some dinner?"

"Probably, but we can eat first."

"As you wish."

After Ink's breakdown, and how vulnerable he had been, I was worried that dinner would be awkward. It was anything but. He peppered me with questions about my world and seemed delighted by some of the mundane things—like movie theaters.

"I want to go there. To your world."

"You've been there."

He snorted. "Let me amend that. I want to go there when I'm not rescuing your boyfriend and running for my life. Better?"

I laughed. "Fair. When I get my abilities figured out, I might be able to take you there. Jay wants me to go back with him when he goes, assuming I'm better at suppressing my abilities. Maybe you can come visit? I'll take you to a movie for sure."

Ink's grin faded. "Why would you want to suppress your abilities?"

"Jay thinks that it's the only way to keep me safe so I can go home. If I don't open portals, Barrington and my government can't find me . . . or so the theory goes."

"You don't sound convinced."

"I'm not sure that I can suppress them enough while I'm sleeping to make a difference. Plus, even if I can, Barrington and the government have enough contacts that I'm pretty sure I'll be running and hiding regardless."

"That doesn't sound like much of a life."

"Jay thinks that—"

"I keep hearing what he thinks," Ink said. "But what do *you* want to do?"

"I haven't figured that out yet. Jay wants to protect me—and he feels like he can't do it if I'm here."

"What if you could protect yourself? Then what would he want to do? What would you want to do?"

What did I want? I was answering what Jay wanted. I was thinking about what Calum wanted. But beyond that, I didn't know. Ink studied me over the rim of his coffee mug, his long fingers tapping.

"What?"

He dropped his gaze to my empty plate. "Ready?"

I got a carton of food for Jay, and we walked to the infirmary in silence. The moon was bright and caught the angles and lines of the tattoos that were peeking out of Ink's sleeve and up his neck. In the moonlight, he looked like a dark angel—a brooding one at that. Beautiful, deadly, and now that I knew where to look for it, sad. The silence seemed weighted somehow, but I didn't mind the quiet. I wasn't about to question it.

He cleared his throat. "I never thanked you for today."

"There is nothing to thank me for."

"No, Fara, there is. You stayed. You saw my demons, the worst of me . . . and instead of running, you sat with it. With me. That . . . that means more than you'll ever know."

I threw my arms around him in a hug, carton of food and all. "I won't ever run. That's not something I'd do to a friend."

He took a deep breath and after hugging me back, he held me at arm's length, his perma-smirk returning.

"I might have to break down more, if it means you'll throw yourself at me."

I rolled my eyes for his benefit. "Whatever."

BLU 25

I ran around the Compound, getting shit done that I had been slacking on the past few days (weeks, months, whatever). I hated doing the everyday things that needed to be done, like laundry and getting supplies from the Admin building. It seemed like such a time-suck, even though I logically knew it was necessary. If I could hire out all of it, I would. I might actually start paying trainees part of my stipend to do my laundry. I sort of enjoyed having it done for me.

At one point during my escapades, I saw Ink and Fara out in the Quad. It appeared that Ink was training her on more defensive maneuvers. What had prompted them to train this late in the day? Maybe she was just a glutton for punishment.

After getting food, I ran into Styx. She was on her way to the mess with Dev and some of the tech operatives. She told me that the Captain wanted to talk to me when I had a second, so I headed toward her office.

"Blu, come in. I'll make this quick. Two things. First, both Styx and Ink know about Jack. You might want to check on Ink later. He didn't handle the news very well."

That was probably why he was out training. Although I wasn't sure why Fara was with him. I'd check on him later.

"The second thing might sound odd—but I need you to go talk to Fara's Agent Hanlon."

"OK. What about?"

"For now, I just want to see how he's feeling, if he needs

anything, and so on. But also to get a feel for what he's planning. If he'd be willing to help with the Barrington problem."

⚡ ⚡ ⚡

When I stopped a young medic in the infirmary to ask which room the agent was in, the clipboard he was carrying clattered to the ground. He looked around, mortified. I couldn't tell if he hadn't heard me coming, or if it was actually me who scared him.

I knocked on the agent's door and heard a voice that I recognized so well telling me to come in. My heart skipped a beat. This wasn't Jyston. I knew that this was going to be strange, probably as strange as it was for Fara to deal with all of us. She was handling it remarkably well, so I could figure it out.

The agent's face went from a smile to confusion to wariness, all within the blink of an eye. His face was still a mess of cuts and bruises, but his eyes were unnervingly fixed on me, and once again the humor that usually accompanied that stare was missing.

"Agent Hanlon, can I come in?"

"Have a seat."

I made my way to the chair in the corner.

"You start to get used to it," I said, because I didn't know if there was something else I should be saying. It was awkward to be looking at someone I had kissed . . . but not really—and who he had kissed . . . but not really. I had a hunch that in the history of all of the universes, this just might be a first.

"Thank you for helping Fara save me."

"It was the right thing to do."

"I owe you all my life."

"I'm sure you'll be repaying it soon enough. We need your help."

He was studying me intently, his gray eyes never wavering from my face. Eventually he looked away with a slight shake of his head.

"Sorry. It's just so strange. You look so much like her that I'm expecting—"

"You're expecting me to smile at you and try to make you feel comfortable, and maybe apologize for something I didn't do?"

He huffed a laugh. "A little bit, yeah."

"Unfortunately, I'm not that nice. They call me Blu here."

"Jay. Although you know my real name. Do you mind telling me how you know that?"

"Maybe another time. I'm actually here to see how you're doing. Sage asked that we wait to come see you until you were on the mend, but he said it was safe to come now. He told Fara the same thing, but she ignored him, apparently."

His jaw twitched, like he was trying to keep a straight face.

"Why do you need my help?"

"How much do you know about our world?"

"Just what Fara has told me. And I've spent some time with Willow, across the hall."

I raised my eyebrows at him.

"She has nightmares sometimes."

"Most of us do."

His eyes flitted over the scars on my shoulders and arms, where the whip had bitten through my skin and the daggers had sliced my flesh.

"Was that the work of Barrington's brother?"

"More or less. His head spymaster."

"I understand that they're coming for my world too. Or at least trying to."

"They're already in your world, Agent Hanlon. Barrington is not going to stop until your world mirrors ours."

"Then I have to go home and stop him."

"You do. But before you do, I just ask that you talk to us about your plans. We have as much of an interest in stopping Barrington as you do."

"I thought it was the Counselor that you're worried about?"

"What the Team is starting to understand is that as long as Barrington is out there somewhere, our world is not safe. He has to die, and you can help us."

He cocked his head like he heard someone coming. The action mirrored what Jyston had done on more than one occasion, so much so that my breath caught.

He turned back to me. "You know that Fara can't stay here, right? It's not safe for her."

"That's not up to you, Agent Hanlon. Or me. That's up to her."

The door opened and Fara was standing there, a smile spreading across her face as she took in the agent. His face softened and he smiled back at her. That was my cue to go.

"Blu, you don't have to go! Really, feel free to stay."

I smiled at her because I was trying to get better at that. "Tomorrow is early training. I need sleep."

"Oh! I want to go too. Do you mind coming and getting me?"

"I thought with your extra training with Ink tonight, you'd be done for a while."

Her face softened into concern. "The training was my idea because, well, I think he needed it. The Captain told him about Jack, and he didn't handle it well. You might want to check on him. Anyway, I need as much training as I can get, so for sure I want to go tomorrow."

"OK, someone will come get you. And thanks for letting me know about Ink."

I left the two of them and walked down the hall. At some point, Fara was going to have to tell the agent that he wasn't the boss of her, but that wasn't my conversation to have. Right now, a spot of worry bloomed in my stomach. Both the Captain and Fara were worried about Ink, which meant that something was wrong. His easygoing demeanor hid some pretty serious demons that I had only seen a few times, but it was enough. How any of us functioned after what we had lived through was beyond me. I guess it was friendship and hope—with a sprinkle of humor—that kept us going. It sounded like Ink could use all three.

⚡⚡⚡

I took in the carnage. Blood on the walls and the floor. A monstrous hole in the wall by the kitchen, and huge chunks of wall over Ink's bed were missing. A chair and table lay in broken pieces on the floor.

"What happened here?"

He didn't look up as he picked up pieces of rubble and put them into his trash. I let him work, not wanting to intrude, but not wanting to leave either, just in case he needed to talk. Eventually he stopped and walked over to the bed, head dropping into his hands.

"I happened here."

"Want to talk about it?"

He looked up at me. "You know Fara says that too? It's weird."

I climbed up next to him on the bed.

"Ink, are you OK?"

"I don't know, B. All I know is that the Captain told me about Jack, and all of the memories of Hastings started rushing back. I was so angry, but I felt so hopeless. I have so much guilt. So much rage. I kept replaying the ambush. Kept seeing Robin's head. The bodies of the prisoners in the prison yard. It was on constant repeat, over and over. I must have come back here and done all of this, because the next thing I remember, I'm kneeling on the ground, and Fara . . . She was holding me to her, and I grabbed her like a lifeline. She helped me pull myself out of that place. She didn't run. She stayed."

"We don't run from our friends, Ink."

He huffed a laugh and kissed my head. "That's what she said."

"We are the same person, you know. I saw the two of you training."

"Yeah, that was her idea. She sort of just knew that I needed to do something to get my mind off it."

"You don't give her enough credit. She might not be trained, but she understands people probably better than any of us do."

He looked around the room. "I could have hurt her."

"You wouldn't have."

"She said the same thing."

"Ink, she might not know you like I do, but I'm sure she knows this, and it's something that I know deep in my bones. There is no one else in this world who I would trust with my life more than you. You don't have it in you to hurt those you care about. You just don't, OK? You're a good person. You just happen to be a pain in the ass too."

"I know I don't say it enough, but I appreciate you. More than you know."

"I know you do. So, what are we going to do about Jack?"

"I guess I punched him in the same eye you did. Hopefully Styx got the other one."

"Are we all going to be OK?"

He paused. "Yeah. I think so."

FARA 26

Blu closed the door quietly and I sat on Jay's bed.

"What was that all about?" He took the food from my hands and placed it on the bedside table. I guess he wasn't hungry. His eyes were troubled, though he was smiling faintly.

"The other Calum—the guy they call Ink here—had a bit of a nervous breakdown and so I helped him, is all."

He arched his perfect eyebrow at me but didn't say anything.

"You know," I said, "every time you make that face, I want to kiss you, and possibly rip your clothes off." I leaned down and kissed his eyebrow.

"Then I need to make that face as much as possible," he said, and he kissed me.

I started tugging on his hospital gown, grinning. "You mean, I can take off your clothes?"

He grabbed my hands. "Not here. Not in a hospital bed."

"Can't I just have a little peek? I mean, I've been staring at your amazing body through your too-tight T-shirts for forever."

"My too-tight shirts?"

"I'm not complaining!"

He chuckled. It was such a low sound that I felt it in my chest. "Please believe me that I want to, Fara," he said. "But I want to be able to take my time. And I can't while I'm here. It wouldn't be right."

I forced myself to shrug, telling my hormones and emotions to get a grip. If he wanted to wait, I'd respect that. I sighed and sat back up, but he frowned.

"Take off your boots."

"OK, Bossy McBosserson."

His jaw twitched. "Take off your boots, please. I would like you to lie with me for a bit, if you would be so kind."

I kicked off my boots and dagger, and snuggled into the crook of his arm. He kissed the top of my head, breathing me in.

"You smell different."

"It's different shampoo than what I have at home."

"No, you smell like cologne."

"Oh, sorry. Why was Blu here?"

"She wants to know what my plans are."

"Do you have a plan?"

He pulled me closer to him. "My big, brilliant plan right now is to get better so I can go back home and see what havoc has been caused. I'm sure Barrington told the department I was dead, or that I attacked him unprovoked or something. So, I need to find out. I'm not good with not knowing."

"What does Sage say?"

"He says two more weeks, but I can't wait that long. I promised him one, and then I have to go—regardless of my health."

"One week? That doesn't seem like enough."

"It's going to have to be. But, in the meantime . . . " He kissed me again, and I felt it all the way to my toes. My body desperately wanted to rip off his hospital gown—but I respected him. He wanted to wait, and so could I. But I couldn't help the moan that escaped as I pressed up against him. His good hand snaked through my hair. He broke it off abruptly, a small smile playing on his lips.

"You're making it hard to be chivalrous."

"Don't be chivalrous on my account."

He held my gaze. Right then and there, I thought I might burst into flames.

"Fara, are you OK with this? In a hospital bed?"

"I'm more than OK with this. I don't want to hurt you, though."

"You won't." He stared directly into my eyes. "Tell me this is what you want."

"This is what I want."

He raised that perfect eyebrow. "Lock the door. Please."

⚡ ⚡ ⚡

We lay in the partial darkness, curled up under the light blanket. I knew I had to find my clothes and go back to my apartment. I knew I was going to be getting up soon to train. I knew that Jay needed to heal and to sleep. But all of that was secondary to this moment. It had been so long since someone had held me, so long since I had felt wanted, that I needed this moment to last.

After Beck and I had sex, he would roll over or get up or really anything to avoid being near me. The sex was usually pretty lackluster, but it was after the act that always hurt me the most. As though I had fulfilled my duty to get him off, so he could go back to whatever it was he wanted to do. That was just one more thing in a long list that showed he was a selfish asshole.

But tonight, with Jay, was different. He was so gentle and careful, as if I was something to be cherished. His was such a solid presence, and he was such a good person, that I found myself wanting to drink it up and savor it. I didn't know what the next few days, weeks, or months would bring, but right now—tonight—I was happy.

I snuggled in closer and felt Jay's eyes on me. As I looked up, he brushed some errant hairs out of my face. Another hair tie had bitten the dust, but at least it was for a good cause.

He sighed. "You can't stay here, Fara."

"I know, I know. Just one more minute."

"No, I mean, I want you to come back with me when I go home."

"Can we talk about this later?"

"What we did just there . . . I just . . . I just care for you a lot, is all, and I'm not good with not knowing. I want to know that you'll come back with me."

"I'm not sure I'll be ready by then. I want to keep training so I can start protecting myself—"

"It's not safe here."

"It's definitely not safe there."

He huffed, frustrated. "We've talked about this, Fara. I can't protect you here. I don't know anything about this place. If we get back to our world, I have friends. I can hide you. I can keep you safe while you work on suppressing your abilities."

"And keep running every time Barrington or the assistant finds me? Always looking over my shoulder, or worrying about opening a portal in my sleep? That they'll take my friends, or you, to get to me? How is that a long-term solution?"

"If you can just suppress—"

"What if I can't?"

"Then you need to try harder."

He wasn't going to let this drop. "Jay, what if the answer isn't to run? What if the answer is to fight? These people can teach me how to protect myself. I just need time."

"Why are you arguing with me about this? Don't you want to go home? Isn't that what we talked about?" He lowered his voice. "Are they pressuring you to stay?"

"No."

"Fara, you aren't like them. You're no warrior. You're sweet and trusting and the most amazing thing that has happened to me in so long. Please." He cupped my face with his good hand and stared into my eyes, pleading. "I care about you too much to worry about you getting killed here while I'm home. I can't do what I need to do and worry about you too."

"I'll be safe here, Jay. You don't have to worry."

"But I will. That's who I am. Just . . . promise me that you'll think about it."

"I'll think about it."

And I would think about it. Going home with him, having him protect me—it made sense. I knew I was at a disadvantage here. I had no training, no skill, nothing to help me out. He was doing this because he thought I was amazing. He was doing this because he cared. This honorable man, this man who came to rescue me, even though it almost cost him his life, cared about me. And I cared about him. A lot.

But.

What he said silently wormed its way into the part of my brain that whispered to my deepest fears. Even though he thought I was amazing, he still didn't think I could survive on my own; that I was too sweet and kind to learn to protect myself. That I didn't have enough fire in me to ever be more than what I was. He didn't believe that I would ever be a warrior. And even if I thought he might be right, it still hurt.

27 FARA

"You know, I'm starting to worry about your pathological cleanliness," a voice teased. It took me a second to register what was happening. I was in my apartment, in bed, and Ink was going through my kitchen cabinets.

"How are you such a morning person?" I grumbled.

"One of the many benefits of being me. But seriously, why is your place so clean? It's weirding me out."

I sat up in bed, trying desperately to figure out why I was so tired. "I don't own enough of anything for it to be messy."

He looked me over. "You look . . . "

I'm sure I was a mess, and part of me was embarrassed that he saw me like this. Part of me didn't care at all and just wanted coffee.

"Don't even go there, Ink. Do not comment on my appearance this morning or I will find something to throw at you."

He grinned at me. "That's more like it. Late night?"

"Something like that."

He stopped opening one of my kitchen drawers midway and raised an eyebrow. Seriously? I was so tired I couldn't even be concerned that all of the men in my life used that expression with me more than was probably necessary. Bastards.

"Well, I hope it was worth it."

I smiled at the memory of Jay hovering over me on his one good arm, asking one more time if I was OK with what we were doing. With his injuries and the size of the hospital bed, we hadn't been able to do much exploring. But he was so considerate during what we were able to accomplish, he made me smile.

I was just going to ignore the conversation we had afterward. I still had a week to decide what I wanted to do. And maybe he was right. Maybe I really needed someone to look after me. Wasn't that what most women said they wanted?

"What was that look?" he asked, finally ending his examination of my kitchen.

"What look?" I headed to the bathroom.

"I've seen you do it a bunch. Your face shows everything you're thinking, and then it just . . . doesn't. It's like it goes away."

I'd pushed down the feelings without even realizing it. Old habits and all. I sighed.

"It's a habit I'm trying to break. Sort of. Because my portal abilities are controlled by my emotions, my mom spent most of my life telling me to put them in a box and push them down. That way, I wasn't opening portals by accident whenever I got dumped by my idiot boyfriend or failed my science test or whatever. I don't even realize I'm doing it most of the time."

"What did you just push down, there? What were you thinking about?"

"About how it is way too early in the morning for you to be this nosy."

He grinned, and turned to leave. "Styx will be by to pick you up for training in a few minutes." He hesitated at the door. "And Fara? I'm not just a pretty face, you know. You can talk to me."

"Your face isn't all that pretty," I quipped, feeling bad because it wasn't true and . . .

. . . And Ink wasn't upset at all. He was grinning like he'd just won the lottery.

"Sweetness, I know you don't really think that. I am quite pretty, and I know you know it."

He left, chuckling to himself. There was coffee and a donut on my table. Bastard.

⚡ ⚡ ⚡

I made it through training with only a few curse words here and there. I was sore from the hours of training yesterday and the *other* activities, and even with ibuprofen, my arm still hurt something fierce. But by the end, I had successfully pulled my dagger out from its sheath quickly and in one motion, without dropping it (which is harder than it sounds), had learned the basics of stabbing someone with it (go for the soft spots like the kidneys. Leave it to the experts to slit throats), and could somewhat disarm Ink. Once again, he had been charming but serious during training, and so when he complimented me on my last attempt to disarm him, I couldn't help but beam.

I wanted food, a bath, and sleep—in that order—but I needed to talk to the Captain first.

"Do you have a second?"

"Of course." She invited me to join her for some food.

Her tray held eggs and an apple. No donut or sugar to be seen. No wonder she was in such amazing shape. Maybe I'd have to reconsider my diet. Later. I would reconsider my diet later, after I consumed the bacon that was staring at me.

The rest of the Team had joined us and were talking quietly. Jack's eyes were downcast, and the others were whisper-yelling at him. But at least they were talking to him. That was a start.

"What can I help you with, Fara?"

I told her about Jay's concerns about his department contacting Calum. "So, do you think if we needed to, we could bring Calum here?" I asked.

She quietly considered it as she ate her breakfast, and I sipped my coffee. I could hear the mumblings of the Team next to me, but I purposely shut them out. This was their fight, and it wasn't my place to interject.

"You pose an interesting problem, Fara. I agree with Agent Hanlon that Calum might be a security risk, especially if Barrington is able to learn more from him about what's happening here. But having Calum here poses its own set of problems. Ink is as recognizable as Blu, so having someone who looks like him will raise quite a few questions, especially since you're already here. And, there's the matter of Dagna's spy. That information could get to the Counselor. So then, what to do?"

I hadn't realized until just that moment how much I wanted her to say yes. I missed Calum, and even though I really was growing to think of the Team as my friends, it wasn't the same as having someone understand me without having to explain myself.

"All right," she said. "If it comes to it, then your friend can come here. But I have some conditions: he stays in your room, and only until the agent leaves, and you take Blu with you when you retrieve him."

At the mention of her name, Blu looked up. "Take me where?"

28 FARA

Back at the apartment, Blu and I discussed our potential upcoming mission.

"So now I just need to open a portal and see if he wrote back. If he's OK, then we don't have to worry about it. If he's not, then he gets to hang out with us here."

I started the process of opening the portal, expecting to see another note, but there wasn't one. Strange.

"That's so cool," Blu said, stepping behind me. "Is that Calum's place again?"

I could hear muffled yelling. Then there was a crash. Something fell on the coffee table: Calum.

"Is that . . .?"

"Shit! Something's wrong." I willed the portal to get bigger.

Two burly arms grabbed Calum around his waist and hauled him up.

"Blu, what do we do? We can't let them take him!"

Jack walked into my apartment without knocking, which seemed to be the way of things around here. "Fara, I was just seeing if you— What's wrong?"

"No time to explain," Blu said, patting herself down, checking her gear. "Want to hop through a portal and save another one of Fara's friends?"

Jack grinned. "Sure! I mean, I didn't have much else to do today since my spy gig is up."

I couldn't see Calum anymore, but I heard another crash. "We have to go now." I motioned toward the portal. "I'll be right behind you."

I kept the portal open as I ran to my bedside table and grabbed my phone. While totally useless here, I couldn't live without it there.

Jack went first, then Blu. I came through last, just in time to see Agent Johnson dragging Calum out the door. Luckily, Agent Johnson did not see me.

"Those were Barrington's goons, right? I'm really fucking tired of those assholes," Blu said, making for the door.

"Yeah, they are annoying. But at least we know where they're headed, right?" Jack said.

"I'm not sure. Barrington is borrowing that house from someone else, so they could be taking him anywhere." I grabbed the extra set of Calum's car keys from a jar next to the door. Of course they were with condoms, and gum; apparently the three things every dude needs when he leaves the house.

Calum's car was an old beater with two hundred thousand miles on it, but it ran better than mine. Ahhh, Voldemort. I missed my POS. Sort of.

Jack and Blu got in after me, Blu bitching about being stuck in the back seat. I would have yelled at Jack in short girl solidarity if we weren't trying to save Calum from Jay's fate. I called Adora and put the phone on speaker as I started the car.

Adora picked up on the first ring. "Fara?"

"Adora!"

"Oh my god, it is you! Fara, honey! I'm so glad I answered. I'm on break right now. I've been so worried . . . and Calum told me what's happening. And what the hell, chica? I mean, portals? Hiding out in another universe? Doppelgängers? And you can electrocute people—"

"They got Calum."

"What?"

"I'm in Calum's car with two of my new 'friends,' and we're following Barrington's baddies. They got Calum, Adora."

"Those fuckers! If I could, I would kick them in the fucking nutsacks until they shriveled up."

Jack and Blu both laughed, not looking terribly surprised as Adora let out a colorful stream of cursing and suggestions as to what hell she'd unleash on Barrington and his men. Styx and Adora were remarkably similar, which was comforting. And weird.

"Girl, I miss you! Does this mean you're back for good?"

I was weaving in and out of traffic at a pace that might be considered a little aggressive. Jack grabbed the car's "oh shit!" handle. I forced myself to slow down. The "sorry that I have a dagger and my passengers look like ninjas, but I was in another universe and now I'm trying to rescue my friend from goons" excuse probably wouldn't work if I got pulled over.

"Not yet," I told Adora. "It's still not safe for me here. But Jay is coming back in a week and wants me to come with him."

"Hot agent man is with you?"

I smiled. "Not currently, no. But he's in the hospital in the other world and we've been . . . talking."

"Please tell me you finally got some."

I sighed. No use hiding it since we were on speaker phone.

"Yes, I did. Last night."

She let out a whoop and I could tell that she was dancing on her toes. Both Jack and Blu were suppressing their laughter

"Did it rock your socks off? Was it good enough to wipe out all memories of bad sex with asshat?"

"It was . . . sweet." I felt myself getting redder and redder.

"Oh girl, that doesn't sound promising."

This was so, so awkward. "It was in a hospital bed, so it . . . never mind. I miss you, my friend. I can't wait until we can catch up for real."

"That doesn't sound like it will be any time soon."

"I don't know yet, so don't keep hanging onto my job. I really appreciate—"

"It's the least I could do. I'll save Calum's too, if I have to. Is he coming with you?"

"That's actually why I was calling you. He is."

"How long will he be gone?"

"A week at most. He'll come back when Jay does, assuming we can get him before they do something to him." I stopped, telling myself to breathe. We'd get Calum back. We would.

"And Adora? Thank you. For everything. I wish you could come with me too."

"If there are hot guys and no Hewitt, then you better bring me along."

I cringed, although Jack didn't seem bothered by it—he just looked at me and winked. "I really don't go by Hewitt anymore," he said.

Adora yelped. "What the fuck? Fara, is Hewitt . . . What?"

I laughed. "It's another story for another time. We're going to go rescue Calum from some baddies."

"You sound so badass right now. Proud of you. Ugh. Hewitt is on his way back to the locker room, so I gotta go. You know he got promoted to assistant manager?"

"When I come back, I'm going to royally kick his ass." And I meant it.

"Make it soon, my friend. This world is darker without you."

I hung up, tears stinging the corner of my eyes. I missed her. But right now, I needed to save my best friend.

"There are so many things I want to ask you about right now," Jack said, then burst out laughing. I couldn't help but join in.

I turned off the interstate and onto the country road. We followed the blue sedan at a distance, but trying not to lose them completely, just in case they weren't taking him to the governor's mansion. This car following thing looked way easier in the movies than it really was. While I tried to figure it out, Blu and Jack peppered me with questions about Adora and my job, but eventually about my asshat ex, because of Adora's comment, and what exactly I had gotten up to with Jay. While it seemed inappropriate to be talking about these things when Calum's life was on the line, it actually made the drive, and Calum's kidnapping, less stressful somehow. Maybe that was why they joked all of the time—it helped with the stress.

"That makes sense now," Blu said after I explained the breakup with Beck. "Every time Dev's name came up, or he showed up, you were trying your hardest to hide."

"I feel bad about that. It's not his fault that his counterpart is the worst."

"And apparently bad in bed," Blu said. "And your experience with Jay was—what did you call it?"

"Sweet," Jack supplied with snort. "Please don't ever tell him that, Fara. His ego will never recover."

I blushed some more, but I didn't have time to feel awkward. The sedan had turned up the drive and stopped at the gated entrance to the governor's mansion. The guard must have been away from his post, because one of the goons was yelling into an intercom thing. But we were in luck—the gate was still down.

I could see Calum banging on the glass partition in the car, and I remembered being exactly where he was, just a week ago. No way to get out of the car, pounding on the glass partition while the goons ignored me. Wanting to escape. I shuddered. We'd figure out how to get him. Somehow.

I stopped the car, hoping that the goons were so preoccupied with their inability to get through the gate that they hadn't seen us pull up.

"Keep the car here and leave it running," Blu said. Jack had already gotten out of the car without my noticing. That was how good of a spy he was—he could just melt out of a car. Was that a teachable ability? If so, I wanted to learn. I watched as he punctured the rear tire of the blue sedan with his dagger. He did it to the other side as well. The goons didn't seem to notice.

The gate was slowly opening, and I started to panic. I had no idea what to do, but luckily I didn't have to do anything. Blu made it to the sedan before it started to drive froward. She held the palmbox to the car door, opened it, and yanked Calum out, shoving him toward his car. They all three sprinted back and jumped in.

It couldn't be that easy. Did Blu really pull Calum out of the car and run away? That was it? I threw the old car in gear and ran up and over the manicured lawn.

"Not to be an alarmist, but you might want to start driving faster, Fara," Jack said. The blue sedan was following us. "I popped their tires, but that won't help if we're dead."

The little car shuddered as I floored it, bullets pinging off the car, one shattering the back windshield.

"I wonder if insurance covers that?" Calum quipped. He grabbed a napkin out of his glovebox and held it to his bleeding mouth. I couldn't tell what other injuries he had—I was too busy concentrating on not killing us—although I could see from the corner of my eye that he had blood down his shirt. When did I get to the point in my life where wondering what combat injuries my friends had was normal?

The gas pedal was right to the floor, but the blue sedan was gaining on us anyway. Their tricked-out sedan was going to overtake us in a matter of seconds. They didn't teach how to outrun bad guys in a crappy car in driver's ed, or at least, I wasn't paying attention if they did. Eventually their punctured tires would go flat, but as Jack said, that didn't matter if we were dead.

"They're gaining on us," Jack said calmly as the goons pulled up next to us, completely ignoring the fact that it was a two-lane road. The passenger window of the blue sedan was down, and the goon in the passenger seat had a gun pointed directly at my head. I slammed on the brakes. They whizzed past us, the bullet that had been meant for me pinging off the front bumper. I switched gears, Calum wincing and looking mildly panicked as his car shuddered and made some horrible noises. I couldn't blame him, but I didn't have time to worry about that. I reversed down the road as fast as I could, away from the goons.

"Not that I'm not appreciative of the rescue," he said, "but is this part of the plan?"

"There is no plan! I'm just trying not to get us killed. Your car isn't exactly made for high-speed chases! I'm improvising."

The goons had made a U-turn in the middle of the road and were closing in. I kept concentrating on driving in reverse. I didn't have to outrun them for long, just until their tires got so flat that they couldn't keep up. Honestly, I wasn't sure how long this could last. Another bullet cracked the windshield right in front of my face.

"That was close," Blu said.

As soon as they got as close as I dared, I slammed on the brakes again, forcing the baddies to swerve in order to avoid hitting our car. I threw it in drive and sped around them, barely missing their bumper. They slammed on their brakes too. A bullet ripped through the windshield, shattering the glass, and lodged in the back seat between Jack and Blu.

I didn't risk looking back.

Calum turned around in his seat. "Their tires finally gave up," he said. He reached for another napkin from his glovebox and slumped in his seat. Whether his injury was from the broken glass or from the goons, I didn't know. I risked a look in my rearview mirror and saw the sedan trying to make a U-turn, but they couldn't do much with the busted back tires. They shot at us a couple more times, but at that point we were too far away for the bullets to hit us.

I let out a long breath.

Never in a million years did I think I would be in a high-speed car chase with guns. In an ancient beater, no less. I never wanted to repeat this experience.

"Great driving," Jack said.

Blu grinned at me. "Maybe we should send you to compete in the PITs," she joked. At least, I hoped she was joking.

"Are you OK?" I asked Calum.

"Yeah, I just bit my cheek when the guy punched me. But I'm all right. Thank you for saving me. But how did you know?"

"It was luck, honestly." I told him what happened.

He turned to Jack and Blu. "Thank you for coming with her."

"No problem. I'm actually starting to like this place," Blu said.

29 FARA

We dropped Calum's car off at The Grill, which was the best I could come up with on short notice. I opened the portal in the alley behind the building, marveling once again that I could do it so quickly now, and we all stepped through into the Captain's office.

She was sitting behind her desk and didn't even flinch when we appeared. I envied her rock-solid demeanor. I was still shaking a bit from our latest escapade.

"You must be Calum."

Blu came forward. "When Fara opened the portal, we saw Barrington's assholes taking him, so we had to move fast. Jack just happened to come along for the ride."

"Of course he did," the Captain said dryly. "Welcome to the Compound, Calum. You're safe here now."

She turned to me. "Fara, I hate to hurry you along, but I have some other Compound residents coming in here in a moment, so can you get Calum back to your apartment? We need to keep him under wraps, at least for now. Ink and Styx should be getting back from their mission soon. I'll have someone come grab you for the debrief after that."

"Thank you, Captain. For everything."

"Just . . . try to remain as unseen as you can, Calum. Oh, and ask Ink for some clothes."

Calum pulled the hood on his sweatshirt up, hiding his features before stepping out onto the short path between the Captain's office and our apartments. The sky was overcast and threatening rain. As we walked past the trees that lined the broken redbrick path, I heard Calum's sharp intake of breath.

"Are those leaves . . . ?"

"The very same."

"Crazy."

Someone was coming down the path. Tall and thin. Silver's platinum blonde hair was in a thick braid that hung over her shoulder. She looked like a runway model. Or maybe a runway model assassin ninja?

She smiled tentatively when she saw us, and then she saw Calum. Her reaction was almost the same reaction she'd had when she first saw me—disbelief and shock.

She wasn't the only one who was staring. Calum was looking back just as intensely, a small smile on his lips. Was he flirting? That would take the cake—to bring my best friend to an alternate universe and get him laid. Ha! She was gorgeous and all.

"Silver—we can't talk about it here," Blu said. "We'll tell you what happened in the debrief. Fara's friend is staying at the apartment. No one else can know. Understand?"

Silver tore her eyes away from Calum and nodded to Blu. "I understand."

"Good. See you in a little bit."

Thankfully, we arrived at my apartment without anyone else seeing us. Blu and Jack left with a promise to bring us food as soon as they could. I didn't know the last time Calum had eaten, but I was always ready for free food.

Calum took the hood of his sweatshirt down and stood in the middle of my apartment, slowly turning around.

"This place is amazing, Fara."

"Isn't it? It's like, the coolest apartment ever. Plus, it's free. And the food is free. And my training is free. Other than this world being a postapocalyptic dystopian sort of hellhole, it's really pretty amazing."

"That's . . . awesome? And scary? I'm not sure how to respond to that."

He took off his shoes, sat on the bed beside me, and hugged me. I breathed his familiar scent in. I was so grateful he was here, even if it was under crap circumstances. I told him so.

"I've missed you too," he said. He kissed my head. "I was so worried about you being here."

"Things are different here, and some of it is scary, but I kind of like it."

"Other than the despotic government and running for your life thing?"

I laughed. "Apparently I have to deal with running for my life at home too, actually more so there than here. So . . . "

"So . . . I'm assuming you have coffee around here someplace, because you wouldn't willingly live in a world without it. Why don't you start explaining this place to me, and the people, and how the food is free, and why you're wearing a dagger. In fact, why don't you start at the beginning and tell me everything?"

We spent the next hour catching up. And, as I explained, I felt the pieces that had been slowly bouncing around my head starting to click into place bit by bit. In my retelling of the craziness that the past couple of weeks had brought, I realized that for the first time in as long as I could remember, I was excited to wake up in the morning. Maybe it was because I didn't have to worry about rent, or food, or my POS car, or Beck, or Hewitt. But maybe it was something more. Maybe it was because I was finally part of something bigger than myself, and these people, who were risking everything to make their world a better place, thought I could help them. Maybe it was because it felt like I was being given the chance to start over, or at least the space to start asking what it was that *I* wanted. I didn't feel like I was just surviving. I felt like I was starting to live. I didn't believe in destiny or fate necessarily, but I couldn't deny that in the infinite number of possible worlds, my powers had opened portals to this one. I couldn't turn my back on them if they needed me. But maybe, just maybe, I needed them too.

With that final thought, the answer to the question that I had been struggling with came into focus with complete clarity. I didn't want to suppress my powers, and I wasn't ready to go home. Not yet. Not until Barrington Park was defeated and I could go back without having to run or hide what I was. And in order to do that, I was going to help the Team in any way I could.

But more than that, I couldn't stand by knowing that I might be able to help but doing nothing. I couldn't just go back to my life and hide while everyone else risked everything. After the story of Hastings; after what had happened to Blu and Jack; after watching Ink fight to get control over his fear and anger; after all of this—I needed to stay and help however I could. And if that meant I needed to learn to wield rather than suppress my powers, then that's what I'd do.

Somehow, the tightness that I had been carrying in my chest began to loosen. I wasn't choosing this to make my parents happy, or Calum or Jay, or because it was the safe thing to do. It was the right thing for me. I was scared shitless, but I knew in my bones that I didn't want to spend my life running and hiding. I didn't want to spend my life having Jay pass me from place to place so that Barrington couldn't get me. I wanted the freedom to be myself—weird portal and electroshock abilities included.

I couldn't go home. Not yet.

As I tried to explain it to Calum, it came out in a torrent of halting words and tears. I knew what I was saying was right, but I still worried about how he would respond. I set my jaw when I was done speaking and met his gaze, which was steady and unreadable.

I was ready for him to tell me that I wasn't a warrior and that I needed to come home. To be safe. I was ready to stand up for myself if I had to.

But he didn't.

He grabbed me in a crushing hug.

"Did Jay really tell you that you aren't a warrior?" he said into my hair. I let the words settle over me. Not a warrior. Not strong. Not able to fight. Too nice. Too sweet. "Then he really doesn't know you at all."

I pulled back to look at Calum.

"Fara, it's true that you worry about other people's feelings more than your own. You push your own emotions down until you don't even recognize them as yours. You let people walk all over you so that you don't hurt them. You don't stand up for yourself. But that's how you've been taught to act, not who you *are*."

A sob escaped my lips, and he pulled me back into him, his arms tight around me.

"You are sweet, and trusting, and kind, but you also just dodged bullets and drove like a race car driver to save me. You jumped through a portal, not knowing where it led, then risked getting captured again to go save Jay. And you would have done it even if you didn't have the help of the Mission Impossible team. Even before then, you stood up to my mom when she was in a drunken rage, letting her berate you time and time again so that I could sneak some clothes and come to your house without her stopping me. Sure, you're not swords and missions and killing people with dental floss or whatever like these guys, but that doesn't make you any less of a warrior. Your strength comes from your absolute faith that helping people is the right thing to do. Jay is very, very wrong about you."

At that, the last tether on my emotions crumbled, and he hugged me to him as I cried.

"Fara, I'm so sorry." I could hear the hitch in his voice.

"What? Why?"

"That I didn't tell you that before. That even for a second you worried I might agree with Jay. That I don't tell you enough how great you really are, and how your strength is what got me through a pretty shitty childhood. Do you really think that I'm your friend because I need to protect you?"

I nodded into his chest. It was my worst fear, that my friends weren't my friends but stuck around because they thought I couldn't survive without them. And worse? That I might agree with them.

His tears started falling onto my hair. "That's exactly the opposite of the truth, Fara. I felt—feel—that I need to prove to you that I am worthy of being your best friend, so I stand up for you. I do it because otherwise, why be friends with me? A shy kid with an abusive, alcoholic mom? Why would someone as smart and kind and funny as you be friends with someone like me? You lent me your strength when no one else did, and then didn't seem to keep any for yourself. I'm sorry I gave you any reason to doubt me. You are my sister in all but blood, and I love you. OK?"

"You are my person, Calum. I love you too."

There was a knock on my door, and without waiting for an answer, Blu and Jack walked in carrying cartons of food. So much food.

Blu stopped when she saw the scene of Calum and me on the bed, wrapped in each other's arms, snot freely dripping down our faces.

"Are we interrupting?"

I choked out a giggle. "No. We're just having a heart-to-heart. Come on in."

"Are you sure?"

"Yeah. We're just talking about how Calum thinks I'm a warrior."

I said it in a lighthearted way, but I forced myself to say it anyway.

"Of course you are," Blu said. "Why wouldn't you think you are?"

Calum answered, a hint of anger in his voice. "Fara's new boyfriend told her that she isn't, and that she needs to suppress her abilities and move back home."

"First, he can fuck right off. Sorry. What I mean to say is that he really doesn't know you, then."

"That's what Calum said."

"Then Calum is smart. At least, smarter than Ink," Blu said with a grin. "Fara, on top of everything badass you did today, you know what's more impressive to me? You moved to a different world—a completely different universe—and not only have you acclimated, but you've done it seamlessly. I'm not sure that if the roles were reversed I could transition and thrive like you are. Truly."

BLU 30

Fara and I left Calum eating tater tots in her apartment and headed for the debriefing. Styx and Ink had verified during their mission that the gate on the end of the trail at Dagna's building wasn't electrified, and it didn't have any cameras or other security measures on it. But it still was too small an opening to herd a bunch of scared prisoners out, especially since we didn't know how many people Jurisdiction had there. The PITs looked more and more like our only option, even though the Captain still wasn't convinced. Either way, it didn't make any of us happy.

Afterward, I dropped her back at her apartment, lost in my thoughts. How were we going to rescue these people? As I headed down the hall toward my own apartment, Jack pulled me aside. "Jyston moved the meeting up. You'll need to go now."

"Now? OK."

Jack stopped in front of my door.

"Blu, I still don't like it. Having the Second Counselor weirdly fixated on you is not necessarily a good thing."

"I'm not even sure that's what it is."

Jack studied me for a moment. "You have feelings for him." A statement, not a question.

I debated what to tell him, but I ended with the truth. Secrets had led Jack to be in this position, and I couldn't be self-righteously mad at him if I did the same thing.

"Jyston was the one who busted me out of Jurisdiction when I was a kid, Jack."

"I thought a Team member did—"

"Me too, but it was him. He wrapped me in a blanket and carried me out. They would have killed him if they found out, but he did it anyway. My gut is telling me that he is helping us, not just because of his fixation, but because he has something else going on."

"If that's not it, and he's setting us up for a trap? Then what?"

"Then I'll do what I have to do. I'll kill him."

⚡ ⚡ ⚡

I drove to the meeting place and parked where Jack had told me to. He had a comm directly linked to me, but otherwise no one knew where I was. I didn't like keeping secrets from the Team, but I wanted—needed—to have this conversation in private. I told myself being here turned the tables and gave me the upper hand. And I almost believed it.

Jack told me that Jyston had picked this spot because there were no security cameras and it was out of the way. There was nothing here but abandoned buildings and rubble, but they were packed so closely together that it made hiding fairly easy. It also would have been a good place for Jyston to kill someone, but now was not the time to worry about that. In a fair fight, he could probably take me. So I wouldn't fight fair.

"Couldn't stay away?"

Jyston had appeared from nowhere, hands in his pockets, a mischievous smile tugging on his lips. He casually walked toward me, and my heartbeat picked up.

"I thought I might remind you that I'm not a mouse in this game."

"Is that why you're here?"

He looked at me with predatory calm, and I forced myself to meet his gaze. I wasn't some teenager with a crush. I wasn't a kid anymore. I was a principal member of the Team, and he didn't scare me. Even if he should, a little.

"I'm here because we need to talk."

"About?"

"What do you mean 'about'?"

"There are many things we need to talk about, Blu. But our time is limited. Dagna is searching for me right now, which is why I needed to move up this meeting." He approached me, tracing my jaw with his calloused hand as he spoke. "If I had known it was going to be you here instead of Jackrabbit, I would have postponed until we had more time."

I jerked my head away, although I didn't move my body out of his personal space. He sighed and dropped his hand.

"Business, then."

"Yes, business."

He sat down on a piece of rubble, his forearms resting on his knees, hands clasped.

"What can I do for you, beautiful Blu?"

"Unless you have any better ideas, Silver and I need to enter the PITs. I don't know any other way to get more information about Dagna's building."

"Alas, I do not have any better ideas. Dagna doesn't seem to trust me very much. Predictably so, since she's trying to kill me. My spies have also been unable to gather further information. I'm afraid her poison has started to work, and the Counselor doesn't trust me as he once did."

His hair hung loose past his shoulders, gently blowing in the spring breeze. He was studying his hands, and while his posture was relaxed, his face was tense and something else. He looked worried. Beneath the humor glinting in his eyes was concern. If Dagna's plan was working and the Counselor thought he was up to something (which he was), Jyston was in trouble.

"Are you OK?"

He started. "Why do you ask?"

"Because you don't look it."

"That is not something a man ever wants to hear, especially from his . . . girlfriend."

"I'm sorry you ever heard Styx say that."

He chuckled. "I'm not. Anyway, yes. I'm fine. I just have more happening than I'd like."

"OK."

"Thank you for asking, though." And he looked like he meant it.

"So, the PITs?"

"I will get you and Silver invited to participate. Meet me back here tomorrow, same time, and I'll have the information you need."

He walked back over to me, standing directly in my personal space again with a smile.

"Jyston?"

"Hmmm?" He was so close that I could see the stubble on his chin and feel the heat radiating off his body. Without thinking, I reached up to tuck a stray piece of hair behind his ear, and he bent so that I could. The corner of his mouth turned up a bit.

"Thank you for your help."

He dipped his head, the move almost regal.

"I must go, beautiful Blu. I will see you tomorrow. Oh, and you might want to ask Ink what they found in the courtyard of Dagna's building."

I was wary. "Why do I need to do that?"

He cocked an eyebrow. "Consider it my first present to you. To commemorate our relationship."

I rolled my eyes for his benefit. "I told you, there is nothing between us."

With lightning speed, he grabbed my face and kissed me, his strong hands gently holding me to him. Unlike the other kisses, this one was less than chaste. His tongue parted my lips, and he tasted of cinnamon and something sweeter. My hands involuntarily threaded through his hair, my body having a mind of its own. He broke it off as quickly as he'd started it, but he didn't let go of my face. He looked at me with a mix of intensity and humor that was sexy as hell.

"Beautiful Blu, tell me again that there's nothing between us."

I couldn't say it and he'd smell my lie if I did. And he knew it. "I'm really not that beautiful, Jyston. I'm not sure why you keep calling me that."

He dropped his hands and backed away. "To me, you are."

31 FARA

Jay was wheeling himself out of the room across the hall, so I opened the door to let him back in his room. He wasn't in a hospital gown, but in the Compound's standard black pants and T-shirt, this one only one size too small. I lamented the lack of access to his ass as I helped him back into bed, although he didn't seem to need much help. All of the clues were pointing to the fact that he was getting better, which meant that he would be leaving soon. In a few days, maybe. He said a week, but my guess was that he'd leave earlier if he could.

He pulled me down for a kiss, but broke off just as it started to get interesting.

"Why'd you stop?" I murmured, kissing his ear and his jaw.

He gently grabbed my shoulders and pushed me up, looking apologetic. "Fara, as much as I enjoyed last night—and I did—I really don't want to repeat it in this hospital bed."

"I enjoyed last night too."

He smiled at me and took my hand. "So, what brings you here?"

"Can't I just come by?"

He gave a soft chuckle. "Haven't we been over this? You can be here to see me, and because you need to tell me something. It's OK that it's both."

"Calum is here."

His humor died. "Tell me."

"Bossy."

"I'm serious, Fara. What happened?"

I told him about the rescue and high-speed car chase. "He's reading my mom's notes and eating tater tots right now."

"Fara, you could have been killed."

"But I wasn't."

He rubbed his face with his hands, and I could tell he was about to start some sort of lecture regarding opening the portal, being reckless, or a myriad of other things, but I stopped him before he could.

"You said that if Calum was in danger, he should hide out here, and that's what he's doing. He's only here until you go back, like we talked about. Then you can help him do whatever it is that needs to be done to stay out of trouble."

"Well, that just confirms that we have to go home soon. Sage said I can start walking with crutches tomorrow if I feel up for it. My tentative plan is for us to leave in three days. Four days at most."

He was still assuming I was coming with him. I knew I wasn't and that I was done thinking about it, but I couldn't get myself to say the words. I still had a few days to tell him and get that figured out. We had time.

He told me about how Sage was working with him on getting his hand moving even with the cast, and how he'd been spending time with Willow across the hall, since they were both recovering and bored. He lamented this world's lack of televisions, and I realized that I hadn't seen any sort of television or radio since being here. Not that I missed it, just that it was strange.

"Fara, are you going to tell me what's wrong?"

"Nothing's wrong."

"You're a terrible poker player, aren't you?"

I snorted. "The worst, but I play anyway."

"Of course you do. So, what is it?"

Not yet. "It's really nothing."

"Do you regret last night?"

"No! I'm really glad about last night. Truly. It's just . . . Today was a bit crazy. I just need a nap is all."

I could tell he didn't quite believe me, but wasn't going to push it. I knew that what I was doing was unfair. I knew I needed to tell him that I definitively wasn't going back with him. That I had decided to stay.

But sitting here in this room, I could pretend that it was just the two of us. I could imagine a life with Jay, making dinner side by side, watching movies and eating spring rolls, calling him bossy while he gently loved me. It would be a safe life, comfortable and something that I had only dreamed of with Beck, knowing full well it would never be a reality with him. But I could see it with Jay. I could see our future . . . if the world weren't so fucked up.

But it was.

My world was in danger, and this world was dangerous. I could open portals and would have to run and hide for the rest of my life, unless something changed. That was the reality. Just for this moment, I wanted to pretend, even if it was selfish. I kissed his gorgeous lips and breathed him in. I would tell him, but not right now. Because I knew that as soon as I told him that I wasn't going back with him, this momentary peace would end. And I wasn't ready. Not yet.

I passed by Ink's door, and it opened to show him standing without a shirt. Again.

"Trying to get a tan?" I asked as I kept walking.

"I thought you were supposed to ask for an escort when you walked around."

Shit. "Sorry! I forgot. I'll do better next time."

He smiled. "You know, if you wanted me in your bed so desperately, you could have just asked me instead of grabbing the other me from your world."

"Could Calum borrow some clothes? You apparently aren't using them."

He laughed as he motioned for me to follow him into his room. It had been put back together, the damage patched up. He even had a new table and chairs. Except for his bed, the rest of the room was clean.

"How did you get such a giant bed?"

"Reputation."

"Seriously?"

He laughed. "No—it came with the apartment. I just lucked out. You got the great window; I got the good bed."

"That seems like I got the better end of that deal."

"Well, you've never been in my bed to judge."

He handed me some pants and a couple of shirts.

"Thanks. He's only here for a couple of days, so this should be good."

"I also have an air mattress, if you need it."

He looked at me like I was supposed to ask for the air mattress now, but I didn't. I'd probably ask for it later, but just watching Ink wonder where his doppelgänger was going to sleep was enough to put a huge grin on my face.

"Thanks again."

32 FARA

I hadn't even made it through the door of my apartment when Calum grabbed me, pulling me across the room to the bed.

"You are never going to believe what I just read!"

I was trying to take my dagger off so I wouldn't impale myself. "What?"

"What if I told you that you don't have just one or two, but multiple powers?"

"What?"

"The notes say that you have multiple powers!"

"How?"

"It's crazy! From what I can understand, when the palmbox toxic light stuff got you or whatever, it gave you every program that was on it at the time. Every fucking one! Your mom didn't know if she had discovered all of them yet when she wrote this—and I'll get to that in a second—but you're like a walking Swiss Army knife."

I sat down with a thunk on the bed. "How many?"

"As of the last entry in that section of the notes, she'd counted four different abilities, but she wasn't sure if there were more and she just hadn't encountered them yet."

"Holy shitballs."

Calum was grinning ear to ear. I couldn't help but smile back, even though I was freaking out. "What are they?"

"According to your mom, there are two main ones. The first is the portal, but she kept alluding to other things you could do with it—"

"I can do *more* with it?"

"I haven't gotten to that point yet, so hold your horses. The second main one is like a souped-up taser, using electricity to incapacitate or kill people."

"That's what I did to the goon?"

"There's more. From what your mom's notes say, she was able to disable a person with shocks through her fingers, since it mirrors the stun program in the palmbox that everyone around here carries. But she also shot lightning once, and she thought that ability might be because this was Barrington's personal palmbox, and the stun program was tricked out."

"Did she say how to do it? Or how to not do it? Or why I've only done it once and by accident?"

"She was still trying to figure it out, and she was pissed because there was no scientific explanation. She wrote that it was like, and I quote, 'the stupid magic in books that Fara likes to read.'"

A laugh burst out of me.

"There's a section on how she had figured out how to create the 'programs' in a palmbox. Or at least the theory behind them. But there's an even bigger section dedicated to how she *couldn't* figure out how it worked in you guys. She said it was like science didn't matter. And that evidently frustrated her to no end."

"I can imagine." And I could. Even though my mom was a peace-loving hippie, she also was a scientist who had to have a reason for everything. The fact that she couldn't find one for why we could do what we did probably drove her nuts.

"I need to get the equations to Styx. She's going to freak out."

"Why am I going to freak out?" Styx said as she walked into my room. Ink, Jack, and Blu were right behind her, all carrying boxes of food. Apparently, we were eating again. Like Hobbits.

Styx stared at Calum. She'd never seen him before.

"Holy shit. Why is there someone who looks like Ink in your bed, Fara?"

"It should actually *be* me in your bed," Ink quipped. I ignored him, telling the blush in my cheeks to take a hike.

Once they had passed out food, introductions were made, and Calum told them what he had just been telling me. They sat in silence for a moment, mouths mostly agape, then all started talking at once. Styx was asking if she could have the notes, and Blu was asking if we had figured out why it made me pass out, and Jack and Ink were wondering if there was a way to safely practice frying someone. Not one of them told me that I shouldn't use my powers or called them dangerous.

"How does it work?" Styx finally asked.

"I don't know yet. They started by accident."

"Your mom's notes said it seemed to be connected to emotions," Calum said, "and what she called 'intent.' She said that because of the thinning membrane, portals were easiest to create. You just got some strong emotions, and a portal would pop up. She said the shock thing was harder, that she found she had to get her emotions up, then intentionally think about hurting someone."

"I guess that sort of makes sense. When we rescued Jay and I shocked the goon, I was panicking because I didn't want him to take me back to Barrington, and I told myself I'd do anything to not have that happen. I guess that was enough?"

"Your guess is as good as mine," Calum said with a shrug. "Your mom didn't even know for sure. She conducted all sorts of experiments and tried to find a logical reason behind the way it worked, but she couldn't. She theorized that it had to do with the neural pathways of the brain, but since she wasn't a neuroscientist, it was a hunch. Her final entry was some notes saying that while it didn't have any scientific basis that she could find, you had to intend to shock someone."

"But why did it make me pass out?"

"She mentioned that for that ability to work, you had to let go of the electricity fast, or it started to work on your own system like a stun gun, shutting it down."

"So now we know that's bad," Jack joked. "You mentioned other abilities too?"

"Her mom found at least two more. The first was lockpicking, and the second was like a fire starter."

The Team burst out laughing, all looking at Blu.

"Weirdly, that's Blu's favorite program on the palmbox," Styx said. "It works like an electric flint—you can start a fire almost anywhere with it. It's how she burned down Dagna's summer cottage and the manor house in Hastings, and a bunch of other places."

"It's not like I'm a pyro—"

Styx smiled. "You are, my friend, but they deserved it."

Blu set fire to all of those things? And now I could set fire to things too? I could pick locks with a thought? The magnitude of this revelation rocketed through me. I was so very lucky that I hadn't accidentally done any of this growing up. My mom's continued vigilance in shoving down my anger now made sense. It never occurred to me to fight back. She was trying to protect me from accidentally hurting someone, or myself. If it didn't occur to me to fight back, then I'd never intentionally think, *You know, I should really set fire to his house.*

Why would I ever think that? But then I remembered when I'd opened a portal in Calum's bathtub. Right before I opened it, I remembered being so angry that I felt I could burn down Beck's place—if he had a place. I remembered it felt like my head was going to ignite in my rage.

Maybe I would have started a fire but for the bathtub. Now that was a thought.

Calum was watching me intently as the rest of the Team talked. "What are you thinking?"

I could feel the panic starting to rise, and a portal starting to open. I thought, *Close*, and it did. Huh. "I'm not sure what to think about this. It's been an absolute miracle that I haven't hurt anybody accidentally, and I'm not sure I want to hurt anybody now. Or at all."

"Just because you have the powers, Fara, doesn't mean you have to go on a killing spree," he said, squeezing my shoulder. "You haven't hurt anyone yet. Or, at least, not anyone who didn't deserve it. So I'm not worried about that."

Everyone had stopped talking. Styx reached up to the bed from her perch on the floor and patted my leg. "Fara, what you can do is amazing, and it might be able to help the Team, should you get control of it. But if you decide that you want to learn how to keep your powers under wraps and never use them, then we will all respect that decision and help you do that. If you decide you want to practice with them so you can become a one-woman team, we will support you with that too. But no one here will ever make that decision for you."

It was my decision. Mine. Not Jay's, or the Captain's, or the Team's, or my parents'. Mine.

⚡ ⚡ ⚡

Once everyone left, Calum and I snuggled down into bed and talked. Even though I had only been gone a week, I had missed him. But it was more than that—other than when we went out to Rick's a few days ago, I hadn't really seen him much the past year because I had stupidly lost myself to Beck, to his wants and needs. I had stopped hanging out with Calum because it bothered Beck—even though he never stopped hanging out with any of his friends. I had allowed myself to believe that you had to sacrifice who you were and what you wanted for love. I didn't want to do that again.

The door to my apartment opened without a knock. Ink was standing in my doorway holding an inflated air mattress and some blankets. I sat up.

"I thought Calum could use the air mattress," he said and dropped it on the floor.

"Thanks. I'd like to go to training tomorrow?"

"Then I'll see you in the morning."

I smiled at Ink. He smiled back, then quietly closed the door.

We got Calum situated on the air mattress. I turned the lights out but left the curtains open so I could see the moon and stars from my window. They were beautiful.

"What was that about?" Calum asked finally.

"What?"

"You and other me?"

"He gave us an air mattress."

"There was a look between the two of you."

"No there wasn't."

Calum quietly laughed. "He shares my face, Fara, so denying it won't work. Plus, you have never looked at me like that. Ever."

"I didn't look at him like anything. We're friends, Calum. That's it."

"That's not what it looked like just now."

"He was here for all of three seconds. There wasn't a lot of time for meaningful glances—even if I wanted to. Which I don't."

"I saw what I saw."

I pulled the covers up to my chin and snuggled down further into my bed.

"Calum, Ink is the resident bad boy. He flirts with everyone—Blu, me, the young women who train with us, the grannies who serve the food in the mess. Even if I had feelings for him, which I don't—at least not like that—I'd be a one-and-done for him. And that's not something I'm OK with."

I could hear Calum chuckle quietly. "You can think whatever you want."

I snorted, done with this conversation. Nothing was going on with Ink. He was a flirt, is all. And becoming a friend. If Calum thought something was happening between the two of us, he was wrong.

"Anyway, I'm with Jay, so this conversation doesn't even really matter."

Calum was quiet for so long that I thought maybe he had fallen asleep. But then he said, "For how long?"

I didn't answer. What I hoped and what my gut was telling me were two different things. I didn't want to think about it.

"What did he say when you told him you wanted to stay here?"

When I didn't say anything, again, Calum rolled over toward me, his face illuminated by the moonlight. "You haven't told him."

"Not yet."

"Because deep down you know."

"Know what?"

"What's going to happen when you tell Jay you're staying here."

"I don't know anything," I said quietly. I didn't want to think that the decision that was best for me might be what stopped our relationship before it even had a chance to start. I didn't want that guilt.

BLU 33

I managed to drag myself to training, even though it was the last thing I wanted to do. Unfortunately, running for my life had become more of a regular occurrence than usual over the past couple of weeks, even for me. I needed to stay in top form.

The Captain had asked that I train Silver separately, since we both knew that the PITs were looking more and more likely. Silver had come to us later than most of our trainees, she had some catching up to do. By nineteenish (since I didn't know my exact age), I had already been part of the principal Team for years, planning and leading missions, but at the same age, she had been training for less than a year. It was a good thing for her to have had the extra time with her family, as opposed to being orphaned when she was small and having to train to kill, but the practical implications meant that if she wanted to be part of the Team, she was going to have to work twice as hard. She didn't seem to mind, and I appreciated her attitude.

As we trained, I caught her watching Ink and Fara out of the corner of my eye. Ink had thrown his head back in a full belly laugh at something Fara had said, and she was grinning at him, her hand resting on his forearm in a comfortable way. They looked like they were enjoying each other's company and had been friends for years. I guess that, in a way, they had. But Silver still seemed hung up on him as she watched them from across the Quad. She'd learn eventually. Or not. Either way, it wasn't my problem.

I ended Silver's training a little early so that I could bathe and sneak away to meet Jyston. I had to help some of the other Team members plan a mission to raid a Jurisdiction storage building later, and I didn't know when I'd next have a chance to bathe. Appearances weren't something that I put much thought or effort into, but I refused to stink. Vanity was one thing—cleanliness another entirely.

Jyston was already there when I arrived. He was dressed in what I considered "Second Counselor attire": a gray suit, white pressed shirt, and no tie. The suit was cut to fit him perfectly, although it still strained over his muscles as he moved. My breath caught, and I told myself to get a grip. I might be a hot-blooded female, but I didn't have to swoon. I was not the lead in a romance novel. I was an assassin, a warrior, and general pain in the ass.

The corner of his mouth pulled up when he saw me, but his eyes were worried. Something had happened between yesterday and today. He handed me a packet of papers, his hand lingering on mine for a bit longer than was needed. I didn't pull away, but he did.

"I don't have much time," he said without preamble. "The PITs are three weeks from today. You and Silver have been entered into the PITs under aliases, and those are the documents you'll need to get into the room prior to the game. You'll need to figure out a way to get out once it's over. I won't be able to help with that. I'll contact you again, before the games, to give you the final details."

He turned to leave, looking over his shoulder as he did. His behavior was unlike what I was used to, and I was about to say something to him when I saw one of Dagna's minions appear behind him. Without a second thought, I unsheathed my daggers.

The minion surveyed us both with a sneer. "Stop right there. Dagna wants you both. Alive."

Both of us?

Jyston stilled. "I think you are mistaken and will be reprimanded for speaking to me in such a manner. Harshly."

In the blink of an eye, I watched Jyston transform in front of me. It was a hundred little things—subtle things. The way he pulled himself up to his full height, towering over me and the minion. The way he shifted his weight and straightened his back. The way he cocked his head at the minion. The stillness that overcame him, the power that radiated from him. But it was his eyes that changed the most—they lost their humor and humanity, and the look that replaced them was purely predatory. In less than a second, he became the cold-blooded killer everyone knew him to be. I didn't recognize him at all. The minion blanched and took a step back.

"Dagna informed me that you are going to be stripped of your title by the Counselor—"

"She was mistaken."

"Then why are you meeting with a known enemy of the Jurisdiction?"

"Did it occur to you that I might be bringing her in myself?"

That made the minion pause, but he still didn't seem entirely convinced. I knew that Jyston could not be seen with me, and if this minion reported back to Dagna, any progress we'd made in destroying her building would be lost, not to mention that Jyston would be flayed alive. I couldn't have either of those things happen.

"Go."

Jyston looked at me out of the corner of his eye, so I knew he heard me.

"Jyston, go. I'll take care of this."

He looked like he was about to argue, but I stopped him.

"You and I both know what happens if the minion leaves here alive."

"There will be more," he said.

"Then you need to hurry."

I didn't wait for him to answer. I stalked toward the minion, a smirk playing on my own lips. Time to get to work.

"Stop right there!" the minion yelled at me.

"You know that never works, right?" I continued to walk toward the minion. "Why would I listen to you, when you want to bring me in for questioning with that sadistic bitch you call a boss? I think I'll pass on your suggestion that I stop, and I'm going to keep coming toward you until I slit your throat."

The minion pulled out a sword. Not ideal—all I had was daggers. I needed to get this over with quickly, and preferably without getting killed. If I died at the hands of this idiot so that Jyston could escape, I'd be pretty pissed off.

I turned one last time to Jyston. He nodded once, then set off at a slow jog in the other direction.

I felt more than saw the minion's blade sweep toward my shoulder. I dodged and, while turning, disarmed the minion like Ink had taught the trainees to do a thousand times. Why they didn't teach that move to minions was beyond me, because it worked every time, but I was glad they didn't. Unfortunately, his sword caught part of my arm in the process, and I wasn't wearing armor. It wasn't a bad cut, but it still hurt like a bitch, and I'd probably need stitches. I kicked his sword out of his reach.

"Dagna is going to reward me for bringing you in."

"She'd reward anyone for that, so don't feel special."

He reached for his daggers and took a swipe at me. He was a tall man, and his reach was pretty impressive.

Normally I didn't care about being short, since it never really hindered what I did with my life, but in situations like this, I wished I had Silver's long arms. If I was going to kill this fucker, I needed to get closer. I was pissed at myself for not having a sword.

The minion went on the attack, and I dodged a flurry of blows. Eventually I saw my opening, feinted, and slammed my dagger into his heart. Or, that's what should have happened. My dagger glanced off his clothes—the minions must have new armor that kept them from getting stabbed. Great. If I lived through this, I'd have to ask Jyston about it. And tell the Team. I just had to live through this. I guess I really did need to slit his throat.

He came on the attack again, and I noted that while his reach was good, his technique was bad. Sloppy training. He was also favoring his left leg—a knee injury perhaps? He was trying to incapacitate me instead of killing me, since he only got his reward if I was alive, even if only just. I saw my opportunity.

This time, when he lunged toward me, I took a calculated risk and dropped one of my daggers so I could grab his arm. I pulled him as close to me as I could, while I swept his leg, aiming for his knee, the cold, metallic scent of the minion surrounding me. My foot connected with a satisfying crunch, and he screamed in pain, dropping to the ground. Using my own momentum, I spun behind him, grabbed his hair to pull his head back, and slit his throat, feeling the familiar pang of sadness when I did. It wasn't that I felt bad for killing him, not really. I felt bad that I lived in a world where one of us had to die.

I didn't wait around to see if anyone else was here. I grabbed my dagger off the ground along with the PITs papers and sprinted to my car. I needed to tell the Team what just happened, even though they were going to be angrier at me than normal.

I'd weather the anger though, because if I had to do it all over again, I would. Jyston had become someone I was willing to protect. Someone I was willing to kill for.

FARA 34

The next morning, Silver gently shook me awake while keeping her eyes firmly on Calum. It would have been funny if it weren't so early. I could tell he was awake but pretending to sleep, maybe because he knew he looked like a model lying there with his long eyelashes resting against his cheeks and the blanket carelessly thrown over his hips. I never knew Calum to be one to flaunt his looks, but then again, he was usually pretty subdued when it came to girls. His last girlfriend had made him choose between her and me, and he chose me. I felt bad when he told me he'd broken it off, until I realized how looney toons she was. Good riddance and all that. He didn't seem to mind. He certainly didn't seem to be lonely, if the smell of perfume on his sheets was any indication.

I caught Silver's eye to let her know I was awake and slowly made my way to getting ready. She left with a smile and one last look over her shoulder at Calum. She was growing on me, even if she didn't bring coffee or a donut. Ink had spoiled me.

Styx came by a few minutes later with coffee and bagels. She looked over at Calum as he got out of bed, and cocked her eyebrow at me. "Silver specifically asked if she could wake you up this morning. And I can see why."

"Her name is Silver?" he asked, trying to look disinterested. I knew better.

"Yep. And from what I understand, she's nineteen and single."

Calum suppressed a grin. Once again, I would laugh my ass off if my best friend got laid here. I guess that would just mean he was multi-universally hot.

I made it through training, and afterward went to breakfast with Ink, as everyone else seemed to have somewhere they had to be. I was going to bring Calum something more to eat, but Silver told me that she would be happy to take him second breakfast.

"Does it bother you?" Ink finally asked over his coffee cup. I was enjoying my last slice of buttered toast.

"That Silver possibly has the hots for my best friend? No. Although it might bother you,. She seems to have traded up—you for him."

"Ouch. Anyway, she's not my type."

"You're not a fan of gorgeous, smart women?"

"I am. Just not that specific gorgeous, smart woman."

"But all other gorgeous, smart women? You don't make any sense to me."

"I wasn't trying to."

"In any case, as long as they don't decide to christen my bed, I don't care. Although, they could probably use your air mattress? My guess is that it wouldn't be the first time it was used in that capacity."

Ink grinned. I took that as a yes.

"Anyway, I'm glad he has some company because I have something I need to do, and I could use your help."

"Whatever you need, sweetness."

I ignored the term of endearment and the blush on my cheeks. "Don't say yes until you hear what I'm thinking. I need to test out my new abilities, but I don't think doing it here in front of everyone is a good idea."

"Probably not." He was still studying me over his coffee mug. "I have a spot or two I can think of. But . . . do I get to come help?"

"I was hoping so."

⚡⚡⚡

We had only been driving for a couple of minutes when Ink pulled off the road and parked under some trees.

"We'll walk from here."

"Where are we going?"

He grinned over his shoulder at me. "You'll see."

We followed a trail through the trees, dead leaves and twigs crunching under our feet. The sun was just making its way from behind the clouds, dappled through the newly budding leaves. It was quiet, though I could hear the faint burbling of water somewhere close. The smell of spring was in the air.

The trail led up a small rise, and as we crested the hill, I saw something out of an idyllic pastoral watercolor. It was a clearing, about the size of a football field, covered in short wild grass that was just peeping up through the ground and surrounded by trees. A stream ran along its leftmost edge, the first hints of wild spring flowers budding along its banks. I was sure in the summer the whole place would be filled with flowers, but the scarceness of them right now accentuated their beauty. Birds chirped in the branches above us, and I half expected deer to go traipsing by. With the sunlight shining down and the soft breeze caressing my face, it was one of the most beautiful places I had ever been.

"This is so lovely," I breathed, turning around to take it all in.

"You like it?"

"How could I not? This is amazing! How did you ever find it?"

"One of my many escape attempts from the Compound when I was young."

"The Captain held you prisoner?"

He chuckled. "No, but I didn't always like the rules she had for us, so I would run away. I was such a pain in the ass. I still wonder why the Captain kept me. Anyway, I'd walk the forests around the Compound and beyond for hours until I'd get hungry or tired, then eventually make my way back. This place . . . Well, it's my favorite spot."

"I can see why. I'm sure the others love it too."

"They've never been here."

"They haven't?"

"It should work for what you need. There's running water just in case you set yourself, or me, on fire. It's surrounded by trees so no one can see us, but it's close enough that should something go wrong, we can get back to the Compound quickly."

"It's perfect. Thank you."

"Ready?"

"As I'll ever be."

"What do you want to start with? Fire? The electricity lightning thing? Lockpicking might be a problem, but we could manage."

"The electricity thing, I think. That sounds like something I should probably get under control before I hurt someone."

He walked toward the edge of the clearing and into the trees as I felt the panic start in my stomach and make its way up to my chest. The thought of unleashing whatever was inside of me . . . I was so afraid of hurting someone. I could still see that goon convulsing at my feet, could still smell his burnt hair and flesh. What if I couldn't figure this out? What if I hurt someone accidentally? Worse—what if I hurt Ink, when all he was doing was trying to help me? I could feel a portal start to open and I clamped it down before it made its appearance. Well, at least I was able to control that, somewhat.

Beneath the panic and fear, there was something else. I wouldn't call it excitement, exactly. Maybe determination? Resolve? I needed to test out these abilities, and this was the safest way of doing it. I'd read my mom's notes and was as prepared as I could be. Having my head buried in the sand for most of my life had done me no good. It had actually led me to this mess. Not knowing was worse than knowing, no matter how painful the lesson.

Ink returned with a giant branch and laid it at my feet. "So, tell me what your mom's notes say about this and how it works. How do you start it?"

"She didn't know much about this power. She wasn't able to get it to work for her very often. I guess I start it like I would a portal, with strong emotions. But then, and she was just guessing, I have to intend to shock someone or something."

"Did she say why she couldn't get it to work?"

"Her theory was because she never wanted to hurt anyone. Ever."

"Sounds like someone else I know." He smiled.

"Oh! Well, my mom was a true pacifist, meaning she believed all war was wrong. She wouldn't fight, ever. No exceptions. I guess her reasons for not hurting someone were sort of philosophical."

"And yours aren't?"

"I don't think so. I mean, I hate conflict. And the thought of hurting someone I care about is almost too much for me to take."

"What about people you don't care about? Like Barrington Park?"

"I'd have no problem frying him."

He huffed a laugh. "Then we have something to work with. So, what did she know?"

I thought about anything helpful she had provided, which wasn't much. Like the portal ability, the first time she used this ability had been an accident. She didn't get into the details of the situation, but I'd been able to piece it together from context. My mom had been out at a bar with some colleagues for happy hour after work, and a drunk guy got handsy with one of the younger scientists. Mom placed her hands on the man to calm the situation down but ended up dropping him to the ground.

After that, she had tried to recreate the situation, but without much success. It wasn't until she accidentally shot the swing set in our backyard with a bolt of lightning (due to my neighbor's vicious dog chasing me) that she realized that the intent to hurt, or at least releasing the intention to not hurt someone, was paramount. She had intended to throw something at the dog to distract it, and ironically ended up throwing a bolt of lightning. While the execution had been more dramatic than she intended, the intent was there. She reluctantly studied the ability later, but because of her disinclination to injure someone, she was never able to do it again.

"I think we just need to wing it."

Ink grinned. "That's more my style anyway. So, what we know for sure is that if you feel the shock thing come up, you have to release it immediately, or you'll pass out. Anything else?"

"Something my mom calls 'intent.' For the portal I just need to use my emotions and it'll open. It's easier if I intend to open it, but obviously that's not necessary, since I open them unintentionally all the time."

The corner of Ink's mouth curved up in an almost smile. "I can see why that might be annoying. So, we just need you to intend to become a walking lightning bolt, and we're good?"

"Sounds about right."

"I have a limited memory of how electricity works from my science classes when I was a kid."

"You had science classes?"

Ink rolled his eyes. "Yes. Contrary to what you might believe, I'm not just some gorgeous hunk of meat who can kill someone but not spell my own name."

I blushed. "Sorry. That's not what I meant. It's just . . . Never mind. Sorry."

Ink grinned. "But you do think I'm gorgeous."

"You're such a shit! You already knew that—not that it matters!"

The perma-smirk reappeared. "It's nice to have my suspicions validated. Anyway, we'll need something to ground you once the electricity comes up, so you don't end up frying yourself . . . or me, for that matter." He stabbed his dagger into the branch. "I think if you hold your dagger, then touch it to the dagger on the branch once you get electrified, that might work. Or not. We're winging it, right?"

Although he winked at me in that off-handed, flirty way that let me know he was enjoying himself, I could tell that underneath it all, he was worried.

"I promise I won't fry you."

"I'm not worried about that."

"Then what are you worried about?"

"Nothing. C'mon. Let's see what you can do."

Ink moved to the other side of the branch as I grabbed my dagger, starting the process of pulling my emotions to the foreground. I could feel a portal opening, but I closed it with a thought. I tried to think about electricity running through me and . . . nothing. I tried again, pulling at the emotions, accidentally almost opening a portal again, shutting it again, thinking about shocking someone, and again. Nothing. I slumped down on the ground. Ink raised his eyebrow at me, then sat down next to me.

"This is what happened with the portal too," I said, as much to myself as to him.

"What?"

"That when I wanted to, I couldn't—and when I didn't want to, I did."

"How did you get it to change?"

"I made the connection that the portals were controlled by my emotions, so all I had to do was let my feelings out and I could open one. Although, it took a while to put it all together."

"We have time. If this other ability is also fueled by emotions, maybe you need stronger ones? What were you thinking about just there?"

"I guess I was thinking about the normal awful stuff that makes me open portals. How my loser ex-boyfriend probably hasn't even realized that I'm not around anymore. How all of my worldly possessions were trashed by Barrington's men. How my job sucks."

Ink listened thoughtfully. At some point, I realized that I had stopped thinking about the horrible stuff and was thinking about how Ink smelled slightly of cologne and something else. How my shoulder was barely touching his arm, but his body heat was warming my skin at that small point. How, even just sitting here, he radiated a kind of coiled energy, like it took more effort to sit still than not. How that was almost the opposite of Jay, who was a rock-solid presence. Why was I comparing them at all?

"You don't sound too upset about any of it," Ink finally said. "I mean, it's all shit that sucks, but you're listing it off like you're going to the market. 'One trashed apartment, one selfish ex-boyfriend who sucked in bed, one bag of tomatoes

. . . '" I couldn't help but laugh, because it sounded ridiculous, and right. "Maybe you've used those thoughts so much that the rough edges have worn off and they don't hurt enough to get you to electrocute someone. Maybe you need to find some more recent hurts, or things that still make you angry."

Maybe he was right. The anger I felt at Beck had taken up a small place in the background, considering everything else that had happened. And with my new apartment here, the loss I felt with my old place seemed secondary. I rifled through the past few days of living at the Compound and found that there wasn't really anything that was making me angry or hurting me. Except . . .

Except that I had yet to tell Jay that I didn't want to go back with him. I had been putting it off. I hoped that our fledgling relationship would withstand something like being separated by two worlds, although I wasn't sure it could. And deep down, I knew why. That wasn't something I was willing to think about yet.

"What are you thinking about now?"

"I really don't want to tell you."

"Why?"

I paused. I hoped that Ink and I were becoming friends, but it was still tenuous. Did I really want to lay all of my dirty laundry out in front of him? There was a piece of me that didn't want him to see my insecurity, my doubts, my ugly inner voice. To say that I was scared that Jay was going to leave me because he couldn't deal with all of this. That I was scared of being alone, of not being enough, of not having a clue what I was supposed to be doing. Ink was surrounded by people who seemed to know who they were and what they wanted, and here I was still struggling to determine where I belonged. If I'd let him see how truly messed up I was, would he still be sitting here with me? Would he still be my friend?

He grabbed my hand, lacing his fingers through mine carefully. I looked at him in profile. He was looking not at me but at where our fingers intertwined. A part of me wanted to pull my hand away, the action too intimate and confusing. It was confusing because I wanted him to hold my hand, and that couldn't be right. He took a breath.

"Fara, that day in my apartment, you saw me at my worst. At my lowest. And you stayed. Please do not insult me by thinking I'll run because you show me your worst. I'm not going anywhere."

My eyes started to sting and my throat closed up. I didn't want to cry over something that had yet to happen—Jay ending our relationship because I didn't want to play it safe and go home. Before I could shut down the waterworks, I realized that I needed to let this pain flow through me, as premature as it might be. I wasn't just sad that things might end before they really began; I was also angry at Barrington Park and his crazy brother for causing all of this, for forcing me into a situation where I was more than likely going to have to say goodbye to someone I was starting to care for. The fact that I might never get to go on that date Jay had promised me, because Barrington would never stop hunting me, ignited my rage further. I wanted to stop him so that I could go back and eat spring rolls with Jay and have sex in a real bed and wake up the next morning and eat donuts. I wanted the life I imagined with him—and even if it never came to life, I wanted the choice of having it. Barrington had taken away that choice. And he killed my parents. I wanted him dead.

Ink dropped my hand with a gasp.

"What the . . . ?"

I felt a weird sensation in my fingers again, like the moment before a shock comes from static electricity, but this time I recognized it.

"Shit! I have it! Now what do I do with it?"

"Quick, grab your dagger and see if you can push the electricity through it—then touch it to the other dagger."

I grabbed my dagger and thought about releasing the energy, but nothing happened.

"It's not working!"

"Don't panic. I know it sounds crazy, but just think 'I intend for this electricity to be released into the dagger.' You have to want it to go there, right?"

I did want it to leave me. It was starting to hurt. I thought as hard as I could that I wanted the feeling to go to the dagger. Why wouldn't it go? My breathing started to increase—I was going to have a panic attack and fry myself again. Fucking great. But then I looked at Ink, worry creasing his face as he made a move to grab me—to steady me.

No.

I couldn't let him touch me because it would hurt him, and I would never intend to hurt him like this. Ever. And with that final thought, I felt the electricity drain out of me like a thousand shards of glass, and then everything went black.

35 FARA

I felt someone brushing hair off my face, their touch feather-light. I heard a voice in the distance, almost like I was underwater and the voice was on shore, barely a whisper. I strained to hear it. It was someone calling my name, gently but with concern. I forced myself to swim toward the voice, holding onto it like a lifeline.

"Fara, wake up. Please. I need you to wake up."

I followed the voice until it sounded closer. I tried to open my eyes, but they were stubborn.

"Fara, you can't die on me. Please, sweetness, wake up."

The voice sounded familiar, and worried.

"I have things I need to tell you. Fara, please."

I found my voice, even if my eyes wouldn't work. "What do you need to tell me?"

It came out muddled and slurred, but I heard the person exhale in relief. I managed to open one eye to see a beautiful face backlit by the setting sun. His green eyes were bright, his dark hair expertly disheveled. Ink looked like a fallen angel, and for a moment my breath caught.

"I needed to tell you that my leg is asleep and I'm hungry."

Confused, I tried to sit up, but a wave of dizziness and nausea stopped me. I laid my head back down. It was resting on something hard. As slowly as I could, I lifted my head and looked around. I was on the ground in the field with my head in Ink's lap. It was dusk. How did I get here?

"What happened?"

"Well, you managed to get the electricity to work, but not before it made you pass out."

"How long have I been out?"

"An hour or two, give or take. If you didn't wake up in the next couple of minutes, I was going to take you to the infirmary. Lucky for me, I don't have to explain to Sage why you were passed out. Again."

"What? Oh my god, I'm so sorry!"

Ink rolled his eyes at me and watched me struggle to sit up. I couldn't get my body to work the way I wanted. Ugh.

"Going somewhere, speedy?"

"Apparently not. I'm so sorry—"

"If you finish that apology, I'm leaving you here."

"What?"

"Fara, you apologize more than any person I have ever met. And none of the things you apologize for are your fault. We knew that testing out this ability came with risks. And considering last time you were asleep for two days, two hours doesn't seem that bad. I don't want to keep listening to you berate yourself, OK?"

I nodded slightly, the motion making my head swim, and I sucked a breath through my teeth. The dizziness would wear off, but in the meantime, I was stuck with my head on Ink's leg, and the sun was going down.

"What were you thinking about that got your ability to work?"

"Why?"

"It might be important."

I shifted slightly, wondering if I should tell him. It felt weird to talk about Jay with Ink. I poked that thought a little, then realized that it didn't matter. He was right—we needed to figure it out.

"I was thinking about how I wanted to kill Barrington."

"Well, that's a good start, although you'll have to get in line. Was that it?"

"And how I want to stay here for a while."

"In my lap?"

"Whatever. At the Compound."

"And?"

Here it was. The thing that I didn't want to say out loud.

"And I haven't told Jay yet that I'm not going back with him."

I tried to shift again and was blasted with a wave of nausea. Stupid ability! Why couldn't it have amazing side effects, like great skin or an amped-up metabolism? Why did it have to make me feel like shit?

"Does he think you are?"

"He assumes I am. Because that was originally what we agreed; that I would come here to get my portal ability under control. And once I did, I'd go back with him and resume my normal life. Or as normal as it could be constantly looking over my shoulder for Barrington or the government to grab me. But once he decided that this world wasn't safe for me, he told me that I needed to go back home and hide so that he could keep me safe. He's leaving in a couple of days and expects that I'll go with him. He says he can't do what he needs to do and worry about me here at the same time."

"Why haven't you told him that you don't want to go? I mean, it doesn't sound like a big deal to me."

"I hope he agrees with you on that. I honestly just don't know him well enough to know how he'll react, which is weird, considering . . . everything. Anyway, it just . . . it sucks, you know? That I may never know what my relationship with Jay would be like, because of Barrington hunting me. We may never have the chance."

Ink brushed some dead grass off my arm. He looked like he wanted to say more, but thankfully he didn't.

"Would you be mad if you were him?"

"I'm not him, Fara."

"I know that. That didn't come out right. What I'm trying to ask is, if I told you that I wasn't going back with you, even though that's what you wanted, what would you think?"

Ink looked out into the forest. He was so still that I was afraid I had crossed some invisible line, or offended him by asking that question, which seemed to be my way lately. The moment dragged on, but then he turned to me, his eyes meeting mine.

"No, Fara. I wouldn't be mad. I'd want you to stay here and get as much training as possible; to learn how to protect yourself and fight, because that's what *you* want to do. I would never, ever try to hide you or your abilities, even if I thought it might make it safer for you. Because that isn't what *you* want to do. And then when you did come back, if you still wanted to kill Barrington, I'd join you in burning that asshole to the fucking ground."

The intensity of Ink's answer, and the way he was looking at me, made me feel like I could do anything. That it wasn't ridiculous that I didn't want to go home; that training here was not a pipe dream; that I could do all of these things and it wasn't wrong, because it was what *I* wanted to do. And what I wanted was just as important as what everyone else wanted for me. More so, perhaps.

"Thank you, Ink."

"For what?"

"For believing in me."

I stopped staring at him, since it was awkward enough to be stuck in his lap, and watched the sun start to set. The colors of the sky changed, deepening into beautiful hues of red and orange, and I told myself that I'd remember this moment. When things were at their worst, I would remember the colors of the sky, and the birds singing in the trees. I would remember that I had made a friend in this world and that he believed in me and told me that I could believe in myself. I would remember.

Ink broke me out of my reverie. "Are you ready to try to sit up?"

I nodded again, this time without wanting to throw up. Ink put his hands under my shoulders and gently helped me up. I wasn't dizzy, which was a bonus, although I felt like I had been put through the wringer. Eventually I was able to stagger to my feet. Ink put his arm around my shoulder, his hand warm on my skin. By the time we made it to the car, I was walking on my own, and although I felt a bit wobbly, I knew I'd be fine in an hour or so.

As he tucked me into the car, he grinned. "Want to do this again tomorrow?"

BLU 36

I started to feel light-headed as I drove back to the Compound. I had ripped part of my shirt off to try to stanch the bleeding on my arm, but the cut was deep and I was losing blood. So much so that I should probably be worried. What did it say about my lifestyle that getting nicked by a sword didn't even make my top five shitty things of the week list? Fucking minions.

By the time I made it to the parking lot by the Quad, I could barely see, I was so dizzy. I turned on my comm.

"Jack?"

"Yeah? I'm glad you're back in one piece."

"That might be premature. Can you send me a medic?"

"Shit! Blu! Where are you?"

"Parking lot."

The next thing I knew, I was in an infirmary bed, my arm hurt like a bitch, and Jack was sitting in the chair in the corner, watching me.

"I will kill Jyston if he did this to you."

"Hi to you too."

"I'm serious, Blu. I'm going to kill him."

My voice came out as a rasp. How long had I been out? "It wasn't him."

"What?"

"It wasn't him, Jack. It was Dagna's minion. Jyston knew he was being followed, and he'd tried to lose the minion, but he found us. The minion told us he was supposed to take us both, which is fucked up. I let Jyston run and killed the minion. They have new armor, by the way."

"What the hell?"

I struggled to get up and find myself some water but gave up. I was still dizzy, although I didn't feel like I was going to die, which was a bonus. Jack stood up and handed the water to me without a word.

"I know. We need to have a meeting with the Captain."

"She and Styx already know you're in here. We're supposed to meet after you wake up and eat."

"Ink?"

"Lucky for you, he had his own medical emergency to deal with."

"What? Is he OK?"

Jack chuckled. "Physically, yes, and pretty pissed at you. It's Fara. He was helping her train in her new ability and she passed out for a couple of hours. Freaked him right out, although he wouldn't say that out loud. Be glad she did; otherwise, he'd kick your ass."

"I'd like to see him try—although I can't blame him. If the roles were reversed, I'd be pissed too. Is Fara OK?"

"Ink had Sage check her out. She's fine, although a bit wobbly. She's talking about trying again tomorrow."

"Good for her. As long as her new boyfriend doesn't try to stop her."

Jack raised his eyebrows at that. "Not a big fan?"

"Not really, no."

"Does it have to do with him looking like someone else?"

I snorted. "No. It has to do with him thinking that Fara is incapable of making her own decisions. But it's none of my business."

Jack looked at me askance but didn't say anything as I struggled to sit up, trying not to put pressure on my newly bandaged arm. I heard a weird buzzing sound coming from Jack. He reached into his pocket and pulled out a comm—but it wasn't one of ours.

"What is—"

Before I could finish, he put it to his ear. "OK. Hang on."

He handed the comm to me. I raised my eyebrows at him, but he shook his head.

"Blu," rumbled a voice on the other end. Jyston. "Are you OK?"

"Just a flesh wound. Nothing serious. Are *you* OK?"

"For now."

"What do you—?"

"I haven't much time. I've cleared up the misunderstanding with the Counselor. I'm assuming that since you are alive, the other is not."

"Correct."

"Good, no one knows then. The Counselor was angry that Dagna authorized that attack on me without his input, so I've bought myself some time, but not as much as I'd hoped. You need to start planning for the PITs, and I have additional information that will be helpful for that. Keep Jack's comm and I'll let you know when to meet."

"OK, bossy."

He chuckled, the sound making me smile in spite of myself. "Well, that's new but not surprising. Unfortunately, for once I'm serious. Please, Blu, if there was ever a time when I needed you to trust me, it's now. I promise you the next time we meet, I will explain everything. But know this: Dagna seems to be accelerating whatever plans she has for the building. You are running out of time."

"OK, thanks. And Jyston? Please don't get yourself killed. I'm actually starting to not hate you."

He laughed again. "That, my lovely girlfriend, will have to get me by until we meet again."

I could hear him click off. Jack watched me warily.

"Don't start."

Jack opened his mouth, then shut it, then opened it again. "All I was going to say is that was the first time, in the years I have known you, I have ever seen you flirt. It was both funny and disconcerting in equal measures."

"Glad to know I'm entertaining you."

FARA 37

"Stop looking at me like that."

"Like what?"

"Like I'm going to fall apart at any second."

Ink turned to me, smirk gone. "That is exactly the opposite of what I was thinking."

"It looks like you're worried about me spontaneously combusting or something."

He barked a laugh. "That'd be a first for me. I'd obviously brag about it for years. About the time I made a girl spontaneously combust just by being near her."

I laughed. Of course he would take it there. "You are definitely thinking about something. I can tell."

"Can you now? Are you basing that assessment on the other me? Or me?"

"Both. And he has a name. It's Calum."

"So is mine. Anyway, if you must know, I was just trying to figure out why you were finally able to let go of the electricity. How'd you do it?"

It was my turn to stop. "I was afraid I was going to hurt you."

"Well, that sounds like the exact opposite of what your mom's notes say."

"I know! It was weird. I saw you reach for me, and I knew that if you touched me with all of that voltage coursing through me, I could really hurt you. And I didn't want that. Honestly, that was the last thought I had before I felt it drain out of me and I passed out."

"Huh."

"Yeah."

We made it to the Captain's office, and before I even opened the door, I could hear Styx yelling.

"And then! And then you go—without backup, I might add—to meet with the Second Counselor—more than once—and don't tell anyone but Jackrabbit—who, by the way, was a double agent for god only knows how long!"

"He's not anymore."

"That's not the point!"

"I know—"

"You obviously don't know! How could you do that, Blu? How could you be so stupid? And Jack, how could you let her?"

"He didn't let me do anything. I chose—"

"And almost got yourself killed!"

"Enough." The Captain's voice cut through the tension, and Styx dropped into her chair, arms folded.

"I agree with Styx," Ink said as he sat down across from Blu. "That was monumentally stupid, even for you, Blu."

"I know. I'm sorry."

The room was quiet as Blu sat, looking at her hands. It was the first time I had ever seen her look anything other than composed, and it was unsettling. I didn't know what happened, but I was going to stay out of it.

The Captain finally spoke. "I believe Blu understands that her decisions were reckless, and I do not think she will do that again."

"I will meet Jyston again. That's not up for negotiation."

It looked like Ink was about to say something, but the Captain held up a hand.

"What I mean is that when you do meet him, you will follow standard Compound protocols, including letting someone—in addition to Jack—know where you are, and taking the requisite gear, including a palmbox and a comm. Is that clear?"

"Yes."

"Then I consider the matter closed. You all can fight it out among yourselves should you choose, but I would say that regardless of her reckless behavior, Blu was able to get information that might prove to be useful—and now she has a direct link to the Second Counselor."

After more moments of uncomfortable quiet, Styx spoke up. "Jack, I understand why you did it. I'm not mad at you, either. Much."

"An apology? That's a first," Ink said with a smile. "Maybe Fara is rubbing off on you."

"I'll take that as a compliment."

The Captain cleared her throat. "Now that we have all gotten that out of our systems, why doesn't Blu tell us what happened?"

After Blu was done, Styx shook her head, saying, "None of this makes sense. Your boyfriend, the second most powerful person in the world, is going to get us into the PITs, even though it seems that he might be in some trouble himself. And Dagna believes that the Counselor is going to strip Jyston of his title? Which means he's going to kill him."

"Boyfriend?" Ink said, half laughing, half . . . Well, not exactly happy.

"That's just what Styx calls him," Blu said, somewhat exasperated.

"Whatever," Ink said. "I still don't trust him. How do we know he didn't set the whole thing up today?"

"I trust him."

"Why?"

She finally looked up from her hands, meeting his eyes. "He rescued me from Jurisdiction. When I was a kid. It was him, Ink. He saved me."

It was deadly quiet in the room. I didn't understand all of the nuance to what Blu had just revealed, but from what I gathered, it was a big deal.

"I always thought it was someone from the Compound," Styx said.

"We never knew who rescued her," the Captain said. "We just found her at the entrance of the Compound, barely alive."

"He wasn't that old, maybe fourteen or fifteen at the time, but it was him."

"Why are you just telling us this now?"

"Honestly? Because I was struggling to believe it. Even though I remember it—I remember *him*—my brain didn't want to admit it. How can I reconcile what we know about all of the horrible things he's done . . . with that? But he did."

"So you risked your life to save his," Jack said.

"Yes. And I'd do it again. Because he did it for me."

"You do realize that means he has known where the Compound is for years and has never revealed its location," the Captain said. "He dropped you off at our door, more or less."

"He also warned us that we're running out of time to infiltrate the building. Whatever Dagna and the Counselor are cooking up in there is escalating. We need to get those kids."

"We will, Blu, but I'm still not convinced that the PITs are our only option. We need to examine the trail more before I make the final decision—"

"But Jyston says we need to start planning for the PITs now. We have less than three weeks—"

"Blu," the Captain said, "I understand that you are eager to help. Especially after witnessing some of the atrocities for yourself. But I cannot risk the Team competing in the PITs unless there is no other alternative."

"I'm at least going to meet with Jyston when he contacts me."

"With the precautions we spoke about, yes. I would ask you to take someone with you, but I know you'd refuse."

"Yep."

"So she can make out with him," Ink muttered.

"You're one to talk."

"That is enough." Even I could tell that the Captain was nearing the end of her patience, which was saying something. "From what I understand, the trail has a good view of the entire building and would be a place for long-term reconnaissance. It's secluded and relatively safe, correct?"

"If you mean seeing heads on pikes in the courtyard as 'relatively safe,' then I would agree," Ink said.

Blu's head shot up. "What was that?"

"I said relatively safe—"

"No, about the heads on pikes. What exactly did you see there?"

"The last time Styx and I were there, we saw at least three in the courtyard, and although it was hard to tell without their bodies, it appears that some of Jurisdiction's finest met an untimely end."

Blu started to laugh uncontrollably. It was more than a little frightening.

"Blu, I'm not sure why you find that funny," the Captain said, sounding as perplexed as I felt.

"It's just . . . Jyston told me that I was supposed to ask Ink what he saw in the courtyard the last time he was on the trail. Jyston said he left me a present to commemorate our relationship."

Styx looked at her friend in disbelief. "What?"

"Instead of flowers or some sweets, he apparently beheaded some Jurisdiction assholes for me."

"That is messed up" was all I could muster. Then I started to laugh at the absurdity of it, and how it really was the perfect present for Blu, in a sick and twisted way.

"Yes, it is. Seriously though," she said as she caught her breath, "my guess is the heads belong to the minions and the driver from the last time I was there."

Styx was shaking her head. "Wow. He really is your boyfriend."

FARA 38

I slept like the dead that night, although Calum said I opened at least one portal while I did so. Having him confirm that I was still opening portals in my sleep, even though I could control them while awake, proved that unless there was something remarkable hidden in my mom's notes, I'd never be able to control the ability completely. That didn't bother me as much as it probably should.

Sage was in the infirmary's lobby when I walked in to visit Jay. He saw me and smiled . . . at least, as much as Sage ever smiled. It was more that his face transformed from super serious to not quite as serious. Considering what he'd been through, the fact that he smiled at all was a miracle.

"Fara, good to see you. Have a moment? Can I walk with you?"

"Sure."

He locked step with me as I made my way to Jay's room.

"Have you met Willow yet?"

Though I hadn't, I knew the Team spoke well of her, and that she was injured during a mission. Something gruesome like almost being disemboweled by a sword. I said as much to Sage.

"That's what I want to ask you about. Willow's injuries are extensive, and they are not healing as I would have hoped. Jay has mentioned in passing that your world has more advanced healthcare available. Is that true?"

"It's possible. I know that our medicines are better—or at least, our access to them is."

"I just hate to think that she's going to be in pain the rest of her life because we were unable to help. If there's anything else we can do, I want to try it."

"I'll help in any way I can. If Jay thinks it'll help her, I'll open a portal and we can go from there. Talk to Jay—he'll know more."

We stopped in front of Jay's door, and Sage patted my shoulder.

"You're a good person, Fara."

"Not nearly as awesome as you are."

I knocked on the door as soon as Sage left, to no answer. Then I heard Jay's voice from across the hall. I hesitated a moment before knocking on the other door. I didn't want to interrupt, but as his . . . whatever I was . . . I didn't think he'd mind. At least, I hoped he wouldn't.

"Come in," said a female voice.

I walked into the room, which was a mirror of Jay's, with a bed, chair, and table. Jack was sitting in the chair, while Jay was in a wheelchair next to the bed. There were crutches resting against the wall behind him.

"I was hoping it was you," Jay said, the corner of his mouth lifting up into an almost smile, which made me grin like an idiot.

"You must be Fara." There was a tiny, frail young woman lying in bed. Her long brown hair hung over her shoulders, and her eyes were almost too big for her face. She was pale and pixie-sized. She reminded me of a doll in the best way possible. How in the hell did she end up wanting to be an assassin? But then again, looks could be deceiving. She could be lethal. Living here, she probably was.

"And you must be Willow. Nice to meet you, finally."

"I've heard so much about you," she said as she waved me in. "Everyone says that you are way nicer than Blu."

Jack huffed a laugh. "That's an understatement."

"Jack!" Willow scolded. "Don't be mean! Blu is always nice to me."

"That's because you're not an asshole, and the rest of us are," he countered.

"I'm serious," Willow said. "You heard what she did to Dev's roommate, Bullfrog, right? Before I got hurt?"

Jack's face contained a grin that said he couldn't begin to imagine what Blu had done.

She leaned in conspiratorially. "Blu overheard Bullfrog saying something really crass to me during training, so she told him to knock it off. When he continued to be an ass to me, she pulled him out in front of the training group, disarmed him before he even knew what was happening, then broke his nose with the pummel of her sword when he got mouthy with her. When he started screaming at her, she just calmly told him that if he ever said or did anything like that to me, or anyone else again, she'd cut off his—her words—'boy parts.'"

She whispered the last part as Jack chuckled.

"Man, I'd love to be able to do that," I said. To bash Hewitt's face in, then walk away to some amazing music would be next-level badassery.

Jay raised a perfect eyebrow at me. "That's not really your style."

"Yet," Jack amended. "Not her style yet. If she keeps hanging out with us, then we might rub off on her."

"I hope so," I said with a grin. "I have a list of people who I dream of punching."

"I have a feeling you'll be there in no time," Jack said, and Willow laughed. But Jay wasn't smiling. What was that all about?

They spoke for a while longer, and I finally gathered up my courage and whispered to Jay that I wanted to talk to him. He nodded, but again without smiling.

"Willow, I think we're going to head back over to Jay's room. It was so good to meet you. Hopefully, I'll get to talk to you more soon."

"Same. I'm looking forward to hearing more about your world. Jay has been kind enough to keep me company, and he's been telling me about some things."

"I'd love to. I'll see you soon."

Jack said his goodbyes to Willow and followed us out. "Ink told me to let you know he'd come get you in a bit for training—abilities, not daggers. He said he needed to get supplies just in case you fried yourself again."

I snorted. "So considerate. Thanks, Jack."

"You know, if you get tired of training with him, I'd be happy to help you with your fire starter abilities."

"I might take you up on that. I want to get the electricity thing down first, since that will be the best one to protect myself with."

I followed Jay as he walked into his room using crutches. He hoisted himself up onto his bed without any help, though he was breathing harder than normal. He was still not smiling, although he grabbed my hand as I sat down on the bed next to him.

"What is it?" I kissed him. He pulled away.

"What do you mean?"

"Something is bothering you. I can tell."

"How can you tell?"

"I just can. What's wrong?"

"It's nothing."

"You just frown for fun?

"No."

"Then spill it. If we're going to spend time together, then I want you to be honest with me."

He sighed. "Fine. But bear with me. I'm terrible at explaining myself."

"I've got all of the time you need."

"You don't, actually. Ink is going to come get you for training . . . and that's part of the problem."

"What? You think that me and Ink—"

"No! I mean, that's not what I'm saying. Really. I'm just struggling to keep up with everything, that's all."

"Keep up with what?"

He breathed out through his nose in frustration. "With how much you've changed, even in the past few days. You're running around with a dagger on your thigh, making jokes about bashing in someone's face with a sword. You just had an entire conversation about training with lightning and fire, for Christ's sake, like that's a normal part of your life."

"It is a normal part of my life here, Jay."

"But it shouldn't be! Not really. Instead of staying in your apartment and reading your mom's notes, you're planning missions and learning different combat techniques. You're going home in a couple of days, but instead of figuring out how to suppress your powers, you're training with them. And it sounds like you've done this before, and hurt yourself?"

"Not badly. I just passed out for an hour . . . or two. But no one was hurt, and I figured out how to get it to work."

"But you're supposed to be figuring out how to get it to stop! And how to stop your portal abilities."

"I can keep the portals under control when I'm awake, but I doubt I will ever be able to control them in my sleep. Even with all of the training and everything, I still opened one last night. Plus, my mom never found a way to stop it."

"Then we need to work harder on that. But . . . it's like you don't even want to."

I took a deep breath. Even though I had already told him my reservations about going home, he wasn't listening. Not really. And to be honest, I was letting him believe that I was going home because I wanted to pretend for just a little while longer. But to be fair to both of us, he needed to know. All of it.

"I don't," I said quietly. "I don't want to suppress any of my abilities. I want to learn how to use them. Safely."

"But when you come home—"

"Jay, I've already told you that I'm not ready to go home. Not yet, at least."

"But I need to go back, and it's not safe here."

"It's not safe for me anywhere until Barrington Park and the Counselor are dead, Jay. It's not safe until we get the palmbox back from the assistant."

He rubbed his face with his hands, and the way he looked at me broke my heart. I really cared for him. He was such a decent, solid guy. The reason he wanted this for me was not because he was an asshole, but because he cared for me. He wanted what he thought was best for us. It just wasn't what was best for me.

"I don't know what to do, Fara. This seems so unlike you. Do you even want to be with me anymore?"

"Yes! I still want this—us—to keep going. I really care for you."

"Then why does it feel like you're choosing missions and combat and the Team over us? Over what we had decided. Over coming home with me?"

I took a deep breath. "Actually, I'm not choosing the Team or anything else. I want to train so that I can learn to use these powers. I am choosing to stay so that I don't have to hide. I want to be able to embrace all of me. I'm choosing *me*. Just me."

"Fara, you shouldn't be using your abilities. It's too dangerous."

"By telling me not to use them, you're asking me to suppress what I am. I don't want to do that anymore. I've done it all of my life because that is what everyone chose for me—because it kept me safe. But now *I* have the choice. I'm choosing the lightning, and the fire, and everything that makes me what I am. I can't hide anymore, Jay. I won't."

He looked like he was going to say something, but I held up my hand. I needed him to understand.

"After my parents died, I didn't have a purpose, other than to make it day by day. Wondering if I could pay rent or eat. Never thinking about anything other than surviving. Allowing myself to be taken advantage of because I pushed my own feelings down so far that I didn't recognize them as mine anymore. But this place, for all of its danger and horribleness, has provided me a purpose. I've finally found a place where I belong."

I thought about my conversation with Ink. About how at that moment I felt like I could do anything. Jay needed to understand that too. "These people accept me. All of me. And not because they want to use me, or because it benefits them, but because they truly believe in me. Can you do that? I know I've changed since we met, and I know this isn't what you signed up for. Can you accept all of me too—weird abilities and all?"

Jay looked out of the window. His brow was furrowed and his mouth was turned down.

"This is a lot to process. I need some time to think. And I want you to reconsider coming home, for me. I can't lose you, Fara. I really care for you."

I wasn't going to change my mind, and I had a feeling he wasn't either. And that knowledge hurt, a lot. But before the tears could fully form in my eyes, there was a knock at the door.

Jay sighed. "Come in."

Ink leaned against the doorframe, but with one look at me, his smirk faded. He turned his attention from me to Jay. "You look way better than the last time I saw you. I'm glad they've been taking care of you."

"Thank you. They have been."

It was uncomfortably quiet. I needed to get out of here. Now. I got up and walked toward Ink, willing my tears not to fall. I didn't have it in me to turn around and say goodbye.

"Hey, Ink," Jay said, "please take care of her. Messing with these powers is dangerous."

"That's the difference between us, agent. I think she can take care of herself."

BLU 39

The Captain wanted me to get a feel for what Jay's plans were. We hoped that he'd be able to provide information regarding Barrington once he left, and Fara hoped he'd be able to smooth over the government's desire to question Calum.

"And if Calum goes back and he's still in danger," the Captain had said, "I think we could risk him living here a little longer. We might even let him out of Fara's apartment." But she was hoping it wouldn't come to that. At least, until the spy was found.

I waved at Sage as I walked through the lobby, then made my way to Jay's door. It was open a crack so I pushed as I knocked.

"Hey there. Got a second?"

"Sure. Come in."

I shut the door and sat on the chair. Jay watched me warily.

"Thanks for talking to me. I hear that you're leaving in a couple of days."

"I'm anxious to get back."

"I'm sure. It can't be easy being here."

"It's not."

He watched me, waiting for me to tell him what I wanted. He looked angry, but it didn't seem like the anger was directed at something I had done. As long as he was willing to talk to me, I wouldn't worry about it.

"Not to beat around the bush, but we hope to partner with you in killing Barrington Park."

"Oh?"

"Yes."

"How do you plan on doing that?"

"With my bare hands, preferably. But I'm not picky."

He didn't smile. In fact, he was frowning. "I mean, what is your plan on getting to him? He has more security and contacts than almost anyone else in our world."

"We figured it would be a shitshow. Really, for now we need you to provide us with as much information as you can get. Once we know enough to formulate a full-scale attack, we will provide a tactical team to kill him."

"Not just bring him back here?"

"No. He needs to die. But we'll worry about that when the time comes, and we know that you can't be implicated in killing him. We just need to figure out the logistics."

He paused, deliberating. "That's why you want to keep Fara here."

That was interesting, and not what I expected. It also wasn't true.

"Not really, no."

"Of course it is. You can't get to Barrington without her."

I sighed. "Jay, it's her decision."

"But you people are pressuring her—"

"That's bullshit, and if you knew us, or her at all, you'd know it."

"You can't do this without her."

"We'd find another way."

"But—"

"You can tell yourself whatever you want, but the truth of the matter is that she wants to stay here and has offered to help. If you think she's so weak that we could manipulate her into doing something that she otherwise wouldn't want to do, then you must have a very low opinion of her. And that's on you."

"That's not what I meant."

"Of course it isn't, but that's what you're saying. Look, what happens between the two of you is none of my business, so I am only going to say this once: Please do not insult her by thinking she's not strong enough to make up her own mind. She says you're better than that. Prove her right."

He didn't respond. Maybe he was thinking about what I said, or maybe he was just done talking about it. Either way, I didn't care. I hadn't come to talk about Fara—not directly, at least. I came here to talk about how the hell we were going to kill a guy in a different universe, a guy who seemed to have as many resources as the Counselor. I needed Jay on our team, and while he didn't strike me as the kind of person who'd withhold help out of spite, I also didn't want to push my luck.

"Can you help us?"

He took a long minute before he responded. "I agree that Barrington Park needs to go. He's a menace, especially if it's true that he wants to turn our world into one like this. I love my home too much to let that happen."

"Good. So what's your first move?"

Jay explained that he needed to find out exactly what Barrington had told his department about him, and what their plans for Calum were.

"And then there's Willow," he finished.

"I heard she's coming with you. I think that's great."

"We're hoping that my world's medicine can help her injuries heal faster. I have a good doctor friend who can help without putting her on anyone's radar."

"Thank you for helping her."

"It's the right thing to do. Plus, if we're going to be working together, she'll be a good asset to have, since she understands this world and its history."

"Is she staying with you or Calum?"

"I have a spare room. Besides, since she'll be seeing the same doctor as I will, it'll make it more convenient. Now, how are we going to communicate?"

"For now, Fara has agreed to open portals a couple of times a day to swap information via letter to Calum's apartment. Calum is currently reading Fara's mom's notes to see if there's a better way, like, if Fara can figure out how to open portals at your place. For now, that's all we can come up with."

"And she's OK with this?"

"It was her idea."

FARA 40

Ink got out of the car, slung a backpack over his shoulder, and started up the trail. I had seen the pack in the back seat, but I hadn't asked what was in it. I hadn't said anything at all—I was just trying to hold myself together. I didn't want to practice my abilities. I didn't want to talk to Ink about how I was feeling. And I sure as shit did not want to think about what had just happened with Jay. But I knew that I was about to endure all three of those things.

It seemed intrinsically unfair that my abilities were linked to horrible feelings. That while mages and superheroes and gods of old could draw up power or mana with a thought (so the stories went), I was stuck having to relive the most horrific experiences of my life in order to drum up enough energy to make them work—even if it seemed all I was able to do was make myself pass out with the effort. I also knew that comparing myself to fictional characters wasn't a good parallel, but at this point I was having a pity party, and logic wasn't invited. Screw logic.

I was also mad at myself for getting so upset over a relationship that had barely begun. It had only been a couple of weeks since I met Jay. This wasn't some love of a lifetime. Our relationship would only have been in the honeymoon stages if we lived in a normal world under normal circumstances. We would have probably gone out to dinner, or maybe watched movies. We wouldn't have had to mount rescues and be tortured. In a normal world, if Jay had broken it off with me after a couple of weeks, I would have been hurt, but I would have gotten drunk with Adora and Calum and moved on, eventually.

But we didn't live normal lives, and I didn't have the luxury of drinking with Adora, so the thought of our impending demise was making me sick to my stomach. I knew that was the conversation we would have tomorrow: Jay asking one more time for me to come home, and me refusing.

I could understand why he wanted me to come with him. Not only was it what I'd said I wanted a week ago, but long-distance relationships—even normal ones—were hard. Throw in despotic rulers and parallel universes and I imagine that they are nearly impossible. But that didn't mean I didn't want him to try, or that I didn't want to try. I just kept thinking that if he cared enough, we could make it work. It was unfair, but I thought it anyway. Neither of us had signed up for this, and holding him to something that he never agreed to—or being mad at him for not changing his mind—wasn't reasonable. But once again—screw logic.

We'd made it to the clearing, and Ink started to unpack his backpack. I glared into the trees, tears threatening to drip down my face. The sun was brilliant on the field, casting sparkling reflections off the creek. More flowers had bloomed since yesterday. The beauty of this place did nothing to soothe my mood.

I was sweating, so I took off my sweatshirt, and I realized that Ink didn't make any comment about undressing—which was unusual for him. I turned to see him watching me, no smirk in sight.

"Want to talk about it?"

"No."

"OK then. Time to get to work. I was thinking about yesterday, and I might have a better way to go about this."

I nodded, not trusting myself to talk yet.

"I know that I don't know you as well as I know Blu, but I think I'm starting to get an idea of how your brain works."

"You'd be the first."

The corner of his mouth tugged up. "Maybe. But I want to try something different. I think that to get this lightning thing to work, instead of intending to hurt someone, maybe we need to reverse that. Maybe you need to intend to *protect* someone. That's how your mom did it with the dog and with the drunk guy. She was protecting someone else. And that's how you released it yesterday. You were protecting me . . . from you."

"And the time I accidentally fried the goon, I was protecting myself."

"Exactly. Honestly, you and Blu are the same in that way. Protecting people is why she does what she does."

He might be on to something. But how do I *protect* someone when I'm just training?

"Any ideas how to do this?"

"We wing it."

"What if I hurt you?"

He smiled at me, the smile that I was starting to recognize but still didn't know what it meant. "You won't."

"How do you know?"

"Because I punched a wall right next to your head, and instead of running, you hugged me. You stayed. Like it or not, we're friends. And you protect your friends."

I wanted to hug him now, but I couldn't bring myself to do it. "I'm ready."

"Good. I have snacks and water just in case you pass out again and I get hungry."

I allowed myself a chuckle. Of course he did. I got my dagger out, and he stabbed his dagger into the branch.

"Remember—the electricity goes into the dagger, then touch it to the other dagger to ground it."

"In theory."

Ink grabbed my chin gently and tilted my head so I was forced to look up at him.

"Stop downplaying your abilities, Fara. You can do this. I know you can. I can tell you're hurting right now, even if you're ignoring it. Channel that."

He dropped my chin and backed away. He was right. As much as I had been subconsciously pushing down what I was feeling about Jay and all the rest of it, I had to face that pain to get this to work. I slowly pulled down my mental walls and started to force myself to feel the bevy of emotions from my conversation with Jay.

I could feel a portal opening, and closed it, concentrating on getting this lightning ability to work. Why was this one so much harder to access? Was it the thinning of the membrane that made the portals easy, but everything else not? Something else?

I let the hurt of the last few hours flow through me, then tried to pull up the feeling of lightning. Nothing happened other than feeling sad and angry. Failure. I tried again, and nothing. I took a deep breath. What was it that the notes had said? About intent? I might not need to intend to hurt someone, but I had to be more intentional about using this ability—it wasn't just going to manifest like the portal. I had to think about wanting to use it. And, while it felt weird, I thought the words "I want to use lightning." I almost imagined that I could feel my brain click to the right program—the lightning program. Weird. The electricity started to build up in my hands.

"Ink, I have it."

He grinned. And took a step toward me.

"Stop! Ink, what are you doing?"

"You need to protect me."

I watched as he took another step toward me.

"Ink, stop! I'm serious! I don't want to hurt you!"

He slowly reached for me.

"Then get rid of the electricity."

"Don't come any closer."

I tried to back up, but my feet were rooted to the ground, and everything was moving in slow motion. His fingers were almost to mine. I wanted him to stop. What was he doing? He could die, and I couldn't live with that. I needed to get the electricity as far away from him as possible. I instinctively dropped the dagger, pulling my hands away from him, and imagined flinging the electricity toward the trees. To my amazement, there was a loud crack as a small bolt of lightning left my fingers and hit a tree on the edge of the clearing. I watched with almost detached amusement as it started to smoke. Then the all too familiar feeling of passing out started to overcome me. Before I gave in to the blackness, my final thought was that I was going to throttle Ink for pulling that stunt.

41 FARA

"I'm going to murder you in your sleep."

I could hear Ink chuckle, although I refused to open my eyes just yet.

"You need to learn your lockpicking ability to make that happen, sweetness."

"Details. How long have I been out?"

"One granola bar."

"We're measuring time in food now?"

"Or drink. Half of one water bottle, or one granola bar. Take your pick."

"I hate you."

"You don't."

"I could."

"You couldn't, even if you tried."

I huffed an exasperated laugh and decided to try to open my eyes. I was dizzy, but not as bad as the last couple of times. Ink was grinning at me.

"I'm serious, Ink. I could have killed you. That was pretty shitty of you to do."

"I had faith that you wouldn't."

"I could have."

"But you didn't."

"Fine. But I'm still mad."

"If that's the price for getting you to shoot a tree with lightning, then I'd pay it again. That was amazing, Fara. Really amazing."

"I didn't mean for that to happen."

"Well, maybe not. But it's a start. And really fucking cool. Now to figure out how to get it so that you don't pass out. Although I kind of like your head in my lap."

I sat up. He handed me an unopened water bottle as the nausea hit but was almost immediately gone. Small steps. Baby steps, in fact. But steps.

I watched Ink watch me from the corner of my eye. "Did you plan that?"

"If I said yes, would you berate me?"

"Yes."

"Then no, I didn't."

"Liar."

"Totally. OK, fine. Yes, I planned that, based on what happened last time. You didn't want to hurt someone, but you would protect me . . . even from yourself."

"Asshole."

"You have to admit that it worked."

I laughed in spite of myself. "True."

"Want to try again?"

"Maybe in a granola bar?"

"What?"

"I thought we were measuring time in food. I would like to try again in a half of a water bottle, or a granola bar."

"Good thinking. That should be enough time."

We ate and drank in a comfortable silence as my body got back to normal. The recovery time was shorter than last time, and considerably shorter than when I fried the goon. Another baby step in the right direction.

"Ready?"

I stood up to make sure I was, in fact, ready, and when I didn't collapse or throw up, I figured I was as ready as anyone ever could be to attempt to shoot lightning.

"Just don't try to touch me."

"Can't promise that."

"Ink!"

"Fara!"

"Seriously!"

"I am serious. If it's the only way to get you to not pass out for a week, then I'll take my chances. I trust you. Start trusting yourself."

I was hoping the threat that he would hurt himself was enough to get this to work. I pulled up the emotions of today again, feeling the ache in my chest and hating the fact that this was what I had to do to make my powers work. If only I had a memory that was happy enough that I could use it. Bummer.

I shut down the portal that tried to make an appearance, then forced myself to switch my brain to the lightning program. After a moment, I felt the click and the now familiar feeling of electricity started to build. Before Ink could make a move to grab me, I tried something new. If my brain was processing this craziness like programs, I imagined choosing the correct program like turning a dial, and I wanted to turn the dial to the "shoot lightning" option. I almost laughed at the silliness of it all, but I imagined an old-school wheel, and envisioned that option. I felt the click, and when I looked at my hands, I saw that the electricity had drained out of me—into balls floating on my palms.

"Holy shit! Ink, look!"

"What the fuck? That's crazy cool! Now what?"

"Ummm . . . I don't know! Try and shoot it? Lay it on the ground? I don't know!"

"Try and hit the tree?"

"I'm not sure how to go about doing that."

"However you went about doing this ball thing would be a start."

I thought of the wheel again, and mentally turned it to "shoot." I moved my arms, one at a time, like I was throwing two balls. I laughed at the sight of the glowing balls hurtling toward the trees, which they hit with a loud crack. The balls, however, did not hit the trees I was aiming at.

Ink threw his arms around me. "Amazing! That was so awesome! You just threw electric balls out of your hands!"

I started to giggle into his chest; then it turned into a full-bodied laugh. All of the tension and sadness and anger and pain and fear oozed out of my skin with my laughter. It felt so good, even if the laughter was bordering on hysterical.

Ink pulled back and looked at me. "Are you OK?"

"You said electric balls."

Ink's eyebrows shot up into his hairline. "That's what you got out of this entire experience? Classic. Anyway, are you all right?"

Amazingly, I was.

"That must be the trick of this," I said, wiping my eyes and plopping down on the ground to drink some more water, Ink following suit. "I think I need to get the charge thing out of me like I did just now. Then I have some more time to figure out what to do with it. Like the first time, when I fried the goon, I think I was accessing the palmbox's normal stun program. And that might come in handy if someone grabs me, but it also puts me on my ass. But for the electric balls, I think I'm accessing Barrington's tricked-out program or something. If I can recreate it, I think that's probably the way to go so that I don't pass out."

"That seriously was one of the coolest things I've ever seen."

"My aim was off."

Ink threw his arm around my shoulder and squeezed. "Can you just enjoy the moment? You managed to do something remarkable, and not die in the process. We need celebratory cheeseburgers or donuts to commemorate the occasion."

"You guys don't have beer, do you? Or whiskey?"

"No. Only the elite have access to it."

"All right, that settles it. The next time I'm in my home world, I'm bringing back booze, and we're going to have a drink together. Or multiple drinks."

Ink's perma-smirk returned. "Sounds like fun. And like a date."

"Ink, you don't date."

"I might make an exception."

"Highly doubtful."

"I'm looking forward to it anyway. Ready to try it again?"

"Why not?"

I tried twice more. The first time, I got the electric balls to work, but before I could shoot them, they disappeared. The second time, I couldn't get the balls to work at all, and ended up passing out for, as Ink put it, a quarter of a cheeseburger, which I took to mean about five minutes.

Eventually we made our way back to the car, having consumed all of the provisions. The setting sun cast an orange glow over the whole forest. The birds were quieting down, and the only noises I could hear were our footsteps on the trail, with the occasional snap of a twig or crunch of leaves. It was like my walk to the clearing had been made by a different person at a different time. I felt so much lighter than when we arrived. So much better.

"Hey, Ink? Thank you."

He turned around, one hand on his car door, the other absently running through his hair. There was no smirk on his face, no teasing or breathy sexpot comment. For just a moment, I caught a glimpse of who he was underneath it all.

"You're welcome, Fara."

BLU 42

It was my turn for surveillance of Dagna's building, and so I drove one of the Compound's trucks to the location the Team had agreed upon, parked under the cover of trees, and made my way up the trail, hoping they hadn't installed spikes of death since the last time I was here. Once again, not the way I'd choose to die.

As I crested the hill, I heard the snap of a twig, and I could see the outline of someone in the dusk walking toward me. I stepped behind a tree and grabbed my daggers.

"It's me," Styx whispered.

I waved at her to stop talking. Even whispers in this sort of quiet carried.

"Don't worry. The surveillance cameras are video only."

"Then why are you whispering?"

"Habit?"

I laughed. "I'm glad you're alive."

"Me too. Although my butt is asleep. By the way, be careful. Minions come to the end of the trail every so often to dump bodies in the grave. You'll see them before they see you, but it startled me the first time it happened."

"Good to know. See you back at the Compound."

"Happy hunting, my friend."

I walked the last few yards to where I needed to be. If I sat at a certain location on the trail, I could see everything without having to move. We were only monitoring the building for seventy-two hours, so we needed to make it count. At least the heads on the pikes were gone. That made me chuckle inappropriately, of course.

Both the front and back entrance seemed to be guarded at all times, and the minions checked the credentials of every vehicle that approached before allowing them entry. The security was tighter at the front entrance, at least in terms of the number of minions, but that didn't mean there weren't heavily armed minions at the back entrance as well. I made notes of everything I saw. Until we got a handle on what was normal for this building, anything could be important. I also remembered something else: surveillance was boring. Like, ass asleep boring.

Lulled by the monotony of it all, I have to admit I jumped when Jyston's comm buzzed. I backed away from the edge of the tree line and farther down the trail just in case my voice carried. I would not get caught—again—for Jyston.

"Jyston, now is not a good time."

"Well, hello to you too."

"I'm serious."

"Where are you?"

"Like I'd tell you."

He chuckled. "So typical. I hear that Dagna took down my present to you. It's too bad you didn't get to see it yourself. I thought it an appropriate gift to commemorate our relationship."

I paused. Did he actually know where I was, or was he fishing for information?

"What do you want?"

He sighed over the comm, and I could visualize the humor and annoyance on his face. It made me smile in spite of myself.

"Have it your way. All business all the time. I really wish you would reconsider your priorities. Now then, I have to be away for a day or two on business. When I return, I should have all of the information you need for the PITs."

"Is this business that you are attending to going to be bad for the Compound?"

"No. I have to take care of some things before we meet is all."

"Just don't die, all right?"

He chuckled. "Good advice at any time."

"I'll talk to you soon?"

"Not soon enough." I could hear the smile in his voice, and as I turned off the comm, I realized something.

The anti-tech didn't affect the comm. We might have a way to communicate for this mission after all.

43 FARA

I opened the door to my apartment to find Silver and Calum making out on the air mattress. I was too exhausted to comment, although I was glad they were clothed—more or less.

"Oh, hi Fara. Um . . . I brought Calum dinner."

I smiled but didn't say anything. Snark wouldn't be fair to her. Anyway, didn't I kiss Jay in Calum's apartment? Turnabout is fair play, and all of that.

"Do you want me to go get you something to eat too?"

"No, thank you. That's very sweet of you to offer, but I just ate about fifteen pounds of granola, so I'm fine."

They both had gotten up and were readjusting clothing and whatnot, and since I didn't want to stare, I went to run a bath. After lying on the ground the past couple of days, I needed to rid myself of the dirt and wayward grass that was sticking to me. Plus, I loved this bathtub more than any human had a right to love an inanimate object.

As I submerged myself in the hot water, I tried to clear my mind, but my brain wasn't having it. What it wanted to think about was the conversation I'd had with Jay. I told my brain to fuck off and dunked my head under the water, but it didn't help. Eventually I gave up. If my brain was going to keep playing our conversation on repeat, I should probably talk to Calum and get his perspective.

I heard the door close as Silver left, and I took that as my cue to get out and get dressed. I walked back into the living area to see Calum sitting on my bed.

"You look tired, my friend," he said.

"I am tired. Exhausted, actually. I got into a fight with Jay, shot lightning and electric balls out of my hands, and passed out. Twice. I've been busy."

There was a two-second pause before he burst out laughing. I couldn't blame him. It did sound a bit crazy.

"Why don't you start at the beginning? I do want to focus on the electric balls part, though."

I told Calum about the conversation I had with Jay.

"The worst part about it," I said at the end of my tirade, "is that I can't blame him, and I can't be mad. I'm hurt and disappointed, but not mad. Who he is—what he is—is what drew me to him in the first place."

Calum nodded slowly. "He needs to protect people."

"Exactly. At first, he was trying to protect the country from me, even though it was ridiculous. I mean, even with the Great Iced Tea Incident, he was trying to protect me from Hewitt. He came to rescue me from Barrington. All of it is geared around this inherent nobility in him."

"It's who he is," Calum agreed.

"And ever since my parents died, that was all I wanted. Someone to look after me, to take care of me, to protect me. But that all changed once I came here and saw what I could be. What I could do."

"Do you want to be like the Team?"

"Not exactly. But I also don't want to hide who I am. *All* of who I am. I've changed."

"You don't owe it to anyone to stay the same just because that's what they want."

"It just hurts. I mean, I think I set a record. Assuming Jay breaks it off tomorrow—which he will—that's two dumpings in as many weeks."

"Then they're both idiots." He put his arms around me.

"You have to say that. It's part of the best friend contract."

Calum softly laughed into my hair. "No, I say that because it's true. If they can't love you for who you are—all of who you are—then they are not meant for you. And that's OK. Like I said before, we're young. There is no rule that says you need to be with someone."

"So says the guy who was just making out with the runway model assassin ninja on Ink's air mattress."

"That's different, Fara. That's just for fun. We both know I'm leaving in a couple of days."

"I'm not built like that."

"Right. Anyway, I love you and think you're amazing and I will be right here to talk to after you have the conversation with Jay tomorrow."

"Thanks. Love you too. Selfishly, I really don't want you to leave."

"Me either. It's weird. I miss seeing scenery other than these four walls, but otherwise, I don't really miss home."

"Maybe once they figure out who the spy is, you can come back and stay."

"I'd like that."

⚡ ⚡ ⚡

Styx woke me up for training the next morning and chatted away as I got ready to go. Ink was already at the trail, Jack was sleeping after taking the overnight surveillance shift, and Blu was at the Quad with Silver.

I hadn't slept well last night. The dread of the conversation with Jay kept popping up and not allowing me to go back to sleep. I eventually realized that trying to predict how this conversation would go was an act in futility, although that realization didn't make the dark hours go by any faster. I told myself that I was strong enough to handle whatever came my way. Maybe if I said it enough, I might start to believe it.

Training with Styx was very different from training with Ink, although just as effective. She was goofy, teasing and dancing around while showing me offensive combat moves that reminded me of *The Karate Kid*.

"Wax on, wax off," I said, then realized she would have no idea what I was talking about. That was one of the detriments of living here—my pop culture references, a staple of my normal conversation, were useless. It was a total downer. My dad was the one who'd started me on peppering everyday conversation with movie quotes and song lyrics, and he would have gotten it. The familiar ache in my heart reappeared. I pushed it down.

I figured I might as well get the conversation with Jay over with. Stewing about it wasn't going to change the outcome. So after training, I got some poor trainee to walk me to the infirmary, taking steadying breaths as I went. Before I could knock on Jay's door, I heard his deep laughter coming from Willow's room. A pang of jealousy shot through me as I listened to her echo his laughter. I clamped that down. Jay was bored, and she was a friend. And to be fair, I had been hanging out with the Team since I arrived here, while he was stuck in his room. It never occurred to me that he might be jealous of the time I spent with everyone else. He'd never said anything, and if he could be that big of a person, I guess I could too.

I took a deep breath and knocked. Willow told me to come in. Jay looked better than even yesterday. He was fully dressed and sitting in the chair, his crutches leaning tidily against the wall. His leg cast had been removed, and he had a medical boot on instead. It seemed weird, considering I was pretty sure that his leg had been broken just a couple of days ago, but then again, I wasn't a doctor, so what did I know? He smiled as I walked in, and my heart gave a flutter.

"Hi."

"Hi, Fara. I'm so glad to see you."

"You too, Willow." I stood there awkwardly. There wasn't a place for me to sit, and I didn't want to be rude and interrupt their conversation anyway. "I can come back?"

"Oh no! Please stay. Jay was just telling me about something called movies. They sound fantastic! I can't wait to see them."

I laughed, remembering Ink's excitement about the same thing. "I think you're really going to love movies. And television."

"You'll have to show me all of it! I'm so excited!"

I paused. Either Jay hadn't told her that I wasn't going with them, or he was still holding out hope that I was.

"I promise I will. As soon as I come home."

She looked at me in surprise.

"You're not coming with us tomorrow?"

"Not this time, but soon. I still have so much to learn with my abilities and training that I need some more time here. In the meantime, make sure that Jay shows you a good time, even if you're there to visit doctors. Don't let him work all of the time."

She laughed. "Deal."

We said our goodbyes, and I followed Jay to his room. He was using his crutches at boss level, and I marveled again at how quickly he was healing. He was apparently very determined to get home.

He got settled into his bed, and I sat next to him, wondering if I should kiss him, or if he would kiss me, or if we'd already moved past that. I opened my mouth to ask how he was doing, but he held up his hand.

"Fara, I've been thinking about what you said ever since you left last night, and since I'm terrible at talking about, well, talking about anything, I want to get it out so I don't forget anything."

He grabbed my hand. I took a deep breath.

"I think I finally understand what you're saying. I have to admit, I was mad at first. I mean, going back with me was what we agreed, right? But that was when we thought you had one ability—portals. Now we know you have at least four, if not more. So I tried to put myself in your shoes, and I realized that I'd make the same choice if I were you."

"You would?"

"I wouldn't want to suppress my abilities. I'd want to know what I could do. I'd want to train here."

He tucked an errant hair behind my ear.

"Except, I probably would have asked you to stay here with me, even if I knew you needed to go home. Even though you're letting me go home. And that bothered me . . . about me. That I would sacrifice your happiness for mine. And that's not who I am, or who I want to be."

I grabbed his other hand, and he gently kissed my knuckles.

"But I also know myself well enough to know that I will worry myself sick every minute knowing that my girlfriend is here and I can't help you. I've been worried ever since we've been here, and I see you every day. I know it's selfish, and I know it's not right, but I'm not sure I can handle being apart from you, not knowing what's happening, or having you call me bossy or tease me about being Agent No Fun." I stifled a snort. "I don't want to lose you, but it might kill me to keep you if you're here."

I buried my head in his good shoulder. "I don't know if I can handle it either, Jay, but I'm willing to try."

He pulled me next to him and wrapped his arms around me. "How can we do this?"

"One day at a time."

"What do you mean?"

"I don't know how long I'm going to be here. Blu and I talked—and I know I'll be opening portals at least a couple of times a day and bringing you back here in a week. I can write notes, and you can stay with me or I can visit you. We'll figure out a way for me to portal out of places that are safe. There are ways to do this. It's not ideal and there is some danger, but it's worth it. You're worth it."

"Fara, that's the problem. You're more than worth it. You're remarkable. I'm the jerk."

"Well, you can be my jerk."

His chuckle rumbled in my hair and I smiled.

"OK. One day at a time."

"Good, since I'm apparently your girlfriend?"

He looked at me, one perfect eyebrow cocked. "As long as that's all right with you."

"It's more than all right with me."

He kissed me. "Another selfish reason I want you to come back with me is so we can do this some more."

"Say the word and I'll stay over."

"Not here."

"I mean, I could learn how to portal to your house for a booty call. I think that's a pretty important use of my powers."

"Did you just call me a booty call?"

"Yes, among other things. I'd ask you to stay with me tonight, but Calum is sleeping on my floor."

"I'm not one for an audience."

FARA 44

Ink and I trained in the clearing until it became too dark to see. By the time I walked into my apartment, I was exhausted and collapsed on my bed. He had promised that someone would bring us dinner, so for a minute, I didn't have anywhere I had to be. It was heaven.

Calum stretched out next to me. "How'd it go?"

I snorted. "It was better than the last two times, but still a disaster."

"How so?"

"Well, out of the half-dozen times I tried to do the lightning thing, I passed out twice, which I guess was an improvement, but still not ideal. The other four times, I was able to get the electric balls to appear, but I'm not sure how. The first time they disappeared after a second. Twice, I was able to throw them at the trees—although I missed what I was aiming at by miles."

"And the last time?"

"Oh yeah. That was the best because I have no idea how it happened," I said sarcastically. "An arc of electricity appeared over my head, connecting the two balls in my hands. Weird, even by my standards. I have no idea what that would be used for, but whatever."

"It doesn't sound like a disaster."

"You should see the tree."

Calum was grinning up at the ceiling.

"What?"

"Could you have imagined two weeks ago that we'd be having this conversation?"

A laugh burst out of me. "Oh my god, no! I was just trying to make enough tips to pay rent and deal with asshat."

"I'm going to miss you."

"Me too. But it won't be for long. I'll come visit. And you said you wanted to come back here."

"I do. Really. I wouldn't mind getting a job here. I could work in the mess hall, or as groundskeeper, or anything, really. There's nothing for me back home, except my apartment. I could sublet it easily."

"And it's not because of the girl you've been sucking face with?"

"No one can take the place of you."

"That's not what I mean."

"I know. But I need to tell you every so often."

"The Captain said that if Jay can't help you with the government, or if Barrington's goons get too forceful, you can come back and stay. Even have your own place. So please, please . . . "

"I won't try and be a hero. Getting kidnapped once was enough for me. But for now, you'll need me to pass notes to your boyfriend."

"We'll figure out another way if we have to, OK?"

He rolled over and hugged me. "OK."

There was a knock at the door, and Silver came in holding boxes of food. She dropped off the food and was about to leave, but I saw the look my best friend gave her, which she returned, and figured I'd give them some privacy to say their goodbyes.

I hadn't even gotten the door closed before they were at it, the food forgotten. I smiled in spite of myself.

I knocked on Ink's door to no answer, although I could hear water running. A bath, maybe? Not wanting to sit out in the hallway, I tried the door—locked. Of course. But I was feeling bolder. Hadn't I just told Jay I was embracing all of me? And didn't that include lockpicking? No time like the present.

I set the food box down and put my hand on the doorknob. How in the hell was I supposed to use my mind to unlock it? Portals and lightning were visual—I could see what I was doing, and it made it easier to envision. But there was nothing visual about unlocking something. Was I supposed to envision a key? Was I supposed to envision the inner workings of the lock? My mom's notes had nothing about this ability, other than she had it. That was it. Not how it worked or how she found out about it. Nada.

I pulled my walls down and released my emotions, this time letting the sadness of knowing Calum and Jay were leaving tomorrow fuel the ability. I imagined the wheel and created an "unlock" option between "lightning" and "shoot." I focused, turned the wheel to the right spot, felt it click, then thought, *I intend to unlock Ink's door.* To my amazement, I heard some of the internal mechanisms click in the knob, and then I could turn the handle. I couldn't believe it.

I'd just broken into Ink's apartment with my brain. Holy shit.

My celebration was short-lived, however, as I turned the knob and the door stuck. Evidently Ink had locked the deadbolt. Crap. I guess he couldn't be too careful with groupies trying to break in. I started the process again. I was so wrapped up in trying to unlock the deadbolt that I yelped when the door swung open. Ink stood in a towel looking down at me with a smirk.

"Hi, sweetness. Might I inquire as to what you're doing?"

"Ummm . . . So, Silver and Calum are having sex in my room. I need somewhere to eat dinner."

"Not wanting a threesome, are you?"

"Ugh, no. We've already established that's not for me."

"So you're trying to break into my room?"

I smiled. "Succeeding."

A huge grin spread across his face. "Good."

He held the door open for me to come in, so I grabbed my food and walked past him. I looked around his apartment, trying to find a spot to eat. His table was covered in clothes and other various things.

"Your best bet is eating on the bed." I raised my eyebrows and he laughed. "Fara, if I were going to try and lure you into my bed, I wouldn't suggest eating there. I'd be more creative than that."

I settled on his bed and opened the box to find some sort of casserole thing. It had peas in it, which I hated, but otherwise didn't look too bad.

"Thanks for letting me interrupt you."

"Not at all. I'm just getting ready for my overnight surveillance shift."

"You won't be training me again tomorrow, then."

"Disappointed?"

"Of course."

He prowled around his room, always restless, always moving. I watched him, trying not to notice the way the towel hung on his hips, or the muscles in his back, or how his tattoos moved over them. He saw me looking and winked, grabbing a pair of the armored pants and a shirt from his closet. He headed to the bathroom to change.

"So how long are you in exile?" he called from the bathroom.

"He's leaving tomorrow. I'm not sure when they'll see each other again, or how long they'll take saying goodbye."

I could hear him chuckling in the bathroom as I took a couple of bites of the casserole. All I could taste was peas, so I set it aside. I was too tired to eat anyway. I was too tired to do much other than sit.

Ink reappeared, clothed. "That's really considerate of you."

"He'd do it for me—at least, if he liked the guy. Definitely not for Beck. Do you need to be doing something? I'm sorry I interrupted."

"Nothing at all. Are you going to eat that?"

"It has peas in it."

"You don't like peas?"

"Never have." I handed it to him. He started eating. "Ink, do you need dinner? I'm sorry—"

"Stop apologizing. And no. This is my second dinner. First dinner was the other casserole. You can stay here for as long as you want. I like your company, you know. And the fact that you can lockpick my door is an added bonus."

"I like your company too." And I did.

He finished my dinner, then went back into the bathroom for whatever reason. It was so quiet in his room, and his bed was comfortable. Like, amazingly so. He wasn't kidding when he told me that he got the good bed. I lay back, letting my eyes close for a moment.

45 BLU

Ink put his finger to his lips as I walked into his apartment. Fara was asleep on his bed.

"It's not what you think," he said in a low voice.

"It's none of my business—"

"Blu, I'm serious."

"Then why is she sleeping in your room?"

"Apparently other me and Silver were going at it in her apartment, so she came over here to eat dinner. She fell asleep when I was in the bathroom. That's it. Really."

Ink looked down at her, his face pensive. I watched him watch her. I sighed. It appeared I knew him better than he knew himself.

"Does she know?"

"Know what?"

"That you love her?"

He stilled but didn't take his eyes off her. "I don't."

"Ink, you can lie to yourself all you want, but you can't lie to me. We've been friends for way too long. It's written all over your face."

He bent down and pulled the covers over her in an act that was remarkably sweet, and completely out of character. Or maybe it wasn't. Maybe he just needed the right person to bring it out in him.

"It wouldn't matter anyway, even if I did."

"Why not?"

"Because I don't . . . We're just friends."

"I have never seen you look at someone like that. Including me. Try again."

He ran his hands through his hair, his eyes never leaving her sleeping face. "What's the point of falling in love when I won't be around to enjoy it, B? When the odds are that I won't get to grow old with someone? That I won't even live to see twenty-five? I couldn't do that to someone. I can't do that to myself."

"She has feelings for you too. She just doesn't know it yet."

"It doesn't matter. Even if she does, it still wouldn't be fair."

"Ink, it does matter. Even if you die tomorrow—which I certainly hope you don't, but even if you do—it would be worth it. To love someone and be loved like that, even for a day. For an hour. It would be worth it because you deserve happiness too."

He kissed the top of my head. "No, I don't."

I'd gone to Ink's apartment to relay a message from Jack—that when Ink went to the trail for surveillance, he needed to park the truck farther back in the trees. Evidently, minions had started patrolling that area. I told him what he needed to know after our heart-to-heart, then left him to his own thoughts, whatever those might be—although I had a pretty good idea.

I made my way to my room, hoping to get a few hours of sleep before training tomorrow. I had stripped out of my clothes and gotten into bed when I heard a strange buzzing. Realizing it was Jyston's comm, I ran across the room to find it in the pile of clothes.

"I thought you were gone on business."

A huff of laughter. "I am."

"Then how . . . ?"

"Let's just say that these comms are special."

"Oh."

"I just want to wish you good night."

"What?"

"Wouldn't it be grand if our lives were that simple? Where it was normal for us to have a chat before sleep? But unfortunately, such is not our fate."

I headed back to my bed as he talked. "I wanted to let you know that your surveillance attempts, while still hidden, won't be for long. Tomorrow morning, they are installing cameras in the area leading to the trail, and possibly the trail itself."

"How did you know?" I settled under the covers.

"I think we've established that I'm not going to reveal all of my secrets. Not yet, at least. But if I were you, I wouldn't risk staying at the trail past dawn tomorrow."

"Understood."

"And Blu?"

"Yeah?"

"Sweet dreams." I could hear the smile in his voice.

I smiled. "Whatever."

I turned off the comm and hauled myself out of bed; I needed to talk to the Captain right away. It was too late to stop Ink from going to the trail, but at least we could stop Jack from relieving him. I just hoped she was still awake.

FARA 46

Once again, I woke up to the bed moving independent of me. I could smell Ink's cologne and mentally began cursing him for waking me up. I opened one eye, expecting to see him dressed and staring at me, but instead, in the faint light of dawn through the curtains, I saw his bare back rise and fall rhythmically with his breath. Why was Ink sleeping in my bed? Then my brain caught up with my eyes and surroundings. I was in his bed. I must have fallen asleep after dinner and slept here all night. And now he was already home from surveillance and getting some sleep. Why didn't he wake me up when he left? Or kick me out when he got home?

"Stop squirming and go back to sleep. Training's canceled."

"I'm so sor—"

"If you finish that apology, I'm never bringing you coffee again. Or donuts."

I could hear the humor and exhaustion in his voice. "Sor—OK."

"Silver is still sleeping in your room and will be for a bit longer, so unless you want to interrupt other me's activities, go back to sleep."

I woke again sometime later, although how much later I wasn't sure. The light was brighter but still rang of morning. I didn't know why training was canceled, and I didn't know when I was supposed to open the portal for Jay, Calum, and Willow. I needed to get up and figure these things out, but I couldn't get myself to move. This bed was really amazing—although I'd never tell Ink that.

He was sleeping on his back, his head turned slightly toward me, his long lashes laying against his cheeks, and his mouth slightly open. Without his pulsing energy, he looked almost sweet. I'd never tell him that either. His tattoos, different from Calum's, were beautiful all the same. I saw a raw spot on his chest—a tattoo that had something recently added to it? Letters in script looped around what resembled Celtic knotwork. I couldn't make it out in the dimness of the room, and I absently reached out to touch it. I yanked my hand back, mortified. I couldn't just rub his chest because I wanted to. My own staring was starting to make me feel like a creeper. It was time to go.

I got up as quietly as I could and tiptoed around the bed. I took one last look at Ink, and pulled the covers over him. I didn't know why, but he considered me a friend. And for that I was grateful. I whispered a quiet thank you as I shut the door.

I stood in front of my own door for a minute, but heard nothing. I opened my door to find Silver already gone and Calum in the bathtub.

"Hello?"

"It's me, Calum. Where's your girlfriend?"

"Getting us breakfast."

"Us meaning you two? Or us meaning me and you?"

"Me and you. She's got training with Blu."

"But Ink told me that training was canceled."

"Yeah . . . about that. How is Ink?"

He stood in the doorway of the bathroom, wrapped in a towel, his eyebrows raised. I rolled my eyes.

"Ink was at surveillance all night. I slept in his bed. Alone."

"And this morning?"

"Nothing happened. He didn't even try."

"Really?"

"Yes, really."

"Well, thanks for giving us some time last night."

"Was it worth it?"

Calum grinned. I took that as a yes.

"Is she at least nice?"

"Honestly? I think you guys could be friends. She's pretty amazing."

"Good."

He went back into the bathroom to change. There was a knock on the door. Silver was standing there with food, Blu right behind her looking all business, and tired.

"We don't have time to chat. Silver and I need to train—but I wanted to let you know that Jay is ready to go home after you finish breakfast. Since we don't know what we're going to find in Calum's apartment, he's asked that you both meet him and Willow at the infirmary, and you all can portal from there."

"Did you call him bossy?"

The corner of Blu's mouth curved up. "Something like that. Anyway, Jack will be by to get you and take you there."

As Calum emerged from the bathroom, Blu turned to my best friend with a smile. "Calum, unfortunately I won't be able to see you off. Hopefully, I'll see you again soon."

He walked over and gave her a hug. She hugged him back stiffly. Eventually she'd get used to our huggie ways. Maybe.

"Stay safe," she said, once she was at least an arm's distance from him.

"I will. You guys take care of each other and I'll see you soon."

He walked over to Silver and wrapped his arms around her, giving her a kiss. He whispered something in her ear.

I hugged Calum as we watched them walk out the door. "You going to be OK?"

"Yeah. Just catch that spy soon so I can come back."

"We will."

⚡ ⚡ ⚡

We made it to the infirmary without anyone stopping us, which was somewhat of a miracle considering the Compound was alive with activity. I was so nervous about someone recognizing Calum on our walk over that I didn't have a chance to really process what I was about to do. My boyfriend and best friend were leaving. And while I hoped everything went to plan and I'd see them in a week, that wasn't a given. I was going to miss them.

The Captain had already circulated a story in the infirmary that she was sending Willow and Jay to some specialty doctors outside of the city center, in secret. That way the medics wouldn't wonder why one minute the two of them were here, and the next they were gone. It wasn't a perfect solution, but neither was telling them nothing. Rumors of two disappearing patients would draw too much attention.

Jay smiled at me as we walked into the small room. With the three of us, plus Sage and Willow, it was crowded. Jay dodged Jack and Calum to hobble over to me.

"You know I'm standing right here, Jay," Sage said wryly. "You could at least pretend to take my advice and use your crutches."

Jay chuckled. "I can't use them at home, so I need to get used to it."

"It's not helping—"

Jay held up his hand. "I know. But I don't have the luxury of time."

He grabbed my hands and pulled me toward the door. "Give us a minute?"

We stepped back into the hall, and Jay bent down to kiss me. "I wanted a minute alone with you before I go. I was hoping for more time—"

"I know. I'm sorry. I slept in."

He rested his forehead on mine, closing his eyes. "You can still change your mind, you know. You can still come with me."

My chest tightened. "You know I can't." No matter how, or why, I was made of fire and lightning.

"I don't have to like it. Please stay safe here, Fara. Please don't be reckless, or go on crazy missions, or anything like that. Please do what you need to do, so you can come home safe to me."

"You be careful too. We don't know who you can trust in your department—or who Barrington has in his pocket. I won't be there to rescue you this time."

He chuckled. "I have a contact at the department, someone I trust. I'm going to reach out to him as soon as I get Willow back to my apartment and settled in."

I sighed. "You know what's messed up? Willow will get to see your place before I do."

He pulled me into his chest. "Well, stay alive so you can come see it. And my plant, Robert, provided he hasn't died while I've been here. We'll get spring rolls too. And go on a real date."

"Deal."

He kissed me one last time and we walked back into the room. I hugged Calum, then Willow.

"Everyone ready? I'll open a portal and you guys can step through. I'll open another one in three hours to make sure things are OK, then twice a day, unless something is needed sooner. And then this time next week, I'll come get you."

Not wanting to put off the inevitable any longer, I let my emotions flow through me and felt the portal open up.

As I told it to get bigger, Calum's familiar coffee table came into view.

"Hey, Calum, did you leave a note for me before you were kidnapped?"

"No. Why?"

I reached through the window to grab the piece of paper. It was a business card, one I recognized. Barrington Park's name was embossed on the front. My hands started shaking. I turned it over.

You cannot hide forever, Fara.

BLU 47

I was in the Captain's office when Jack and Fara came in. She told us that Willow, Calum, and Jay were back in her world, then handed the Captain a piece of paper. She was paler than usual, shaken, and with good reason. So, Barrington was going to play mind games. Fine. She was safe here for now and had a team of people willing to kill and die for her. Plus, according to Ink, she could fry his brains out.

So Barrington could fuck right off.

The Captain told us all to meet back in her office in three hours so that we'd be present when Fara opened the next portal. Planning to take a nap before the shenanigans began, I'd just made it to my door when Jyston's comm buzzed.

"Change of plans. We need to meet soon. Today. Now."

He sounded worried . . . and something else.

"I have to be back here in three hours."

He told me a place to meet and assured me that it was safe—at least, safer than out in the open. I already had a comm and a palmbox, so I commed Styx to let her know where I was going and who I was meeting. I felt virtuous for doing the right thing and told Styx that. She laughed.

"Say hi to your boyfriend for me."

⚡⚡⚡

Jyston was already in the abandoned building, sitting on a concrete block that had been some sort of wall. He was armed to the teeth, his hair pulled back from his grim face.

He started speaking without looking up. "Do you know where the PITs are held?"

"In the stadium in the city center, right?"

Jyston's plan for getting us into the PITs was just insane enough that it might work. He gave me some suggestions as to how to handle the negotiations prior to the PITs, which might lead to the driving jobs that could get us into Dagna's building. But he seemed to be distracted. His face was drawn and the usual mischievous glint in his eyes was gone. He spoke without stopping, like he just needed to deliver all of the information. Like he was running out of time.

"Jyston, what's going on?"

His eyes searched my face, and I let him. I tentatively sat down next to him. I could feel the heat of his body warm against my arm.

"You can trust me, Jyston. If you're in trouble, I might be able to help."

He was so quiet that I thought he wasn't going to tell me, our bodies pressed together in the cold, abandoned building.

"After the PITs, I'll have to go into hiding. And I probably won't be able to communicate with you before then."

"You're leaving Jurisdiction?"

"Yes."

"Is it because Dagna's plan has started to work? The Counselor believes her lies about you?"

"They aren't all lies. She has figured out that I'm not exactly what I seem—although she is unaware of the depth of my duplicity."

"What are you talking about?"

He took a deep breath. "She has figured out that my intentions are not necessarily in Jurisdiction's best interests; that I have been actively working against her. She suspects that I've been working against the Counselor as well. But she doesn't yet know my biggest secret. And she cannot know."

"What secret, Jyston? What's going on? Will you tell me?"

He slowly turned his head to look at me, his cool gray eyes landing on mine, mere inches separating us. "I watched Barrington Park slaughter my parents because my world did not contain the weapons he and the Counselor sought."

"Your world?"

"Yes. This horrible world is not my own. I am from a different universe entirely."

48 FARA

The next three hours were going to be the longest in my life, which was saying something. Waiting to see if Jay and Calum were safe, or if they had been ambushed by Barrington's men, or maybe even my own government. Waiting to see if they needed help of any kind, but not being able to do anything about it. Yet.

Watching Jay go through that portal was hard. How were we going to make the first (known) interdimensional relationship work? It had sounded possible when it was theoretical, but reality sucked more than I thought.

And then there was the threat from Barrington Park, which was buzzing through my mind. How did that note get into Calum's apartment? Did he know we'd been passing notes, or was it a guess? I had so many questions, but only one answer: he knew how to scare me.

I walked around my apartment restlessly, hoping the movement would settle my nerves. Maybe making coffee would help.

"You're reminding me of *me* right now, which is freaking me out a bit. May I ask why you are looking through all of your kitchen cabinets, repeatedly?"

Ink was leaning on my doorframe, complete with perma-smirk and unreasonably tight black shirt. I wasn't in the mood for his banter.

"I think I need coffee."

"I was actually just stopping by to see if you wanted to go with me to the mess. But if you're too busy rearranging your plates, I understand."

"It would probably do me some good to get out of this room."

"Missing other me, are you?"

I glared at him as we made our way into the drizzle of the spring day. Ink was watching me out of the corner of his eye.

"Want to talk about it?"

I definitely didn't, so I reached into my pocket, pulled out Barrington's business card, and handed it to him.

His teasing manner disappeared. "Has the Captain seen this?"

I wasn't sure I could speak without crying. The more I thought about it, the more freaked out I was. Barrington (or one of his goons) broke into Calum's apartment and left the card. How did he know to do that? As if sensing my distress, Ink stopped in the middle of the path and took my hands in his. His green eyes were bright.

"I'm not worried about this, Fara."

"Of course you aren't. Barrington Park doesn't want you; he wants me! Or at least, he wants what I can do. And even if he did want you, you could kill him in one hundred different ways without breaking a sweat. Which I can't. He already kidnapped me once, Ink. I can't get caught again."

"Fara, I don't mean to be an asshole, but I think you're missing the point."

I jerked my hands away. "What? That a sadistic megalomaniac wants to keep me as his personal interdimensional bus service?"

"What's a 'bus service'? Anyway, what I mean is that even if he kidnaps you again—which he won't—you'll escape."

"How? Another rescue mission? I can't put you all in danger to save my life."

"That's not what I mean. Although you'd have to tie Blu to a chair before she allowed you to stay a prisoner. Fara, you don't have to stay anywhere you don't want to be. You can just portal out. If someone grabs you and your combat training doesn't get you out or you can't stab them, you shock them, then portal out. If you can't portal for whatever reason, use your electric balls and fry the bastard. You can unlock any locked door. You could burn the entire building down, if you thought hard enough about it. You aren't helpless anymore, and unlike the rest of us, you have a built-in escape route. You're nearly unstoppable, so stop thinking that you can't take care of yourself, because you can."

"What if he takes Calum again?"

"Then you walk in like the badass you are, grab Calum, and portal out. Flipping Barrington the bird on the way. I might even help."

I let his words settle around me. He was right. I had been so focused on what happened last time—that feeling of helplessness and fear, and the way Barrington tortured Jay—that I hadn't stopped to think about what would happen if they tried to kidnap me today. I was stuck thinking about myself as I was before all of this. But I wasn't her anymore. I was stronger. Braver.

And Ink had reminded me of that. Again.

I threw my arms around him; his now familiar smell wrapped around me. I stood there, breathing him in, listening to his steady heartbeat. After a moment, he rested his chin on top of my head and pulled me closer.

We stood like that for long enough that we were getting furtive glances from people walking by. But weirdly, I didn't care. He always managed to make me feel like I could do anything. And standing there, hugging him, I felt like I could almost believe in myself. Eventually, I forced myself to step out of his embrace.

"Not that I'm complaining about a beautiful woman throwing herself at me, but I have to ask, what was that for?"

"To thank you." The words came out quieter than I intended. His face softened only a moment, but as quick as it came, it left.

"For what?"

"For not being as much of an asshole as everyone seems to think. Including you."

"Um, thanks?"

"Really, though. Of all the universes I could have escaped to, I'm glad I came to this one, and you're in it. Thank you for believing in me."

He ran his hands through his hair. "It's my pleasure, although at some point you need to start believing in yourself."

"Why would I do that when I have you around?"

He started walking down the path again, eyes ahead. "Because I won't be around forever to remind you."

49 BLU

Jyston looked down at the ground, the only indication that he had just revealed his biggest secret to me.

"Tell me," I said.

"Are you sure? Not to sound overly dramatic, but it will change everything."

"Yes, I'm sure."

He took a deep breath and stared off into the abandoned building, as if searching for the words in the rubble.

"Where to begin? Well, I suppose when Barrington murdered my parents. He showed up out of thin air, demanded weapons, and when my parents didn't produce what he required, he used lightning to kill them. He then opened a window in the air and walked through. He did always have a flair for the dramatic."

"I'm so sorry, Jyston." I saw the rage and pain in his eyes. "How did you end up here?"

"I came through after him."

"You just followed him in?"

"Yes."

"How were you not caught?"

"I'm just that good. Even at that age." He raised an eyebrow at me, and I barked out a laugh. "To be fair, it wasn't some grand plan. I wasn't really thinking of much other than killing him for slaughtering my parents. So, I followed him, the window closed, and I found myself here, in this world. Eventually, I stole some minion's clothes and pretended to be one of them."

"That's—"

"—nuts? I agree. But Jurisdiction was so eager for minions that no one ever asked where I came from or why I was here. All they cared about was how well I followed orders."

"That really is nuts."

"Truly. Anyway, I didn't seem to have any other options. I needed to kill Barrington. It was—and is—something of an obsession. So, I had to get close to him. After a brief time assessing this cesspool of a world, I figured being a minion was the easiest path to doing so. He was always surrounded by security, and they're a paranoid bunch."

"They should be."

"More than they know. Anyway, I bided my time, plotting and planning his murder."

"And training as a minion."

"Which was less than delightful. But, after a couple of years, I was a fairly formidable warrior. The Counselor took notice and put me on his security detail."

He wasn't bragging. From what little I knew, he was actually downplaying his abilities.

"You couldn't have been that old."

"I was ten when I came through. Twelve when I started working directly for the Counselor."

I was barely older than that when I joined the Team. "I've heard the rumors."

Jyston chuckled. "Some—actually, most have been exaggerated. I'm afraid to even ask, but what have you heard about me?"

Most of the stories were horrible. How many were true, and how many cultivated by Jyston himself?

"Lots of things, actually," I said. "Like, once when you were barely a teenager, you defeated ten adult minions, one by one, in the combat ring—and the only reason it wasn't more was that no one else would challenge you, since those you defeated were . . . I believe the word was 'eviscerated.' Is that an exaggeration?"

"Let's just say that I took my aggressions out that day on those who deserved it."

I snorted and he waved me off. "It was all part of the plan. Anyway, I just kept waiting for the right opportunity to kill Barrington. But as they say, all the best laid plans go to shit, or something like that."

"That I *really* understand."

"We are more alike than you know, beautiful Blu."

I leaned into him a little, and he nudged me, leaving his body pressed against mine.

"The day I planned to kill Barrington started perfectly. I had been called to the Counselor's chamber to await his arrival from another world. I was going to follow him to his own rooms, kill him, steal his palmbox, and use it to go back home. It sounds so foolish and simple now, but at the time, it seemed foolproof."

I knew how this part of the story went because of Fara. "But Barrington never returned. He got stuck in another world."

"Unfortunately, yes. Which caused me no small amount of ire. At that moment, my dreams of avenging my parents' deaths came to a very frustrating halt. But fate has a way of working itself out. Because of a little girl with bright blue eyes, I found another purpose."

I stilled. "What little girl? What are you talking about?"

"If you would do me the honor of letting me finish my saga . . ."

"Fine."

He chuckled. "Thank you. I'll try to keep it brief, although you will need to allow for some poetic license." He shot me a lopsided smile, which was amazingly cute.

"Get on with it, Jyston."

"As you wish. To get away from the Counselor and the horrible things he had me do, I would wander the empty spaces of Jurisdiction's headquarters, feeling sorry for myself. It was not my finest moment. On one particularly appalling day, I collapsed near a cell in the dungeon. As I sat there in the dark, dank cold, lamenting my life, there was this tiny girl with the brightest blue eyes I had ever seen. She startled me. I hadn't realized anyone was there because she was so quiet. And then she did the most remarkable thing. She reached through the bars of her cell so she could hold my hand and told me that no matter how bad it got, I would be OK. It was you, Blu."

"I don't reme—"

He held up his hand. "Please, I'm almost done. I promise." I snapped my mouth shut. He gave me a sad smile. "The next day, I was ordered to sit in on an interrogation. When I walked into the room, the same little girl was chained to a chair. After what Dagna did to you that day, I promised myself that I would destroy Jurisdiction so that no one else had to go through that. I might not be able to kill Barrington, but I could destroy everything he ever cared about. I would make Dagna—Jurisdiction—the Counselor—pay for what they did to you. To everyone."

"That's why you rescued me."

"Yes."

"Thank you seems inadequate."

Jyston tucked a piece of hair behind my ear. "I'm not sure you should thank me."

"What? Why?"

"I didn't exactly rush in to save the day. It took me so long—too long—to get you out. I think back to that moment in the interrogation room quite often, wondering if there was something I could have done that would have saved us."

Jyston ran his knuckles over my cheekbone, lingering to cup my face for a moment. I took his hand and laced my fingers through his, earning a shadow of a smile. I understood about moments like that. And the nightmares they bred.

"Well, thank you anyway."

He dipped his head. "Where was I? Oh yes. Destroying Jurisdiction. In order to thoroughly thwart them, I had to climb the ranks, whatever it took. Once I got into this position, I tried to derail some of the worst of Jurisdiction's plans, but Dagna, ever the pariah, seemed to block me at every turn. I realized I needed help, and since I had spies watching you, I knew that you would be a good person to help me."

"You had spies watching me?"

"Not closely, but I generally knew when you were doing things. Like, I knew about the time you burned down Dagna's summer cottage."

"She deserved it."

"Yes, she did. But considering that escapade of yours—and everything else I knew you had done—I needed a way to approach you that did not end in you trying to kill me."

"I'm still surprised I haven't killed you yet."

Jyston raised an eyebrow at me. "Honestly? Me too. But I'm glad you haven't."

"The day is still young. Is that why you talked to me at the High Governor's ball?"

"Yes. I had planned on contacting you earlier—as you sat on top of the building waiting for me to leave for the High Governor's party. But I was thwarted by Dagna. Again."

"I saw her show up."

Jyston shuddered, as if reliving some horrible memory. "Yes. When she got there, she let slip that her minions were going to capture you as you waited for me to leave. I obviously couldn't allow that to happen, so I asked her who was providing her with information. She said she would give him to me for a price."

"What price?"

"I let her seduce me."

He searched my face, like he was waiting for me to condemn him for what he did with Dagna. But how could I? He did something that he obviously thought was horrific in order to save Jack—and me. I squeezed his hand to let him know that he would find no judgment from me. I was grateful. If the roles were reversed, I hoped that I was brave enough to do something as horrible to help my friends.

"Later, Jackrabbit told me you would be at the ball. And you know the rest of the story. Although, I must admit that even if I hadn't planned on meeting you there, once I saw you in the crowd, I still would have sought you out. I'd recognize those eyes anywhere. But now they're attached to a beautiful, fierce woman who, for whatever reason, has decided not to kill me."

His eyes met mine, and I looked at him. Really *looked*. His shoulders were rounded and lines creased his forehead. The half-smile playing on his lips was gone, as was the mischief in his eyes. He looked tired and . . . sad. I felt like he was allowing me to see who he really was.

"Jyston, what is it?"

"I'm exhausted. I've been playing this game for almost twenty years, and I can see it's coming to an end. Dagna suspects me."

"Then we'll kill her."

He chuckled. "That *would* be a good start. But I don't think it will be enough. I don't want to go into hiding, but I'm not sure how much longer I can keep this up. And as much as I would like to play the hero and finish this by myself, I can't."

"Jyston, why are you telling me all of this?"

I let him kiss the corner of my mouth. "Because I care for you, like it or not. But also because I trust you—more than anyone else in this godforsaken world. What you do with the information is up to you, but I'm hoping it helps you to trust me too. It was a calculated risk. I can't do this alone anymore, Blu. I need your help." He knelt in front of me. "Will you help me?"

As he stared into my eyes and awaited my response, words escaped me. What Jyston just told me was beyond anything that I could have conjured in my imagination. He was from a different universe, like Fara and Calum. His parents had been killed by Jurisdiction, just like mine had. He had done horrible things in order to make this world better, just like I had. We were on the same team, and he cared about me—and he was on his knees asking for my help.

Before I could think too much about it, I grabbed him and kissed him. After his initial surprise, he wrapped his arms around me, and after what seemed like eternity and no time at all had passed, I broke off our kiss and took his face in my hands.

"I will help you. For your parents. For mine. For everyone."

Jyston kissed me gently once, then looked into my eyes. Even though the mask was completely gone, his gaze was no less lethal. "Together?"

I kissed him back, unable to keep the wicked grin from my face, a promise of what was to come. "We will burn the whole fucking thing to the ground."

ACKNOWLEDGMENTS

I took a huge leap of faith writing *A Choice of Lightning*. I hadn't released *Running in Parallel* yet, and I had no idea how any of this was going to turn out. I still don't, really. But having the help and support of amazing people kept me writing and continuing this story. I'm so thankful for them. For you. So, in no particular order, thank you:

To my remarkable beta readers: Tiffané, Andrea, and Kirstin. Not only for the hours you spent reading and bringing your thoughtful perspectives and insights to this story, but for your friendship. You guys are the best. To Jim: beta reader number one. Thank you for all of the support you give so that I can continue pursuing this dream of mine. I couldn't do this without you. To Jennifer: for reading random snippets and book blurbs, and discussing plots over beers and cheeseburgers—which is the best way to discuss anything, really. To Matt: for patiently explaining how guns/bullets/car chases actually worked, just to have me ignore most of it and go rogue. I really appreciate your help with everything; any bending of the laws of physics is totally on me. To my editor, Kathrine Kirk: you are awesome! Your insightful changes and comments helped bring the best out in this book and my writing. I can't wait to keep working with you. To my mother: for your unending love and support. Saying I'm glad that you're my mom is the world's biggest understatement. To my kids, Alex and Charlie: for reminding me what bravery, compassion, humor, and fun look like. I love you three thousand.

Finally, thank you to *you*: the reader. I couldn't do this without you. Reading my books. Recommending my books. Posting pictures of my book at various locales on social media. Leaving reviews. Sending messages of support. Asking me to speak at book clubs. Because of you, I was able to keep going. Because of you, I'm turning this dream into a reality. I know I repeat myself, but you guys truly are the best.

Peace and Love, KOT

Made in the USA
Las Vegas, NV
16 February 2022

43979794R10182